THE BALLAD

OF

BABY BLUE

A Novel by Celeste Sutton

The Ballad of Baby Blue

Copyright © 2025 by Celeste Sutton

This is a work of fiction. Names, characters, places, and incidents are either the product of the author's imagination or used fictitiously.

Cover design by Amy Dudek

Interior design by the author

First edition, 2025

Published by Dark Ink Press

For more information, visit: www.celestesutton.com

For anyone who's ever been called strange—

and quietly took it as a compliment.

She walked through the Hollow with moss in her hair,

A girl with a secret, a name she won't share . . .

The river ran dry and the sky turned to flame,

But Baby Blue crossed, and she left us her name.

∞

—Appalachian folk song, origin unknown

Prologue

Four-year-old Blue had just curled her fingers around a mug of milk when the thudding began. The low ceiling trembled, dislodging clumps of dirt. The candle flame jumped, frantic in the dark. Blue saw terror in the face across from her. Her breath hitched. The mug tumbled from her hands, and the soil drank up the milk in an instant.

"Oh!" she exclaimed.

"Shh, it doesn't matter."

The earth above them shook from heavy footfalls. Voices boomed. Dirt rained down, snuffing out the candle and plunging her underground home into darkness.

"Go." Hands gripped her, shoving her toward the warren's tunnel. Blue's ankle twisted, and she yelped.

"Sorry! Crawl. Go deep." The voice was urgent, breathless.

"But—"

"Don't let them find you! If they do, play dead. Just like we practiced."

"But—"

"I'll be right behind you. I promise." A fierce hug, a final kiss, and pressure urging her forward. "Go, Blue. *Go!*"

Blue crawled blindly, the scent of damp earth thick in her nose. Above her, hounds bayed and feet pounded. Men shouted, their angry voices crashing together.

"This way!"

"Git 'em!"

"Flush him out and shoot him dead!"

Daylight punched through as portions of the den collapsed. Blue glanced back just long enough to see a man's black boot, an enormous wet nose, a frenzy of scrabbling paws.

She pressed on. Her stomach churned and terror consumed her. Then—

A bang.

A flash.

An anguished howl.

Silence. Abrupt, unnatural.

Then a raucous cheer.

Blue squeezed her eyes shut, pressed her back into the soil, and curled up as tight as a pill bug. *Play dead, play dead, play dead.*

She heard the men leave—and the dogs with them. Still, she didn't move.

Time stretched and shrank. She needed to pee. Still, she didn't move.

Much later, she heard the thud of boots. Blue's people didn't wear boots. A lantern flickered, then flared, its beam cutting through the dark. Blue trembled. Her people didn't use lanterns, either.

Hands, rough and firm, lifted her. A voice rumbled near her ear. "The other one called you 'Blue.' That your name?"

Blue shook, too frightened to answer.

A new roar, different this time. Not voices. Not hounds. Something bigger. The world lurched—she was moving fast, then slow again, then was bounced, churned, and spat out.

Starlight. A luminous moon. Then warmth. Water. Fingers scrubbing her skin. A smell—sweet, foreign. Flowers, but not flowers. Another thing wrong.

She wanted to disappear.

Her deerskin tunic was never returned. She was dressed in soft fabrics and placed on top of something thick and cushioned. A bed. But not like the bedding she knew—no packed straw, no fur. Not terrible, but strange.

The days that followed were a tangle of waking and sleeping, of a woman's strange face and words she barely understood. Her home was gone. Everyone she loved was gone. Four-year-old Blue was alone in the world, except for the steady presence of the woman sitting beside her bed.

When Blue stirred, the woman was there. When she blinked back into awareness, the woman was there, her brown eyes filled with worry.

"You have to eat," the woman said one day. Her dark braid fell over her shoulder. Her voice was soft but firm. "It's not what you're used to, but it'll help you get strong."

She eased a spoon through Blue's cracked lips.

"There now," praised the woman. "Good job, Blue."

Blue stiffened, and her throat ached when she tried to speak. "How . . . how did you . . ."

She felt unfamiliar to herself, a terrifying, dizzying sensation. She clutched the blanket wrapped around her, an anchor to keep her from going under.

"How do I know your name?" the woman guessed. "The person who left you with me wrote it on a note pinned to your blanket."

Blue looked down. The blanket was pearly gray and softer than the cattails by the stream, softer than anything she had ever touched.

"They left this, too," the woman said, gesturing at the strange silver object resting on the nightstand.

It was there every night when Blue went to sleep, and it was there every day when she woke up. It was small with a rounded end, engraved with curling vines and leaves. She picked it up once, to study it, but dropped it immediately when it chimed.

"What is it?" Blue asked.

"Why, it's a baby rattle."

"A rattle?" Blue repeated, the word strange on her tongue. Bones rattled. Dried seed pods rattled. This thing only sang.

"It was with you when you came," the woman said—too quickly. Uncertainty flashed over her features, and then she squared her shoulders and nodded. "It was. Really. It's very nice, Blue. Whoever left it with you wanted you to have something special—that's what I think."

Blue wasn't sure if that was true. But the *rattle* was hers now. Later, perhaps she would make it sing again.

"Anyway, I'm Margie," the woman said briskly, as if to move the conversation along. "And I know this must be confusing, but I'm glad you're here."

That evening, Margie placed a wooden tray over Blue's lap, bearing a plate of food and a tin cup of milk. The scent hit first, sharp and familiar. Blue kicked out ferociously, upending the tray and sending the milk—and everything else—flying.

"Whoa!" Margie exclaimed, stepping back.

Blue pressed her spine to the headboard, heart hammering.

"I'm sorry," Margie said. "I didn't mean to startle you."

Twilight was settling, shadows creeping into the corners of the room. Margie moved toward the wall and reached for something.

"I'm going to light the lamp, just so you know," she said. "Just so we can see each other—"

"No!" Blue cried, but the flint had already sparked. The sudden flare filled the room, harsh and alien. Blue inhaled sharply, compressing her rioting emotions into a single crackling surge of energy. With a snap of her chin, she flung it outward.

The oil lamp shattered with a bang.

Margie screamed. Glass and soot rained down.

She stared at Blue. Blue stared back, chest rising and falling fast. Tears welled up and spilled over. She hadn't meant to scare Margie. And—too late—she realized that Margie hadn't meant to scare her, either.

"Oh, honey," Margie whispered. She righted the fallen chair and sat beside the bed once more. A shard of glass clung to her sleeve, and she plucked it off, setting it on the windowsill.

"So, you do have magic," she murmured at last.

Blue's breath hitched.

"You're only the second fae I've met," Margie continued. "I wasn't sure how much to believe."

Fae. Blue furrowed her brow.

"That's what you are," Margie told her. "And I'm a mortal." She laughed awkwardly. "You do know about mortals, don't you?"

Blue was at a loss. How was she supposed to know what she knew?

Margie exhaled. "Well, we'll figure it out. We have to."

Blue hesitated, then—tentative, cautious—reached for Margie's hand.

Margie's fingers curled gently around hers, a fragile thread between them.

Weeks passed, and Blue's broken ankle healed under Margie's care. So did her heart—mostly. Sometimes she still woke up sobbing, but her nightmares came less frequently. The past blurred, softened, dulled. Her old life became a foggy thing, a story she almost remembered, like something that had happened to someone else. Forgetting was a gift: a soft gray blanket shaken and fluffed, drifting down like snow to cover what once had been.

By fall, Blue was used to Margie's bright, tidy cabin. She grew accustomed to the clothes Margie gave her as well. She especially liked her "overalls," as Margie called them. They were part trousers and part top, with straps that looped over Blue's shoulders and hooked onto bright brass buttons. The fabric was soft but durable, and the pants legs didn't rip even when Blue scrambled up and down the rocky outcroppings that surrounded the cabin.

Blue had been taught that mortals didn't have magic, but they did, she thought.   Lantern magic. Pillow magic. Overalls magic.

Then the thought slipped away, and with it, eventually, all recollection of who might have told her such a thing.

10

She wanted to know, but at the same time, she didn't. It hurt, poking at those wisps and whirls of who she used to be. As time passed, she let them float away.

And anyway, Blue had plenty to distract her. Blue's first home had been a hidden warren in the valley's low crook, whereas Margie's cabin perched high on a ridge, where the sky stretched wide and bold. Every time she stepped outside, the view startled her with its beauty, as if the world had opened just for her.

Through the seasons, Blue explored every crag and cliff, every sunny glade and shady nook and rushing stream. She bathed in the river and dried off on warm slabs of stone. In winter, when snow piled too high to go out, she curled up by the fire with a book.

Margie taught her to write her name and trace letters with a calligraphy pen dipped in ink. The paper was coarse, the words clumsy, but Blue loved the scratch of the nib and the mystery of words coming to life. She listened when Margie spoke of a particularly bitter winter and the sickness that had followed, the long, cruel years when mortals had turned on the fae and driven them from their homes. The Hard Times, those years were called. But the Hard Times were over, mainly.

Down in the valley, the town of Hemridge sat squat and small—a smudge of roofs and chimneys half-swallowed by trees. Now and then, someone in need of herbs or salves made the climb up to Margie's door. When they did, Blue stayed out of sight.

"They look at me like I'm cursed," Margie said. "But when their babies won't stop crying or their lungs get tight, suddenly I'm worth the walk. And, I suspect, some of them just want a peek at you."

"*Me?*"

"We have my mother to thank for that. She's been telling anyone who'll listen about her wayward daughter's bastard child."

"What's a bastard?"

Margie cupped her cheek. "A word used by people who want to feel superior—and nothing worth troubling yourself over."

Margie said it was just as well that the folks in Hemridge thought Blue was her blood daughter. Still, it was safest for her to stay out of sight.

Blue didn't mind. If ever someone appeared on the steep path—first just a speck, then slowly taking shape—she scaled a tree as easily as any squirrel and spied on the outsider from above. She watched them huff and puff on the last stretch of the trail, lingering at the edge of the clearing before working up the nerve to step onto Margie's land.

"She's not going to eat you," Blue muttered. "What do you think she is, a witch?"

They probably did. Mortals were fools.

As the years passed, Blue grew taller, faster, stronger. She also grew . . . odder. Or perhaps just better at noticing Margie's sidelong glances.

Like the time Margie caught Blue juggling stones—not with her hands, but her mind.

"Blue!" Margie cried.

The stones dropped. One struck Blue's cheekbone.

Margie rushed to her, flustered. "Sweetheart, I'm so sorry —"

"I'm fine," Blue said, waving her off. She was thirteen now, and she neither needed nor wanted Margie fussing over her.

"But—Blue!"

Blue tried to be patient, knowing that Margie saw herself as the adult and Blue as the child. But Blue wasn't a child, not anymore.

"I said I'm *fine*," she repeated.

Margie's arm lifted, then fell. Her mouth formed a shaky smile. "Your pain tolerance is remarkable," she observed, almost casually. "Most people, after being hit in the face with a rock, wouldn't be nearly so calm."

Blue touched her rapidly swelling eye. "I don't enjoy getting hit with rocks, if that's what you're suggesting."

"Of course not."

"I'm tough, that's all."

"That you are." Margie gestured at Blue's feet, slender and tanned and marked up in slashes from healed cuts and scrapes. "I can't take two steps on gravel without hopping— not when I'm barefoot—but you can run straight up the mountain without shoes."

"And?"

"And nothing." Margie's voice softened. "I'm not criticizing you, Blue. I'm in awe."

Which, somehow, was worse.

When Blue was fifteen, Margie came up behind her as she lay by the side of the stream, crooning to a school of trout. The trout swam closer, swaying dreamily in the current. Blue imagined them flipping over and offering their bellies up for a scratch, and, one by one, they did.

Their skin was cool and slick beneath her fingers, a lovely

sensation. Blue felt the whisper of their muscles shifting, the ripple of water gliding between them like breath between bodies. For a moment, the world held still—until Margie gasped, breaking the spell and sending the fish darting off in silver flashes.

"Did you make them do that?" Margie whispered.

"I didn't *make* them," Blue said irritably. "I offered. They accepted."

"I see," said Margie, though Blue could tell she didn't. "Can you . . . do you . . . communicate with all animals?"

"Sometimes. It depends. Mainly birds and squirrels, I suppose." Blue shrugged. "They cheer me up when I'm feeling down."

"The squirrels."

"And the birds." Blue hesitated. "Is that bad?"

"Nooo," Margie said. "But people need other people as well."

"I have you. You're my person."

"And you're mine," Margie said, though her voice caught faintly on the words.

Still, Blue spent most days not with Margie but on her own, exploring the mountains. She memorized every curve of the mountain, learned the names of plants, and knew which animals would meet her gaze and which would slink away. She knew how to survive. She knew how to be alone.

And yet, sometimes, when the wind tugged at her hair or a wren sang a mournful tune, a strange ache would bloom in her chest, a sorrow without a name. At times like that—when her throat locked tight and she missed people she couldn't quite remember—she'd go to her room and find the silver baby rattle and curl her fingers around it, holding on until the ache began to fade.

But most days were good, and the bad ones passed like storms, rough for a time, but over soon enough. She tried not to think about the past. She refused to imagine the future. The present was enough. It was a tightrope stretched across the mountain, and yes, it was precarious— but she told herself nothing bad would happen as long as she didn't look down.

Her balance shattered the summer she turned seventeen, when Margie's old telephone rang, sharp and metallic and merciless. Blue startled. She had almost forgotten the thing existed, anchored high on the kitchen wall, an old wooden thing with a horn-shaped mouthpiece that no one ever used.

Until now.

Margie went rigid. The batter spoon sagged in her hand, forgotten.

It rang again.

When Margie answered, her face was pale and set. She turned her back and murmured too low for Blue to catch her words. When she hung up, the receiver clattered.

"That was my mother," she said. Her hand found the back of a wooden chair, gripping it tight. "She had a fall. She needs me to go to her."

Blue's stomach knotted. "Go where?"

Margie grimaced.

"To town? You have to go down the mountain and into *town*?"

Margie didn't answer.

"How long?"

"She'll need me for a while. A month. Maybe more."

The room tilted, then almost as quickly snapped back into place.

"I'll go with you," Blue pronounced.

Margie shook her head. "Absolutely not. The people in Hemridge . . ."

The people in Hemridge. Mortals, Margie meant. Mortals who would gawk at Blue—or worse—if they recognized her for what she was. Margie knew it, and Blue did, too. She felt the weight of it press against her ribs.

But the townsfolk would stare at Margie, too. Blue knew that the townsfolk thought it wasn't right for an unmarried woman to live on her own, high up in the mountains, and certainly not with a child to raise. They'd already judged Margie once for choosing the life she had. They'd judge her all over again if she came down the mountain and left Blue behind. After everything Margie had done for her—raising her here, keeping her safe—letting Margie go down the mountain on her own felt like cowardice.

Also, though she was reluctant to admit it, Blue was curious about Hemridge—just a little. What was it like? She imagined brick storefronts and wide dusty streets. Cars with roaring engines that coughed out smoke. There'd be young people, too. People her age. Girls her age. Girls who didn't juggle stones or speak to birds when there was no one else to talk to.

Blue didn't *care* about those girls. They would be silly, vapid creatures, surely. And yet . . . and yet . . .

"I'm coming with you, Margie," she pronounced.

"Oh no, you're not!" Margie said with a laugh of disbelief.

"I'm not letting you go alone. You don't even *like* your mother. You've told me so often enough."

"There's not much to like, I'll give you that. Being nasty to others is the only thing that brings her pleasure."

"I can handle a nasty old woman," Blue said. "I can handle the townspeople, too."

Margie studied her, lips pressed thin.

"I'm going with you, and that's final," Blue said. She gave a sharp nod. "So. When do we leave?"

Margie smiled bleakly. "Tomorrow."

The word landed harder than Blue expected. Not some far-off day but the next sunrise. *Tomorrow.* Her bravado held, but only just.

"Right," she said at last, forcing the word past the tightness in her throat. "Then we should start packing."

Chapter One

Blue stood at the foot of the bed, arms crossed as she watched Margie fold the last of her shirts. The suitcase yawned open, its hinges rusted and lid scuffed from a life lived rough. It looked like it belonged to a different world—and maybe it did.

"Blue, you need to move more quickly, please," Margie said. "Stop watching me and get busy with your own things." She flapped a hand at the pile of clean clothes she'd laid at the end of the bed. "Choose what you want to bring. It's warmer in the town, sometimes downright muggy. You'll need light shirts, trousers, maybe a dress."

Blue stared at her. "A dress? I don't own a dress."

"Then I'll buy you one at Taylor's." Margie's voice was curt enough to make Blue raise her brows. If the prospect of returning to Hemridge made Margie this uptight, Blue had a feeling that town life might prove to be worse than she imagined.

Then again, maybe Margie's mood had less to do with Hemridge itself and more to do with the woman waiting for Margie to return back home. The few times Margie had spoken of her, it had been with the tight, clipped tone of someone wary of disturbing an unhealed wound. Margie's mother was a pillar of the church, Margie had said. She had friends in high places, the kind who ran "restoration homes" for wayward youth. She believed there was only one right way to be and that those who didn't see things her way were afflicted with sickness and wickedness, stained by a shame that had to be scrubbed clean.

Margie had clawed her way free of all that once.

Now she was marching back into it—and Blue was going with her.

"Do I really have to call your mother *Grandmother*?" she asked.

"For appearance's sake, yes." Margie said. "If I'm your mother, which is what everyone believes, then she's your grandmother."

"Only she's not."

"Yes, Blue, I know that," Margie snapped.

"Sheesh," Blue said. "No reason to bark."

Margie sighed and bowed her head. When she lifted it, she looked hard at Blue and said, "I'm sorry. I'm in a foul temper. But Blue, please, don't fight me on the little things. We need to show a united front, and that means doing what I say."

Wordlessly, Blue grabbed a pair of overalls and tossed them over to Margie. She wasn't in the best of moods herself. Packing meant leaving the mountain and the trees and the sky that had always made room for her. The fae had always thrived in the wilderness. They weren't made for neighbors and streets and spires.

"If she's supposed to be my grandmother, maybe she should've acted like one," she muttered.

"My mother only plays by her own rules."

"Why has she never visited?"

"She did. Once. You were very little."

"What—she didn't like what she saw?"

"She didn't like mountain life. Said only a fool would settle down this far out." Margie's mouth pinched. "She never forgave me for leaving Hemridge."

"But 'Hemridge is a den of hypocrisy,'" Blue countered, throwing Margie's words back at her.

Margie snorted. "It is. Or was. Or at least that's how I've always thought of it. But mortals like my mother have lived by the same rules for so long, they've forgotten how to question them."

"Then we should remind them."

"Absolutely not."

"If we keep quiet, then we're hypocrites, too."

Margie pinched the bridge of her nose. "Oh, for heaven's sake." She shut the suitcase and regarded Blue in a way that made her itchy.

"What?" she demanded.

"You can't do magic in town. Not ever."

"Gee, really?"

"Mortals don't trust magic, and they fear fae who can wield it."

Blue's stomach turned. "They think we're wicked. That I'm wicked."

"That's not what I said."

"It's what you meant. I know how hated the fae are."

Margie's frustration crumpled into something smaller. Wearier. "No, Blue, you don't. Not really."

At this, Blue faltered. She'd heard stories, of course,

reports that had cut through the static of Margie's radio before Margie had rushed to turn it off.

The fae woman found floating in a millpond after stepping too close to town.

The hunter who'd come back raving after spending a night in the hills, swearing he'd been hexed. His wife had blamed the pretty fae girl down the way, and the pretty fae girl had vanished before sunrise.

The farmhouse that had burned to the ground. The fae boy who'd been doused with gasoline and set on fire, because someone, once, had seen him wandering around those parts, whistling like he hadn't a care in the world.

"You'll have to pass," Margie said quietly. "That means no trout spinning, no lamps exploding, no flying cups of milk—"

"I only did that once."

"It scared me."

"It scared me, too."

They stood in silence.

Blue reached up and traced the tip of her ear. "Mortals may be thick, but they're not blind. These will give me away."

"Not if no one sees them."

Margie crossed the room and rummaged in the linen closet, where she kept her sewing kit.

Blue stiffened. "You're not going to ask me to clip them, are you? Because I'm telling you right now—"

"Don't be silly." Margie turned around, a blue bandana in her hands—soft with age, the edges fraying. She stepped forward and folded it into a strip. "Tie it just so and it'll cover the tops of your ears. No one'll look twice."

No one would look twice. Right. Unless they did and decided to take offense at the color of her hair, the set of her jaw, or the confidence of her gait.

Blue fought not to scowl as Margie placed the bandana across her head and knotted it beneath her hair.

"It suits you," Margie said.

"Oh, well. In that case."

"You don't have to come, Blue," Margie reminded her. She put her hands on her hips. "You can stay right here at the cabin. Doesn't that sound nice?"

"It does," Blue acknowledged. "I'm coming anyway."

Margie glanced at the clock. "Well, if there's anything else you want to pack, now's the time."

The bandana pressed tight against Blue's ears. She yanked it off and stalked to her room, where she stuffed a few things into her rucksack: her soft gray blanket, a hunk of obsidian, and the silver rattle. She added her "toiletries," a la-di-da word Margie had never used before today. Already, town ways were creeping in.

She caught her reflection in the mirror. Reluctantly, she picked up Margie's bandana and tied it back in place. She made sure it covered the tips of her ears, but didn't tighten it as much as Margie had.

It wasn't hideous. The blue brought out her eyes.

She hated it just the same.

Could she still change her mind? *Should* she? Other mothers might not leave a seventeen-year-old girl to fend for herself on top of a mountain, but Margie wasn't like other mothers. And Blue wasn't like other girls. Surviving on the mountain wouldn't be an issue. Surviving on the mountain would be a breeze.

Surviving in town, beneath the grandmother's roof, sounded more like sinking slow and silent, lungs tight, waiting for the dark to finish what it had started.

But if Blue remained at the cabin, Margie would be stuck with her mother on her own, and it would be Blue's fault. Which meant she couldn't stay behind.

She sighed, knowing there was more to it than that. Securing food, water, and shelter would be simple on the mountain, yes. But the prospect of being completely alone —not just for a night but for days, maybe even weeks— unlocked a hollow place inside her where reality felt as flimsy as falling dirt.

So she'd go. Not because she had to. Not because it was noble. But because she knew what it felt like to be left behind.

She wouldn't let it happen again.

Chapter Two

A girl lived in the house next door.

Blue watched her from the grandmother's kitchen, tucked slightly behind the frothy yellow curtains that matched the yellow teapot on the stove and the woven yellow rug beneath the breakfast table.

The whole house was smothered in yellow. Blue had come to realize that she might just hate yellow. She definitely hated the grandmother, and the grandmother hated her.

"She's an ugly thing, isn't she?" the old woman had said two days ago, when Blue and Margie had shown up at the door. She'd waved them impatiently into the house and looked Blue up and down from what she called her "invalid chair." It was basically a rolling throne, this chair—an enormous iron-framed contraption with spoked wheels and carved wooden armrests.

"Maybe it's for the best, if we're going for verisimilitude," the grandmother had added, shifting her gaze to her daughter. "You're no beauty yourself, Margaret."

Margie had prepared Blue for this on the long trudging walk down the mountain. "She'll try to provoke you," she'd warned. "Making people cry is her life's greatest joy. Don't give her the satisfaction."

Her words had reached Blue, but dimly, as she had been busy saying her goodbyes. She'd promised the meadow daisies she'd see them soon. She'd assured a worried bluebird that, really, she wasn't even leaving. The mountains were forever, she'd reminded herself. They were part of Blue, and Blue was part of them. And if town life became unbearable—truly unbearable—then she'd hightail it out of there. She didn't want that to happen. She wasn't planning on letting it. But if worse came to worst, she could always change her mind and leave.

Margie had talked all the way down the road, filling the air with words about the grandmother. "There's no love lost between us, I'll tell you that. She branded me a 'sympathizer' years ago." She'd snorted. "A sympathizer, as if that's a bad thing! What's the opposite? A hater?"

"Yes," Blue had said flatly.

The word had hung there. For a moment, the trees themselves had seemed to hush.

Then Margie had drawn herself up, her voice roughening with resolve. "We're survivors. We've survived blizzards that cracked trees in half. We survived that time the pump gave out, and we hauled water by hand for six weeks. We can survive her."

When the bus had picked them up at the lonely crossroads—nothing around but gravel and silence— Margie had gone silent. The ride might've been interesting —maybe even thrilling, with its hairpin turns and sudden drops—but Blue had already decided to hate it, and she'd found plenty of evidence to back her up. The way the houses had seemed to spring up from the earth the farther they traveled. The way the air had thickened, losing the crispness of the mountains and taking on the stink of motor smoke and too many people.

Then, too soon, they'd arrived at the grandmother's yellow house, where there were too many new smells, new textures, new sheets on a new bed. There was the disorienting sensation of being *placed* somewhere, rather than choosing to be there. Blue had been uprooted once before, landing at Margie's bruised and broken. The memory had softened over the years, but this—being transplanted again—had awakened old and unsettling emotions.

Up in the mountains, there was no question of belonging. Blue fit because there was no *other* to define her against. No measuring up, no proving herself, no pretending to be something she wasn't. She was part of the woods, just like the ferns, just like the rivers.

Here, in this prissy house with its prissy yellow curtains, she most definitely didn't belong. Because she was fae and the grandmother was not, and mortals and fae had been enemies for as long as anyone could remember. It was in their blood.

Through the kitchen window, past the yellow lace, Blue stared at the girl who lived next door—the mortal girl with mortal blood. She was about Blue's age but puny, the kind of girl who'd be no good at climbing trees or swimming against the river's current. Pale curls tumbled over her face and hid her expression, which Blue guessed would be snooty or stupid or both.

Something about the girl's posture—shoulders hunched,

arms drawn close—pricked at Blue, though. It was almost as if the neighbor girl felt awkward, too. As if, like Blue, she didn't belong in this dumb town either, even though everyone around her was just like her.

Margie had once told Blue that, whether fae or mortal, people needed other people. Blue had rolled her eyes, because she had Margie and Margie had her, so that was that. But sometimes—just sometimes—Blue had felt a quiet sort of ache.

A funny, unwelcome thought slunk into her mind: She wouldn't mind a friend.

At the house next door, something was happening. The girl's mother was pushing her out the door. Down the steps. Onto the sidewalk.

The two were coming their way. *She* was coming their way, this blonde-haired girl who wasn't for Blue, no matter what strange aches stirred within her. The girl was a mortal and would no doubt find Blue repulsive.

Blue made up her mind then and there that she didn't care. That *she* found the neighbor girl repulsive, so what did it matter anyway?

Behind her, Margie and the grandmother squabbled.

"No eggs, no bacon," the grandmother said petulantly. Margie was making a grocery list, and the grandmother wanted her to cross off multiple items. "I prefer toast for breakfast. Just toast."

"Fine," said Margie. Blue heard the scratch of pen on paper. "I'll add bread for toast, which Blue and I will eat alongside our eggs and bacon."

"You'll get fat, Margaret."

"Yes, Mother. Noted."

"'Noted'? What is that supposed to mean?"

"It means, 'Yes, I heard you. I'm going to get fat.'"

"How nice for you, not to care. You'll never get a husband, not if you're fat."

"Noted," Margie said.

The girl and her mother were halfway up the driveway now. Blue's stomach twisted, resentment pressing down on the softer thing beneath.

"You have visitors," she informed the grandmother.

"I most certainly do not," the grandmother replied. "My neighbors have enough sense to leave me alone."

"It's a woman and a girl. They're from the house next door."

"*Oh*," the grandmother said in a knowing voice. "Well. That changes things."

"How?"

The grandmother studied Blue, eyes sharp. "The inhabitants of Hemridge won't know what to make of you, will they?"

Blue knew what the grandmother was doing—baiting her, toying with her—but it didn't stop the sick feeling from spreading in her gut.

Margie joined Blue at the kitchen window and pushed aside the yellow curtains. "*Mother*," she said. "You have *got* to be kidding."

The old woman set her hands on the wheels of her invalid chair and shoved, inching toward the front of the house. She carried a bell within a hand-sewn pouch fastened to the chair's armrest, a small metal bell with a wooden handle that she rang anytime she wanted something. It chimed as her chair bumped over the uneven floor.

"Why didn't you tell me?" Margie demanded.

"You didn't ask," the grandmother replied.

The doorbell rang.

"Quick, Blue, your bandana," Margie said.

Blue grabbed it from the counter and tied it in place.

The grandmother smiled her sweetest smile. "What a lovely surprise," she called as she rolled toward the entryway. "Margaret? Blue? Do come meet our guests!"

Blue dragged her feet.

The grandmother prodded her forward. "Go on. Tell them your name."

"I'm Blue," she said flatly.

The neighbor girl didn't reply, and Blue almost snorted. What was this, some weird custom where mortals just stared at you, silently judging?

The girl's mother jabbed her. The girl jumped.

"Oh! I'm Evie," she said. Her wide eyes skated over Blue's bandana, then down the length of her, landing on her bare feet. She clasped her hands behind her and took a dainty step back.

Heat bloomed in Blue's chest. She wasn't *surprised* that this was how it was going to be, that one quick assessment was all it took for Evie to reject her. It stung nonetheless.

"Noted," Blue said and turned away.

Chapter Three

Other than her dog, Windsor, Evie had exactly zero friends.

And Windsor was dead. Evie's sole friend was her dead dog.

She used to have her brother, Jax. Jax wasn't dead, but he and Evie were no longer close the way they used to be.

Jax would say they'd grown apart because he'd grown up, but for heaven's sake, he was nineteen, not ninety. He continued to fart at the dinner table, the Brylcreem he'd started using made him look shiny, not suave, and he still crowed when he thrashed her at checkers—though he only bothered to play her when there was no one else around.

He hadn't grown up. He'd just grown away.

A year ago, he'd been short and chubby, his eyes hidden behind thick glasses. Then, practically overnight, the glasses had disappeared, the baby fat had melted, and he'd shot up four inches. He'd started doing pull-ups in doorways and shoveling down eggs like his life depended on it. Then Silas Bratton had taken Jax under his wing, and that was it. Jax had swapped sneakers for boots, jokes for scowls, and his normal voice for a new one that mainly grunted.

"We used to make fun of Silas," Evie had reminded him last week as Jax had laced his boots before heading to Silas's yet again.

"Yep," Jax had acknowledged.

"You called him a cap-gun cowboy."

Jax had grunted and grabbed his rifle.

"Can I at least come with you?" she'd asked, desperate for the company, even if it meant watching Jax and Silas plink tin cans off a fence post.

"Are you kidding?" Jax had said. "No way. Old Man Bratton's house is no place for a girl."

"Oh, please."

"He's almost always drunk, and when he's drunk, he goes on these . . . tirades. You wouldn't like it."

"Why, because I'm a *girl*?"

Jax hadn't answered. He hadn't needed to.

Lately, everything came down to the fact that she was a girl, and girls didn't get to go where boys went. Didn't get to know what boys knew. Girls were instructed to sit up straight and keep their dresses clean and make small talk with "proper young ladies" like Trink and Cookie, who passed around lipstick samples and whispered about which boys they wanted to marry.

Nope, thought Evie, stealing a line from Jax's new vocabulary.

Which left her on her own. Miserable. Only instead of letting her be miserable in peace, her mother had dragged her to the house next door to meet cranky Mrs. Freeman's mountain relatives.

Evie and her mother perched on a stiff yellow sofa, facing Mrs. Freeman's daughter and granddaughter, who sat on an identical yellow sofa. Mrs. Freeman, in her hulking invalid chair, commanded the head of the space, her chair groaning as she inched the wheels forward and back.

The invalid chair made Evie nervous. So did Mrs. Freeman.

She stole a glance at the granddaughter, who had a narrow face, spiky energy, and straight black hair tied back with a blue bandana. When the granddaughter caught Evie looking at her, she bulged her eyes as if to say, *Yeah? And?*

Evie quickly looked away.

From her quick appraisal, she'd seen that the girl was roughly her age, though she had the kind of curves that made Evie painfully aware of her own flat chest. Not that Blue seemed to care. Blue wore loose, boyish clothes and didn't carry herself like someone trying to be looked at.

The only other thing Evie knew about Blue was that she—and her mother—weren't very conventional. Blue's name alone told Evie that much.

"*Blue*?" Evie had repeated when her mother had told her earlier that morning. She'd been slouching against the bathroom door, watching her mother paint her face.

"I'm sure Margie took pleasure in picking the most outlandish name she could," her mother had replied, flicking mascara onto her lashes. "She always fancied herself too good for the rest of us. That attitude certainly came back to bite her."

"How?"

"There was . . . an incident. In Rosmond, where Margie went to college. It's not a story I care to repeat, but let's just say I'd rather be a realist with a clean conscience than an idealist with blood on my hands." She'd applied a pale pink lipstick, pressed her lips together, and checked for smudges. "Afterward, Margie ran off to the mountains, declaring herself done with humanity. Next thing we knew, she'd had a baby, and to this day, no one knows who the father is."

Now, in the stale air of their neighbor's living room, Evie's mother spoke out in a voice that made Evie cringe.

"The mountain air certainly agrees with you, Margie," she said. "And just look how tan you are!"

What she really meant, Evie knew, was, *Gracious, she looks like she's been working in a field.*

"How was the trip down the mountain?" Evie's mom continued. "You look exhausted."

"*Mom*," Evie said under her breath.

Her mother feigned embarrassment, pressing her fingers to her breastbone. "Goodness, how rude! Margie, I apologize. I simply wasn't thinking." She lowered her voice conspiratorially. "When people tell me I look tired, I always want to say, 'Yes, thank you, I am well aware!'"

Evie wanted to die.

Her mother laughed. "But don't you worry. You'll be back to yourself in no time."

"Oh, I think I'm still me," Margie said, pleasantly enough.

Blue, however, gazed at Evie's mother murderously, which seemed to amuse Mrs. Fairchild. She cackled and rocked back and forth in her steel chair.

"Now, Margie, I know you fancy yourself a simple country girl, but town life does have its perks," her mother pressed on. "Taylor's carries beauty creams now, and there's one that works wonders on sunspots. Porcelana

Whitening Cream, it's called. I bet it would brighten you right up."

"And if she doesn't want to be brightened up?" Blue asked. Her voice was low and raspy.

"Blue, please," said Margie.

"Growing older shouldn't mean giving up," Evie's mother declared. "With a little effort, any woman can make the most of what she's got."

Mrs. Freeman cackled again.

"I exercise, I eat well, and yes, I take care of my skin," Evie's mother said, just a touch too defensive. "I consider it an investment."

"As you should," Mrs. Freeman said. "What happens to a woman who loses her looks? Nothing, that's what. Not a blessed thing."

Blue touched her mother's arm. "Margie, can I go to my room?"

"What? Oh. Yes, of course," Margie said. "Take Evie with you, why don't you?"

Blue stood and turned to Evie. "Evie," she said with terrifying politeness, "would you like to come to my room?"

Evie drew into herself. Blue radiated nothing but hostility, and it wasn't like she was pretty enough to get away with it. Her face was too narrow, her features too sharp.

Her eyes, though. She had the most extraordinary eyes Evie had ever seen. A clear, brilliant blue, like rain on a sunny day.

"I . . . ah . . ." Evie tried to speak, but her mouth had gone dry.

"For heaven's sake, just go," her mother hissed.

Everyone was staring. Everyone but Blue, who was already taking the stairs two by two.

Evie forced her feet to move, the carpet swallowing the drag of her worn lace-ups.

Chapter Four

Up in her second-story room, Blue took Evie in properly. She was slight and skittish, with pale curls, awkward arms, and no figure to speak of. She wouldn't last a day in the wild. She'd be eaten alive.

"Were you named after your eyes?" Evie blurted when the silence between them evidently became too much for her to bear.

Blue looked at her askance. "Was I named after my *eyes*?"

Evie blushed.

"Were you named after yours?" Blue asked.

"My eyes are brown."

Blue waited.

"And...my name is Evie."

"Oh, that's right," Blue said blandly, as if the introduction downstairs had been so unremarkable she'd simply forgotten. "Sorry."

Evie blushed and crossed the room, staring out the window with her arms folded tight.

Blue felt a stab of guilt, which made her irritable. How was she supposed to have answered Evie's question?

Should she have explained that she'd been abandoned on Margie's porch, a note pinned to her blanket? *Her name is Blue, and she is precious beyond measure,* the note had read. *Please take care of her.*

Blue dropped onto the floor beside the bed and leaned back against the frilly pink coverlet. While the kitchen was an explosion of yellow, her room was an overload of pink: pink curtains, pink decorative pillows, even a pink lace doily draped over the dresser like a veil.

At the cabin, Blue's quilt was patched by hand and smelled faintly of woodsmoke. It wasn't fancy, but it was warm. And there wasn't a doily in sight.

"I just meant that your eyes are striking," Evie said from the window. Her voice was cool, which Blue deserved.

"Thanks," Blue replied in an equally frigid tone. She hated the awkwardness that hung heavily over the room. She hated how out of place she felt in this frilly house, and she hated that she cared. Most of all, she hated the mortals who made it so that she had to care. Well, all but Margie.

Evie, though? Blue loathed Evie with her stupid remarks about her "striking" eyes. So why was Blue's body sending her signals that suggested something else?

Evie turned from the window and returned to where Blue was, lowering herself carefully onto the foot of Blue's bed. The mattress hardly moved, that's how controlled her movements were. "Why do you call your mom Margie?" she asked.

"Because that's her name."

"Sure. But most kids call their mom *Mom.*"

A memory flickered in Blue's brain. Not Mom, but something similar. *Mum? Mam?* It slipped away before she could catch hold of it.

"Not me," she said.

Evie looked perplexed, and Blue could tell she didn't understand. But she smoothed her features and said, "Right. Okay."

She was trying, Blue could tell. It was annoying.

"Have you lived in Hemridge your whole life?" Blue asked, because she, too, could try. She might not enjoy it, but she could do it. She cut Evie a quick glance.

"Mmm-hmm," Evie said. "There's me, my brother Jax, and my dad, but he's out of town." What sounded like pride crept into her voice. "A machine broke at another paper mill, and they needed my dad to install the new one."

A paper mill. Blue knew about paper mills. And textile mills. And matchstick factories, where girls spooned phosphorus into tiny boxes and prayed their teeth wouldn't rot away. Places like that had driven a wedge between the fae and the mortals long ago.

"We're the same species. We share the same history," Margie had said. "But somewhere along the way, mortals chose a different path."

While the mortals went off and built things, the fae stayed close to the old ways. They listened to the hush of the forest, watched the stars for signs, read meaning in bone and flame and seed. Their magic was in the soil, in the rhythm of the land, in the knowing.

Mortals preferred hammers to hush. They had laid roads across roots, run wires through branches, carved the land to fit their hands. And slowly, they'd stopped believing in magic. And soon after, magic had stopped believing in them.

For a time, it hadn't mattered. Mortal and fae had coexisted, wary but willing.

Then a strange and bitter season had fallen across the land—too little rain, too many mouths. Crops had withered in the fields. Livestock had given birth to still things. In the villages, infants had sickened without reason. One by one, the cradles in the homes of mortals had fallen silent.

In the hollows and glens where the fae kept to the old ways, however, the gardens had grown, and the babies had lived.

The mortals had noticed—and grown angry. Afraid. Whispers had turned to suspicion. Suspicion had soured to blame. *They hoarded the luck,* the mortals had said. *They stole the blessings meant for us.*

It hadn't mattered that none of it was true.

"Mortals and fae are the same where it counts," Margie had explained. "The way we love. The way we grieve. The way we long for things we've lost." Her gaze had gone distant, and she'd seemed not just defeated but heartbroken. That had been the only word Blue could put to it.

Then Margie had blinked, cleared her throat. "But fear is a disease. It turns neighbors into strangers. And mortals? They're riddled with it."

Blue looked at Evie.

Riddled with disease.

"A paper mill, huh?" she said. "What do they make?"

"Well, paper."

Blue raised an eyebrow. "Just *paper*? Nothing specific?"

"They make whatever they're contracted to make."

"Like what? Calendars? Playing cards?"

"It depends. First, they make pulp into paper. After that, the paper can be made into all sorts of things."

"'All sorts of things,'" Blue repeated. "How about cigarette papers? Does your father make those?"

Evie frowned. "My dad's an engineer."

"So he runs the machines that make the cigarette papers, which folks roll their tobacco in, which poisons the air once they light up and start smoking."

Evie chose not to respond, because she knew Blue was correct. At least, that's how Blue interpreted it. The look in Evie's eyes, however, could have curdled mayonnaise.

"You do know that animals breathe in that poison, too?" Blue continued.

"It's not just cigarette paper," Evie said. "Most of what's made at the mill is turned into Bibles and toilet rolls, so unless you plan to recite the Bible from heart and wipe with leaves and moss, maybe get off your high horse?"

I'm fine wiping with moss, Blue thought, though her heart was beating fast and once again she felt hot all over. *And the last thing I need is a rulebook filled with "shalls" and "shalt nots."*

A chime interrupted them—the grandmother's bell ringing from downstairs. *Ting-ting-ting! Tingtingtingtingting!*

Blue stood. "I have to go. I'm being summoned."

"Summoned?"

"The grandmother has a bell. She rings it like she's calling down the wrath of God."

As if to prove her point, another round of bellfire pierced the air.

"Coming!" Blue called.

At the bottom of the stairs, the grandmother sat hunched in her wheeled chair, half lost in shadow. When she spotted Blue, she seized the bell and rang it with fresh fury.

Blue stood where she was, one hand on the banister.

Evie slipped by and darted down the stairs, her shoulder barely brushing Blue's as she passed. She said nothing, but Blue caught the twitch of her lips—possibly sympathy, but more likely relief at being able to escape.

Chapter Five

Blue couldn't sleep.

The mattress was too soft. The pillow was too hard. The sheets were absurdly smooth, as if they'd been boiled and ironed into submission. Blue kicked them off in a fit of annoyance.

She flipped onto her side. Onto her stomach. Onto her back. She stared at the ceiling, which had been nubbly in the daylight but developed craters in the dark.

She missed her bed, her pillow, her familiar scratchy sheets.

She missed the cabin's beamed ceiling, the window she could crack open to hear the night's hush. She missed the stars. Where were the stars?

She sighed and rolled onto her side, hitching her knees up and tucking both hands beneath her cheek. Nope, still no good.

Maybe the town air was keeping her awake. She pictured the paper mill, its giant chimneys puffing out clouds of dust. Maybe microscopic scraps of toilet paper and Bible pages were drifting through the night, clogging her lungs, clinging to the walls of her throat. Maybe that was why she felt off, like her body was rejecting this entire place.

She rubbed her arms. What she needed was her soft gray blanket. Except—she'd left it downstairs.

Blue bolted upright—what if the grandmother came across it? That mean old biddy would toss it out without blinking.

After dinner, she'd called Blue over and *smelled* her, insisting there was a new and unpleasant odor in the house.

"Mother!" Margie had exclaimed, yanking Blue away from the old woman's grasping hands. "Blue is cleaner than you are. She swims in the river every day."

"You allow the girl to swim in the river? It's a wonder she hasn't drowned!"

"The current is only dangerous along Graveyard Fields. Blue knows better than to swim there. And do you think you could call her by her name?"

The grandmother had harrumphed. "It's not coming from her. The smell. At least not directly." She'd flapped a hand at Blue. "Go get your things. Collect them and bring them here."

"Blue, don't," Margie had said tensely.

But Blue had, wanting to prove the old lady wrong. She'd marched upstairs, gathered her things, and placed each item in front of the unyielding grandmother, who'd been forced to admit that neither Blue nor her belongings had been the source of the smell.

In the end, it had been Blue who'd stridden across the dining room, pulled the heirloom sideboard away from the wall, and fished out the pitiful corpse of a mouse, holding it by the tip of its tail.

It had been at least three days gone and stunk to high heaven. The summer heat had cooked it where it sat.

"Don't just stand there!" the grandmother had barked. "Take it out back!"

When Blue had returned from the garbage pail by the woodshed, Margie and the grandmother had been in the middle of a fresh bicker. Blue had slipped upstairs before they'd spotted her, leaving her belongings behind in her haste.

She needed to reclaim them, especially her blanket.

She swung lightly out of bed, crept down the hall, and started down the stairs. Before she reached the bottom, voices stopped her—words not intended for her ears.

"The girl has no place here," the grandmother said. "She's not one of us, Margaret."

"You asked me to come, and I came," Margie said. "I told you Blue would be with me."

The grandmother huffed. "Did you see her with that thing? Just picked it up like it was nothing! One rat sniffing out another, I suppose."

"Mother," Margie said, "you smelled the mouse first."

"Dirty, dirty girl. And to have her in my house—"

"A house *you* allowed to become overrun with vermin. Blue didn't bring the mouse in."

"You could have had a child of your own!" the grandmother burst out. "A real child!"

Blue went rigid.

"Oh, Margaret," the grandmother went on, her thin voice trembling. "Things could have been so different."

Margie answered with a long sigh. "You can't change the past, Mother. No matter how much you wish you could."

Blue turned and dashed upstairs, throwing herself onto her bed and burying her face in her pillow. Muffled sobs tore out of her like baby bats, blind and panicked. They slashed her with tiny teeth. They stole her breath with flapping wings.

She hated the grandmother.

She hated Margie for coming here to take care of the grandmother, and for forcing Blue to come, too. Not that Margie had. She hadn't. But still.

Most of all, Blue hated herself for . . .well, for all of it, she supposed. If Blue weren't here—if Margie hadn't found her, kept her, raised her—none of this would be happening.

There would be no tight smiles over cold tea. No grandmother's eyes, sharp as pins, measuring every inch of Blue like she was assessing something foul. No cloying sweetness hiding barbs, no prayers muttered under breaths, no talk of *trials* and *unnaturalness* disguised as concern for Margie's well-being.

Without Blue, there would be no need for pretending. No need for Margie to lie.

And without Blue, there would be no need to fear what would happen if Margie's lie cracked open—and that fear was well founded. The grandmother was the only townsperson who knew Blue was fae, and yet the grandmother filled the house with hatred so toxic it made Blue's eyes water. If one old woman could ooze such malice, what would it be like if everyone knew?

The thought hollowed Blue out, and a fresh round of sobs shook her body. Her pillowcase clung to her cheek, sticky and mean.

She hadn't *asked* to be fae. She hadn't *asked* for ears that needed hiding or magic that needed binding. But that didn't matter, because the truth of it was that her existence made things complicated. Her truth, if spoken aloud, would make things impossible.

She didn't want Margie to twist herself into knots just to make room for Blue.

She didn't want knots at all.

She wanted . . .what did she want?

She just . . . if only . . .

Sleep took her before she could solve the riddle, and a nightmare dragged her to a dark place behind locked doors. The grandmother, on the other side, hissed, "Stay where you belong, girl."

Chapter Six

The following morning, Blue sipped at her orange juice more from habit than thirst. She hadn't slept much and felt soft in the middle, like a plum that had dropped from the tree and landed hard.

"What's going on with you and the woman next door?" Blue asked, eyes fixed on Margie. The grandmother sat silent in her wheeled chair. Blue didn't so much as glance her way. "The way she looked at you yesterday? It was like she wanted to spit nails."

"I'm sure she didn't," Margie said. The circles under her eyes suggested she hadn't slept much, either. "That's just how Nicole is."

"So Nicole's a dried-up, spiteful prune. Got it."

"Her *name* is Mrs. Carpenter, and she's a fine piano teacher. Gives lessons to all the neighborhood children," the grandmother interjected.

Blue could only imagine how fun that must be, sitting on a hard bench next to Evie's mother and a metronome. She rolled her eyes.

The grandmother rapped her bony knuckles on the table, making the dishes jump. "Up in the mountains, Margaret may have let you do as you pleased. But you live in town now, so don't you sass me, girl."

"How did I sass you? I didn't say a word!"

"Well, Blue, you just did, didn't you?" Margie set a platter of eggs and bacon on the table, then squeezed Blue's shoulder—a wordless plea for peace. "Don't be impertinent to your grandmother."

"She's not my grandmother," Blue said, just as the grandmother sniffed and said, "I am *not* that girl's kin!"

Blue turned her gaze to the grandmother. *I have wiped your bottom, old lady,* she thought. *You are wrinkled and withered and weak—and still you think you're better than me?*

"Pass the preserves," the grandmother commanded. When Blue didn't jump to do her bidding, she snapped her fingers. "Not tomorrow. Now."

Blue waited for Margie to speak up and scold the grandmother the way she'd just scolded Blue, but Margie only reached across the table, took the jar, and set it in front of her mother herself.

"Wait," Blue said. "I have to mind my manners, but she" —she jerked her head at the grandmother—"can call me 'girl' and snap her fingers at me like I'm a dog?"

"I'll talk to you however I please," the grandmother pronounced while spreading a meager layer of preserves onto a piece of toast. A strawberry plopped onto the bread, glossy and red. She flicked it off with the tip of her knife. "You may be under the misapprehension that the rules of society don't apply to you, but you're still under a mortal's roof. *My* roof."

Blue turned to Margie, her mouth falling open.

"My mother has been very generous over the years," Margie said wearily. "She's given us a lot of financial support."

"She's paid for the right to insult me? That's what you're saying?"

"We're guests in her home, Blue."

"We're here as a favor! She begged you to come!"

Margie held up a hand. "Her house, her rules. Discussion over."

The grandmother looked smug as she took a bite of toast, chewing for an inordinate amount of time before patting her mouth with her napkin.

She pinned Blue with her birdseed eyes. "You asked about Nicole Carpenter. Her husband was Margie's childhood friend. He was sweet on her. Wanted to marry her. Margie broke his heart when she left for college and then stayed on for that teaching job out in Rosmond."

"What teaching job?"

"I taught at the college," Margie said. "Botany. I loved it."

"That wasn't all you loved," the grandmother said dryly.

Blue glanced back and forth between them. "What else?"

"Not what," the grandmother said. "Who."

"A boy?"

"A girl," the grandmother said, drawing back like the word tasted foul.

Margie didn't answer right away. She only cupped her hands around her coffee mug, as if the heat might steady her. "Layla," she finally said.

Blue frowned. She'd never heard Margie speak of any "Layla."

"Layla was bog-bred, just like you," the grandmother

said.

"Fae," Margie said tightly.

"She didn't belong in Rosmond," the grandmother pushed on. "The *fae* had their own dirt to squat on."

Margie closed her eyes.

"But Margie kept her little fae girl tucked away. Hid her from all those prying eyes."

Blue turned to Margie, bewildered.

"Oh my. Did you not know?" the grandmother said. "My Margie was a blood traitor long before she brought you in out of the cold."

"Mother, that's enough."

"A mortal who shares a bed with a faerie isn't just shameful. It's betrayal, plain and simple. Margie betrayed her own kind without a thought for the possible repercussions."

"*Mother.*"

"Of course, Margie herself was betrayed in the end. Layla turned on her. Threw Margie to the wolves to save her own skin."

Margie pushed back from the table. "Mother, you are a cruel woman," she said, striding from the room.

Blue's heart thumped fast, but she had to know. "What happened?" she asked, once Margie's footsteps faded.

"She was picked up in town," the grandmother said. "Layla. She'd ventured out for a walk, thinking herself safe since it was past sundown. But someone spotted her, and she was brought in and questioned by the Virtue Board."

Blue said nothing, barely breathing.

"She cracked, of course. The Board promised her mercy in exchange for truth, and so she pointed them straight to my Margie."

Blue pictured it—the knock at the door, the quiet horror of Margie's neighbors, grim and self-righteous, stepping over the threshold with folded arms and tight mouths.

"'That's her,'" the grandmother said, mimicking a sweet, false voice. "'She's the one.'"

"What did they do to her?"

"Layla? For heaven's sake, girl. I don't know and I don't care. They let her *live*, I suppose."

"No, I meant Margie. What did the Virtue Board do to Margie?"

The grandmother sniffed. "Oh, nothing so dramatic. They ruined her, is all. Stripped her title. Drove her from the college and made sure no one in polite society would so much as spit in her direction. Margie could have fought back, mind you. She could have stood in front of the elders and confessed her wrongdoing."

The grandmother's eyes took on a faraway look. "Things would have blown over eventually, if she'd owned up to her sins. But Margie ran instead. She fled to the top of that godforsaken mountain and left her own mother behind."

The grandmother lifted her toast, then put it back down. She pursed her lips. "Abe helped her build that cabin of hers. Spent hours hammering and sawing while Nicole stayed in town, pregnant with their girl."

She turned her attention to Blue, and the mist of memories lifted from her gaze. "That's why Nicole and Margie aren't friendly, since you asked."

Blue frowned. Somewhere in the grandmother's story, there was a warning. Blue saw it in the hard cast of the old lady's features. But of what?

"What do you think of the daughter?" the grandmother inquired. She took a sip of coffee and kept her eyes on Blue.

"Evie? Nothing."

"You didn't like her?"

"Not much to like. She and her mother both talk too much and act like they're better than everyone else."

The grandmother lowered her mug. Her elbow knocked against her wheelchair, and the bell in her side bag gave a faint chime.

"Well, what do you know," she said. "Seems we've got something in common after all."

Chapter Seven

When Blue had told the grandmother she didn't like Evie, it hadn't been a lie. All those pale curls, those big brown eyes always ready to water—like a puppy worried it was going to be kicked. No, thank you.

She liked Evie's mother even less. Who was Nicole Carpenter to pass judgment on Margie? Of course Nicole's husband had once wanted to marry Margie. Any fool would've. And so what if her husband had helped Margie build her cabin, leaving Nicole alone in town with her big pregnant belly?

Blue had lived through worse. She'd been four when someone had left her on Margie's porch, a mute and terrified child with her name pinned to the blanket draped around her. Did anyone hear her complaining?

Blue didn't like thinking about Nicole Carpenter's gussied up hurts, and she certainly didn't enjoy dwelling on her own painful past. So she thought about Evie instead. Spied on her, if truth be told.

For days now, Blue had watched Evie from her upstairs window. She knew Evie's morning routine by heart. A little before nine, which was when her mother's first piano student arrived, Evie slipped out the side door. Always careful, always quiet. She cracked it just wide enough to slide through sideways, clutching a book in one hand and a metal pitcher in the other. There was something furtive in the way she moved, like she knew she wasn't supposed to be doing whatever she was about to do.

Blue found her behavior interesting, despite herself.

Once outside, Evie walked over to a wooden fort in the corner of the yard, something her father had probably built years ago when Evie had been little. It was constructed from rough planks and had two levels, with a rope swing on one side and a ladder on the other.

First, Evie tossed her book onto the upper level of the fort. Then she moved on to the next step in her ritual: pouring birdseed from the pitcher into the hanging feeder. Sometimes she brought scraps from the kitchen, too— crusts of bread, leftover pancakes. Those she put out for the squirrels on a flat board nailed to a post.

Then she climbed onto the raised fort and stayed there, not going back inside her house for hours.

Other kids went into Evie's house. Lots. They filed in one by one, half-hour shifts of off-key piano playing that filled the neighborhood with discordant noise.

Blue didn't blame Evie for wanting to stay away, but why did she hide out in that silly fort rather than go somewhere else? There were plenty of kids in town—three on the grandmother's street alone. Two houses down lived Trink, who was seventeen like Evie, and her sister Bronwyn, who was one year older. Their place was always full in the summertime, with girls in gingham frocks with bouncy ponytails coming and going, vanishing inside for hours and reappearing with flushed cheeks and bright eyes.

Why didn't Evie join them?

If Blue had wanted to—which she didn't—she supposed she could knock on Trink and Bronwyn's door and be let in, handed a glass of sweet tea, and ushered into the parlor like she belonged there. But the thought of sitting in a room full of girls, trying to catch up on their stories and laughter, made her feel tired before she'd even begun.

Anyway, Blue had her own routine. Once she was done watching Evie, Blue slipped out the grandmother's back door, crossed the yard, and hopped the split-rail fence at the edge of the property. From there, she vanished into the trees, where she could do as she pleased and no one expected anything from her at all.

Once, on a narrow trail that led to one of her favorite waterfalls, she'd rounded a bend and come face-to-face with Evie's brother, Jax. He was older—nineteen, Blue'd heard the grandmother say—with a lean, loose-limbed build and a masculine energy that unsettled her.

Blue had stopped short, instincts flaring.

Jax hadn't done anything at all. He'd just kept walking, like the path belonged to him. "Hey," he'd said, easy as anything.

"Hey," she'd replied, voice even. No big deal. Still, her hand had drifted up to her bandana, checking that the fabric had been snug over the points of her ears.

Now, in the bedroom at the back of the grandmother's house, Blue checked the clock that sat on the chest of drawers. It was two minutes before nine, which meant Evie should be outside.

Where the heck was Evie?

Ah. *There,* slipping outside at last, book in one hand, pitcher in the other. She wore a pale cotton dress, the hem brushing her calves, and white socks that she'd rolled neatly above her Mary Janes. She scattered birdseed into the feeder, then laid what looked like leftover dinner rolls on the squirrel plank.

That was it. Blue couldn't take it anymore.

She jogged downstairs, fetched a tin of roasted walnuts from the pantry, and hopped the fence into Evie's backyard.

"You're doing it wrong," she announced.

Evie startled, and the pitcher jerked in her hands.

Blue gestured at the feeder. "Those rolls. They're for the squirrels?"

Evie nodded.

"Squirrels don't like bread. They'll play with it, but they won't eat it."

Evie looked at Blue as if she was an idiot, or that's how Blue read it, anyway. "It's always gone the next day," she pointed out. "I'm pretty sure they do."

"Just because it's gone doesn't mean the squirrels ate it."

"Well, *I'm* not sneaking out for the joy of day-old rolls. Are you?"

Blue opened the tin of nuts and scattered a handful onto the feeder. "Squirrels like nuts. Acorns, too." She pressed the lid back into place and handed the container to Evie. "Here. For next time."

Evie accepted the container hesitantly. "Thanks," she said, like she half meant it at best. She glanced at the feeder. "If the squirrels don't eat the bread, who does?"

"Oh. Bears, probably."

"*Bears?*"

Blue gestured at the mountains. "This is their home."

Evie gestured at the space around her. "This is my backyard."

"Which you oh-so-kindly keep luring them to visit. Bears love day-old rolls."

Evie paled.

What a baby.

"Bears only mess with people if people mess with them," Blue said. "Don't try to pet one, and you'll be fine."

A squirrel leapt from a tree branch to the squirrel feeder, grabbing a nut with its little paws and nibbling at it happily. A second squirrel joined the first. There was a bit of angry chitting and the swishing of tails—big, white fluffy tails—but the two worked it out and settled down.

"They do like the nuts," Evie said.

"Told you."

She watched them for a bit, her lips curving into a smile. "They're so pretty. Don't you think?"

Blue shrugged. She liked squirrels just fine.

"In other places, squirrels are brown," Evie said. "Brown and sometimes grey. Did you know that?"

Blue gave the squirrels on the feeder a second look. They were as white as snow, just like every other squirrel Blue had ever seen. White fur, white tails, and inquisitive brown eyes. So what was Evie talking about? Was she making a joke at Blue's expense, a jab to see how gullible Margie's unschooled hillbilly daughter was?

"No, really," Evie said. "Hemridge is the only place in the world with white squirrels." She tipped her head from side to side. "Well, maybe Brevard and Rosmond too. I doubt squirrels care much about county lines."

"Neither do I," Blue said under her breath.

"What's that?"

"Hmm?"

"I missed what you said. I didn't hear you."

Blue jerked her chin at the two squirrels on the feeder and said, more combatively than she intended, "Do you have more squirrel wisdom to share, or can we move on?"

Evie's eyes widened, then narrowed. "You brought up the squirrels. Not me."

Blue felt her cheeks go warm.

"Seeing a white squirrel is *supposed* to bring good luck." Evie tapped her lower lip. "But you know what? I'm not convinced."

And with that, she spun on her heel and strode away.

Chapter Eight

Blue bowed her head and cursed her awkwardness. Her inability to interact even somewhat normally with a girl her own age. *She* was the one doing it wrong, not Evie, and she wasn't talking about the care and feeding of squirrels, either. Blue, it seemed, was doomed to do everything wrong, always.

Evie was halfway to that silly, childish fort she still hid out in. Blue jogged to catch up with her.

"About Margie," she said, because this was what she'd really come outside to talk to Evie about. She'd given it some thought and had settled on an explanation that felt plausible. "Yes, she's my mother, but she wants us to be equals. That's why I call her by her first name."

Evie paused, her foot on the bottom rung of the fort's ladder. "How can you be equals when she's the parent?"

"What do you mean?"

"She's the mom. You're the kid."

"I'm seventeen."

"Okay, but to her, you're still the kid. She's still in charge, right?"

"No. Maybe. Margie asks me to help out, and I do." Blue

made a *pff* sound. "The grandmother, on the other hand, bosses both of us around."

"I can see her doing that. She's..." Evie's brow furrowed, as if she was searching for a polite way to say something which was surely impolite.

"A witch," Blue said for her. "I despise her."

"Is that why you call her 'the grandmother' instead of 'Grandmom'?" She climbed to the raised floor of the fort and dropped into a sitting position, twisting so that she could talk to Blue face to face.

Blue barked a laugh. "I'd rather eat my own foot than call that woman 'Grandmom.'"

A ghost of a smile crossed Evie's face.

Blue hoped that meant she was moving back into Evie's good graces. She nodded at the fort and said, "You spend a lot of time up there. I guess you like being outside?"

"Usually, I'd go to the library—it's cooler in there—but they're shut for the summer."

Blue squinted. "Y'all don't have a fan?"

"We do."

"Then—"

"My mother teaches piano lessons. I can come in for lunch, but I'm meant to stay out the rest of the day till supper."

Blue gestured with her hand. "So you sit up there the whole time? Don't you get bored?"

"Not really."

"What if you get hungry?"

"No snacks between meals."

"What if you get hurt? Can you go inside then?"

"Only if there's a cup of blood or more."

"You're kidding."

Evie's expression said she wasn't.

"A cup of blood," Blue marveled. "How would that even work? Are you supposed to carry a measuring cup wherever you go?"

Evie shrugged.

"What if you have to use the toilet?"

"I hold it."

Blue let out a whistle. "So you hide out here and read all day. Sheesh."

"It's not *that* bad," Evie retorted.

Blue thought it was, especially the hiding bit. She scratched the back of her neck, working her fingers up under the knot of her bandana, hiding them as Margie had insisted. Hide, hide, hide. Always hiding.

After hearing the grandmother's story about Margie and Layla, Blue had gone straight to Margie, pressing for answers. She had expected anger, maybe sorrow. What she'd gotten was silence, and then, "Layla clipped her ears. Tried to pass."

The words had made Blue reel. *Clipped* her ears. Not covered them. Not tucked them beneath scarves or bandanas. No, she'd cut them. Shortened them. Made parts of her own body disappear.

Blue had pictured it: the clumsy blades, shallow breath, blood running thin as sap. All in the hope that glances would slide past instead of sticking. All to move through mortal spaces without turning heads or drawing whispers.

But it hadn't been enough. Someone at the college had found out. There were always watchers. People who made it their holy duty to sniff out the unnatural and drag it into the light.

"Threatened to report her to the Virtue Board," Margie had said, her mouth tight.

Blue had never heard of the Virtue Board before the grandmother mentioned it, but it wasn't hard to imagine. The members would have been town elders and church folk, men in starched collars and women in stiff bonnets who met in back rooms to decide who was right and who was wretched.

Rather than subject Layla to the vigilante justice of such a group, Margie had taken Layla in. She'd hidden her and loved her for nearly six months, and during those months, they'd lived like ghosts—curtains drawn, footsteps soft, every knock at the door a held breath.

How grueling it must have been, staying cooped up in Margie's small apartment day after day. And now, here was Evie, cooped up in her own backyard! Although, at least she was outside. At least she could see the sky.

Still, it had to get awfully hot with no trees for shade. And boring, even if Evie wouldn't admit it.

Blue felt a flicker of pity—but the feeling was short-lived, incinerated by a flare of anger.

Yes, Blue pitied Layla. Pitied Layla and Evie both, maybe. But Layla had betrayed Margie. She'd broken under pressure and offered up the person who had protected her. And Evie—skinny, awkward, mortal Evie—wasn't the one who'd made the rules, but she belonged to the group of mortals who did.

Was that Evie's fault? Maybe not. But mortals didn't have to hide what they were. They didn't have to clip away pieces of themselves just to walk the streets without drawing stares.

Mortals didn't get hunted. They did the hunting.

Blue stood taller. "Your mother doesn't allow you in the house, and the library is closed for the summer, so you sit out here in the broiling sun all day." She was doing it again, shifting into combat mode. She couldn't seem to stop herself. She cocked her head and said, "You don't have any friends, do you?"

Evie's mouth fell open. Then she snapped it shut and blinked rapidly. "That's rich. *You* go traipsing off into the woods every day, all by yourself. How is that any different?"

"You've been watching me?"

"You *just* told me that you see me out here every day," Evie said. "I don't think you get the moral high ground here."

She made a good point, annoyingly. Blue took half a step back.

"Day after day, you climb the fence and disappear into the forest," Evie went on, "but never with anyone else. I'd say you're the one with no friends."

"It's not the same. I love the forest!"

"Then why are you here, with me, instead of communing with your precious trees?"

"Good question!" Blue strode to the far fence, the one that separated Evie's backyard from the wilderness beyond, and swung her leg over the top rail. Her heart drummed in her chest.

She heard Evie make a frustrated sound. A moment later, she called, "Blue, wait!"

Blue glanced back to see Evie jumping to the grass from

the fort's ladder. She crossed the lawn, hands clenched at her sides. The swish of her dress around her calves had a fury to it.

"I *am* bored. And hot," she proclaimed. "And I've read *Little Women* at least ten times."

Blue raised her eyebrows. "*Little Women*?"

"My book. It's . . . actually very good."

"If you say so."

"I do. But today I'm not in the mood."

"Ah."

Evie stood there. She seemed to be nearly trembling. "Well?"

"Well what?" If Evie was waiting for an invitation, she'd be waiting for a long time.

"Can I come with you or not?"

Chapter Nine

Tall grass brushed Blue's shins as she led Evie through the field that bordered the forest. With every step, the town felt farther away. With every step, Blue breathed more easily. Once the houses disappeared from view, she felt almost fully herself. *Almost*, but not quite—not with Evie walking alongside her.

She wished she'd thought more about what she was wearing. Her overalls were fine—and far more practical than Evie's dress—but the shirt beneath suddenly felt too thin. The fabric clung to her in ways she hadn't paid much attention to that morning. Now, she felt sharply aware of how much she was revealing.

She crossed her arms over her chest, then scolded herself for being ridiculous and dropped them to her sides. Then she tried not to think about bodies at all, and certainly not about Evie's—not about the way her dress nipped in at the waist or how the pale hollow place just beneath her collarbone caught Blue's eye when Evie turned her head.

Sunlight streamed through the leaves, turning everything glossy green. Overhead, blue jays squabbled good-naturedly, and from a low branch, a snow-white squirrel flicked his bottlebrush tail.

Sorry, can't play, not now, Blue told him.

The squirrel scolded her and scampered off.

At least Evie didn't feel compelled to fill the silence with mindless chatter. That was good. Unless . . . it wasn't? Was Blue so dull that Evie didn't think it worth the effort to try and make conversation? Blue lengthened her stride to escape her thoughts, appreciating the distraction of exertion as the trail grew steeper.

Evie fell behind. From the shortness of her breath, it was obvious that she wasn't accustomed to this sort of exercise. Blue felt a bloom of vindication—*Ha! You in your dress and your silly shoes!*—followed by a pinprick of guilt and the deflating acknowledgment of shame. It had taken courage for Evie to invite herself along, and it took determination to pretend that everything was fine and dandy when clearly she was struggling.

Blue paused, feigning interest in an intricate spiderweb that hung between two branches. When Evie caught up, she pointed at the upper corner, which seemed to blink in and out of sight.

"Take a look at how thin the silk is," she said.

Evie frowned, breathing hard. Then her face cleared. "I see it now. At first I couldn't!"

"Yeah, you can only see it when the light hits it just right."

Evie nodded.

"It makes me wonder what else we're not seeing," Blue went on, mainly for the sake of letting Evie catch her breath, but also because it was true. "What's visible, what's not, and where's the line?"

"It depends on how much attention you're paying," Evie said. "Don't you think?"

"Yeah, I guess. Orb weavers—those are the spiders that make these webs—I figure they like it that way. A web like this, it's hard to see even if you're looking for it."

She knew she was rambling, and yet the words kept spilling out. "This web would have been spun this morning, given how intact it is. Which means that yesterday's web didn't come down till after dark. Which means that this lucky spider"—she nodded at the tiny creature holding still near the web's exterior—"probably caught a mosquito or two, since mosquitoes are most active after dusk."

"Oh yeah?" Evie said. "Neat."

Neat. Now Blue felt dumb for her impromptu discourse on spiders and invisible webs.

"I mean it," Evie said. "It's kind of wonderful, actually, that you know this stuff."

Blue smiled, but kept her lips pressed tightly together.

They resumed hiking, with Blue taking care to maintain a slow and measured pace. She enjoyed having someone to walk with. She especially enjoyed having *Evie* to walk with—Evie, who'd earned bonus points for listening to Blue's spider soliloquy and saying it was kind of wonderful, actually.

It was *possible*, Blue acknowledged, that she'd misjudged Evie. What she'd mistaken for snootiness might have been simply shyness. Awkwardness. What Blue sensed in Evie today was . . . curiosity, in a good way. An open heart and a willingness to give Blue—and the forest—a chance.

"Wow," Evie said when at last they crested the hill. The meadow unfolded before them, golden roses stretching as far as their eyes could see. Bluebells and hollyhocks provided pleasing pops of contrast, and from farther away came the babble of a creek. "How did you find this place?"

"Find it?" Blue gave her a funny smile. "I didn't. It's just . . . it's always been here."

"It's so lovely, like something out of a book."

Blue laughed. "It's better than a book. We're *in* it. Come on, there's more."

They had to descend a ravine to get to their destination. Normally, Blue would have launched herself into a run, spreading her arms for balance and racing gravity to the bottom. With Evie to look after, she picked the way down step by careful step.

When Evie wobbled, Blue shot out a hand to steady her.

"Thanks," said Evie.

"Of course," Blue replied. Evie's skin was warm and soft and made Blue's stomach dip. When she let go, it was with regret.

They reached the bottom of the ravine, and Blue held a finger to her lips and modeled how to move quietly through the overgrown field. She stopped just shy of a clearing and nodded at two deer—a mother and her speckled fawn—who stood alert in the tall grass. The doe's ears flicked forward, muscles tensed, ready to bolt. The fawn stilled beside his mother, liquid eyes fixed on the girls.

Evie made a hushed sound of wonder before pressing her hand to her mouth.

Blue's heart swelled.

To the deer, she said, *She's with me. She won't hurt you.*

The doe eased her stance, though her gaze stayed sharp. The fawn looked to his mother and twitched his ears. With a slow dip of her head, she granted her permission.

He stepped delicately forward to sample Evie's scent, and Blue felt the effort Evie put into holding still. Her brown eyes shone, and Blue, glancing at Evie slantwise, thought them even more luminous than the fawn's.

The doe gave the fawn a nudge—*that's enough now*—and the pair turned and bounded off.

Evie watched them go, and Blue watched her watch them.

When they'd vanished into the trees, she turned to Blue and said, "I can't believe that really happened! I've seen deer before—of course—but not up close. Not like that. And not just one but two!"

Blue almost said, *That's what you get for staying in your backyard,* but the words caught in her throat. Evie's expression was radiant, and the warmth of her gaze made Blue dizzy. Her blond hair glowed like a halo around her face, and there was something about the line of her neck, or maybe the way her lashes caught the sunlight, that made Blue quickly look away, then back again.

"There's a stream up ahead," she said, pretending her voice didn't sound tight. "If you want, we could dip our feet in."

Evie captured her lower lip between her teeth and studied Blue.

Blue's pulse stuttered.

Evie nodded, a smile blossoming across her face. "Yes, let's."

Chapter Ten

A band of worry tightened around Evie's chest every morning, loosening only when she spotted Blue, usually in overalls, always barefoot, hopping the fence that separated Mrs. Freeman's yard from Evie's. It wasn't that Evie didn't trust their friendship. She did. Blue had lived next door for a month now, and after those first awkward days when they'd circled each other warily, they'd slipped into an easy rhythm, spending practically every waking moment of their days together.

And the days were glorious. With Blue, Evie felt alive in a way she never had before, as if a new part of her had quickened and unfurled. She knew—or at least really, really hoped—that Blue felt the same, and she thought there was a good chance Blue did because of the way she grinned whenever Evie said or did something that amused her. It was the cutest grin ever, with just the tiniest scrunch of her nose. You couldn't fake that kind of grin.

Likewise, when they were walking in the woods, Blue had a way of bumping Evie's shoulder that wasn't just a normal, boring shoulder bump. (Evie doubted anything having to do with Blue could ever be normal or boring.) If Blue wanted to emphasize a point she was making, she'd veer toward Evie until their shoulders touched.

"Don't you think, Evie?" she'd say. "Don't you think so?"

Sometimes they walked for several paces like that, arms lightly touching, then bouncing apart, then coming together again.

If Evie *didn't* agree with her, or pretended not to rile her up, Blue growled and careened into Evie on purpose so that both of them stumbled and fell and landed together in a tangled, giggling heap. One time, in the meadow of golden roses, Blue propped herself up on one elbow and smiled down at Evie, who was stretched out on her back beneath her. Their hip bones touched, and the lean length of Blue's left leg pressed warm into Evie's thigh, which was bare because her skirt had hiked up. Blue was wearing a pair of trousers she'd cut off above the knee, so her thigh was bare, too. Partially, anyway. Skin met skin, and Evie felt a rush of yearning she'd never felt before.

"Hi," Blue said softly, her lips inches from Evie's.

"Hi," Evie whispered. She wanted to touch that line on Blue's lower lip. She didn't, of course, but she wanted to— and she refused to feel bad about it, either. Instead, she reached up and pushed Blue off balance so that she fell onto her back beside Evie. Two girls in a bed of roses— that's what they were. Evie imagined they were flying through the sky on a magic carpet, and she felt so full of joy that she could hardly breathe.

Theirs was a friendship like no other. It was special and precious and rare. And *that* was what made her worry: the fear that, for whatever reason—a summer cold or the grandmother falling into a particularly evil mood—a day might come when Blue didn't hop the fence and grin her adorable grin. Evie would probably die if that ever happened.

Well, no. She wouldn't *die*, and thinking like that was just plain silly. Still.

Evie understood, conceptually, that other girls' friendships were surely nice enough—in their way. Trink no doubt enjoyed braiding Cookie's hair or swapping sewing patterns or whatever it was the two of them liked to do. Same with Bronwyn and her new friend Eliza, who had only recently moved to Hemridge from Rosmond. Eliza styled her hair in loopy spiral curls, and now Bronwyn did, too. Evie's mother remarked that Eliza probably owned one of those iron rods you heated on the stove and pressed your hair around, which sounded dreadful.

But if Bronwyn and Eliza enjoyed curling their hair together, then why not?

Their friendship didn't hold a candle to Evie's and Blue's, that's all. Nobody's did. In fact, if Evie could scroll back through time all the way to Noah and the Ark—and all those animals lining up two by two—she would bet a nickel that no two souls, human or animal, had ever experienced a friendship as deep and true and real as the one Evie shared with Blue.

Jax had teased Evie once—only once—about Blue.

"You've got a crush on her," he'd said, grinning like an idiot. "You do. Admit it."

Evie had gone hot all over. Not just in her cheeks. Everywhere. The back of her neck, her palms, even behind her knees.

"Take it back," she'd snapped, lunging at him. She'd

pummeled his chest with her fists, landing soft, frantic blows. "Take it back, Jax!"

"Whoa—whoa!" He'd laughed, more startled than mean, and caught both her wrists easily, holding them above her head. "Calm down, Eve. I was only joking."

But Evie couldn't calm down. The heat inside her had boiled over in a wild, miserable rush. Tears had sprung to her eyes before she could stop them, fat and furious and sudden.

Jax had let go at once, stumbling back like she'd burned him.

"Jeez," he'd muttered, face going beet red. He'd tugged his ball cap lower over his forehead. "Are you having—" He hesitated, eyes darting. "Your . . . you know. Girl stuff?"

The moment the words had left his mouth, he'd looked horrified with himself.

Evie had swiped at her eyes, mortified and seething. "No, *Jax*. And you don't get to say that, *Jax*."

"Okay! Okay." He'd backed up a step, hands raised. "Forget it. Dropping it. Totally dropped."

He'd bolted, leaving Evie standing there, her chest heaving, throat thick.

For a long moment, she couldn't move. Couldn't think. Her skin had felt too tight, her head too full, because Jax had been wrong. Her feelings for Blue weren't about that. Not in the way of boys and girls and *Ooh-ooh! Look who's holding hands!*

What she felt for Blue was deeper. Stranger. When Blue was near, Evie's whole body felt tuned to her—like a plucked string, vibrating so that the note lingered on and on.

Yes, Evie wanted to touch Blue. Yes, she noticed her mouth, her skin, the way her hair spilled like a waterfall halfway down her back.

But it wasn't just want. It was *need.* An ache that lived somewhere too deep to name.

And it didn't belong in Jax's stupid jokes or silly whispers or giggles behind cupped hands.

It belonged to her and to Blue alone.

One day, Blue showed Evie how to squeeze nectar from honeysuckle blossoms and licked up the drops like sugar thieves. Another day, Evie taught Blue how to make crowns out of flowers, and while Blue was better than Evie at nearly everything, Evie was the undisputed queen of dandelion crowns. Her fingers, deft from years of forced piano practice, could weave together a necklace, a crown, and an anklet before Blue could manage even a bracelet.

Evie draped Blue in flowers, and although Blue acted grumpy—of course Blue acted grumpy—Evie caught her ducking her head to hide a smile.

And when Blue smiled?

When Blue smiled, the world held its breath, and everything was dewdrops and fireflies and the splash of cool water.

This, Evie told herself in these moments, pressing the feeling deep into her bones. *This is what happiness is.*

Chapter Eleven

Another thing Blue did, when Blue and Evie were hiking, was stopping short for no reason that Evie could discern. Blue would take in their surroundings with a slow, sweeping gaze, and then she'd turn to Evie with shining eyes.

You see it, don't you? Evie read in her blue eyes. *How impossibly lovely it all is?*

Evie did. The jack-in-the-pulpits with their striped green hoods, the blood red flicker of a cardinal's wing, the pansies nodding their upturned faces like mischievous schoolchildren. Blue's hand would find Evie's, and she'd weave her fingers through Evie's smaller, softer ones. Both girls would lift their faces to the sun because they were pansies, too. They were everything, everything, and for the first time in possibly her whole life, Evie grasped that she was part of something bigger.

When they got too warm from the hot summer sun, they'd splash in the creek or slip into one of the many swimming holes Blue seemed to know by heart. Evie felt self-conscious about what they did at first, but she told herself that her cotton brassiere and underwear covered just as much skin as any bathing costume.

Blue, to Evie's surprise, didn't wear a brassiere.

Actually, no, that part wasn't surprising at all. Evie had already noticed.

What *did* surprise Evie was how easy Blue was in her body, shucking off her shirt, her shorts, and the rest without a moment's shame. Then *splash*—just like that, she was neck-deep in the French Broad River, where there was nothing to hide because there was nothing to see. The river water was brown from silt and mud, and grew more so when they plunged in, their movements churning up the bottom and sending gold filaments dancing to the surface.

The only thing Blue didn't take off when the two girls went swimming was her trusty blue bandana. She never took her bandana off, ever.

"I have *a lot* of hair," Blue explained when Evie asked. "If I didn't tie it back, it would drive me nuts."

"Wear it in a ponytail," Evie suggested. She thought of the iron rod Eliza probably had, the one she probably heated up on the stove and looped her hair around to make curls. "Or you could curl it."

"Curl it?"

"Mmm-hmm. That's what girls do these days. Well, some do. They put an iron rod on the stove, and when it's hot, they wrap their hair around it."

Blue regarded her, dumbfounded. Then she shook her head as if to clear it. "*Why?*"

Evie had been hoping for exactly that reaction, and so she laughed.

"What?" Blue said.

"Nothing. You." She flicked water in Blue's direction.

"You're funny, that's all."

"Why? Because I don't want to cook my hair?"

"Yes. Exactly," Evie said. She adopted a sniffy tone and paraphrased her mother's opinion on such matters. "A smart young lady makes the most of what she's got—even if it involves hot-ironing her hair. Beauty is power. Don't you know?"

The way Blue's face fell suggested she didn't. And now Evie felt terrible. Blue hadn't lived in town all her life like Evie. She wasn't bursting at the seams with "girls should do this" and "girls should do that"—nor did she spend her days rehearsing smiles or smoothing skirts. She didn't shrink herself to fit into anyone's idea of "proper," and Evie was glad she didn't!

"Blue, I was teasing," Evie cried, breaststroking closer. "I could give a . . . a . . . ." She swiveled her legs to stay afloat, heart pounding. "I could give a rat's ass whether you curl your hair or not!"

"A rat's ass?" Blue repeated. "To whom?" She said it with perfect formality—*whom*—like a girl quoting from a book. A book on rats and their nether regions.

"I don't know. To no one," Evie said. "All I mean is that I like your hair the way it is."

"Well, good, because I don't want a rat's ass," Blue said. "I don't want a rat's anything. Not the ass, not the—what do you call the front of a rat?"

Evie blinked. "The . . . face?"

Blue grimaced. "Nope, I do not want a rat's face." Her eyes glittered. "I don't want its upper body or its midsection, either."

Evie's mouth dropped open. "You—!" Then she caught on

and gave Blue a proper splash. "You're awful!"

"Rat's ass!" Blue cried. She lunged forward and dunked Evie beneath the water. Evie shrieked and spluttered when she surfaced. Then she grinned wickedly, dug her fingers into Blue's shoulders, and returned the favor.

~

Later, they floated on their backs and watched the clouds drift by. They were big white fluffy ones, and when the water caught their reflections, they gathered and bumped up against one another. Evie felt like a drowsy shepherd tending to a flock of watery sheep.

"Evie?" Blue asked.

"Hmm?"

"Why don't you go around with Trink and Bronwyn and the other girls in town?"

Evie swished her arms through the water and thought about how silly that question was. Overhead, the sky stretched wide and blue, and beside her—just there, her friend's face turned toward her—Blue searched her expression with eyes the same bright shade. Dazzling. That was the word. Why would Evie choose to spend time with Trink and Bronwyn when she could float in the river with Blue?

"They're nice enough, I suppose," Evie said. The words came out loose and untroubled, as if the river had swept away all things sharp. Sunlight flickered on Blue's skin in little ribbons, and all the rules of the world felt far away. Evie wished she could float here forever, buoyant and free. "But they're not you."

"And your mother . . . does she mind?"

"Mind what?" Evie asked, though already that delicious

freedom was slipping away. She knew what Blue was asking.

"About me. Us. That we're friends."

Evie turned her attention to the sky and tried to radiate neutrality because, as a matter of fact, yes, Evie's mother did mind about Blue. Evie. Them.

Her mother called Blue a *wild child* and described her to Trink's mother as *feral*.

Evie aspired to be feral. She was out here swimming in the nude, wasn't she? Practically in the nude, at any rate! The situation seemed suddenly ridiculous, and Evie burst out in a fit of giggles when Blue said, dourly, "So that's a yes?"

"Oh, who cares?" Evie said.

"Let me guess," Blue continued. "I'm not ladylike enough."

"You're not *ladylike* at all."

"And I don't wear . . . crinolines."

"No one wears crinolines! Do you even know what a crinoline is?"

Blue turned her head. "Do you?"

Evie had a vague notion that it was something like a bustle, but she didn't know exactly what a bustle was, either. What she did know was that she admired the way Blue stomped barefoot over gravel without a flinch and how she always knew which way was north. How she moved through the forest like she belonged there and how she was never bothered by the yellow-eyed creatures that sometimes watched them from the underbrush.

"You know what, Blue?" Evie said. She brought her palm down flat against the water, sending a slap across the surface. "You're right. My mother doesn't think you're ladylike enough."

Blue raised an eyebrow.

"But guess what? She doesn't think I am, either. I only wear dresses because she makes me. I hate shopping. I *loathe* the piano. I can't promenade, I can't do-si-do, and last summer, when my partner tried to swing me, I knocked over a lemonade table."

Blue gave her half a grin.

"The last time I did needlepoint," Evie went on, "I bled all over the pillow I was making, which was the size of a postage stamp. I was supposed to be stitching dainty pink roses all over it. In the end, I gave up and stitched in the ugliest red cabbage you've ever seen."

That got a laugh—a real one.

"And I have terrible posture."

"No, you don't."

"According to my mother, I do."

Evie felt something at her ankle—the lightest touch, a nudge from Blue's foot beneath the water.

"You only hunch when she's around," Blue said. "The rest of the time, you carry yourself like . . ."

Evie held her breath.

"Like a princess. Like someone who knows how special she is."

All of Evie's nonsense about needlepoint and do-si-dos was knocked clean out of her. Blue's words settled in their place.

"People used to call me a princess when I was little." She gave Blue a quick, shy glance. "Because of my hair, which is the only thing my mother likes about me. At church, people would make such a fuss over my *golden curls*, my *princess* hair, that I thought my mother would faint from the excitement."

Blue snort-laughed.

"If my mother could conjure up a daughter made entirely of bouncy blond curls, she would," Evie said.

"Well, that would be spooky, so I'm glad she can't. Your hair *is* beautiful, though."

"So is yours."

"Nah."

"It is!"

"Yeah?"

"Yes, you goose. What's that fairytale about the two sisters, and one of them had black hair and the other had blonde?"

"'Snow White and Rose Red'?"

"Well, we're like them, just without the little folk."

"What do you have against little folk?"

Evie considered this, then shrugged. "Nothing, I guess. They can stay."

"I'm sure they'll be pleased to hear it. Although I think they live in a different fairytale about a different Snow White."

"Too bad for them," Evie said.

"More room in the fairytale for us," Blue agreed.

Chapter Twelve

After they dried off, Blue led Evie to a tucked-away spot where they picked the most delicious elderberries Evie had ever tasted. That afternoon, while her mother was out running errands, Evie rolled out dough and baked an elderberry pie as a surprise.

At dinner, her mother cut into it and asked, "Where did you get the berries?" She hardly paused before answering herself. "Wait. Don't tell me. You were tromping through the woods with Margie's daughter again."

"Blue doesn't tromp," Evie protested.

Her mother tutted. "I do wish you'd find a more suitable friend."

Evie sighed. *She* wished her mother would get over her obsession with "suitability." And that her dad would hurry up and get back from Tennessee.

"The pie's great, Evie," Jax said, digging into a third slice.

Her mother humphed, but even she helped herself to seconds.

~

Blue knew that Margie felt the same way Evie's mother did about her friendship with Evie: that it wasn't a good idea.

"I just worry," Margie said. "What if you're offered a glass of milk? What if you eat a spider?"

"I'm seventeen," Blue said stiffly. "Do you honestly think I'm going to accidentally eat a spider?"

"Just yesterday, I saw you lick your foot," Margie countered.

"I had a splinter. I don't lick my feet in front of Evie."

"So you change who you are when you're around her? What kind of friendship is that?"

A hot ache leaped into Blue's heart. She glared at Margie, furious at her for pretending not to understand.

Margie stared back, unyielding.

"I'll be back for supper," Blue said tightly, striding out of the house before Margie could call her back.

Evie's room was smaller than the one Blue slept in at the grandmother's and was far less frilly. A quilt stitched with stars lay over the bed, and wooden shelves sagged under the weight of books. Blue traced a finger along the spines, still fascinated by the strange pull they seemed to have on Evie. As far as Blue could tell, they were only words on paper, nothing more. Evie, however, insisted they were doors into unseen worlds.

"What's this one about?" Blue asked, tugging free a book titled *Wuthering Heights* and turning the battered cover toward Evie.

Evie's face lit up. "It's about a love so wild it ruins everything." She sat cross-legged on her bed and leaned back on her palms. "About people who can't stay where they belong, no matter what it costs them."

Blue slid the book back into its place. "Sounds

exhausting."

"Oh, but it's *so* good. Honestly, Blue, you should borrow it and give it a try. Junior year English is no joke, and *Wuthering Heights* is one of the books Mr. Campos is likely to assign. He has a reputation for giving pop quizzes."

"Not to me," said Blue. "The grandmother's getting stronger. By fall, Margie and I will be back in our cabin, thank goodness." At Evie's hurt expression, she added, "I'll still see you. It just won't be at school."

She flopped facedown onto Evie's bed and wiggled forward until her torso dangled over the edge. She groped beneath the frame until her fingers found the oversized book Evie had stashed down there, a collection of diagrams, figures, and illustrations called *A Factual (and Fearsome) History of Faeries.*

It was a book for adults, the preface boasting that it was a "scholarly work based on decades of robust and rigorous analysis." Evie just liked it for the pictures, she'd confessed to Blue, some of which were explicit and gruesome. Blue hated it for the same reason.

Even so, she pulled the book free and heaved herself up with it clutched against her chest. She scooched across the mattress and settled in next to Evie, opening the creaking spine between them.

"Oh, fun," Evie said, leaning in until her shoulder pressed against Blue's. She turned the pages slowly, the familiar illustrations leaped out at them, dark, spidery figures with crooked wings and eyes like pinpricks. One creature grinned wide, showing sharp, triangular teeth that jutted outward at odd angles.

"If my dentist saw those teeth, she'd order a mouthful of

wire straightaway," Evie remarked. "Total bogglin mouth."

Blue nearly corrected her—*faerie*, not *bogglin*—but the thing on the page wasn't a faerie. It was a creature born from a mortal's nightmare and captured on paper, propaganda that supported the mortals' party line: Faeries, bad; humans, good.

The next illustration was even more gruesome. It showed a pale, translucent creature, thin as paper and buck naked, its ribs protruding like fence slats. Evie shuddered and turned the page.

Eventually, they reached the worst picture of all, a rendering in dark oil paints of a hunched boy with pointy ears and crinkled wings. His skin tanned and leathery, stretched over his bones. His toes were fused together. His skull bulged, but he had no eyes, just dark stains where they should have been.

He was crouching over something plump and wormlike, his fingers digging into its bloated white flesh while the plum stains of his missing eyes stared through the drawing at whoever was on the other side.

"Ugh," Evie said with a shiver. "Can you imagine?"

"These pictures are fake," Blue said. "You know that, don't you?" Looking at them—especially with Evie—made her stomach twist. So why did she do this? Why keep coming back to this book, this page, this pointless self-inflicted cruelty? She should burn the damn thing, not sit here leafing through it with Evie like it mattered.

"He's staring right at us," Evie whispered in an *ooo, spooky* voice.

"Actually, he's not, because he doesn't have eyes." Blue jabbed the picture. "Also? He isn't real, Evie. None of them are."

Evie shrugged. "My dad says fae folk do exist."

"They do. But they don't look like that."

"How do you know? Have you ever seen one?"

Blue snapped the book shut and shoved it back under the bed. Spots of light swam in her vision.

"Also, you shouldn't say 'bogglin,'" she muttered.

"Right. It's a slur. I get it."

Only Evie didn't get it. If she did, she wouldn't wonder out loud if faeries had plum-pit eyes and feasted on bloated albino worms.

Regular worms, on the other hand?

Blue bowed her head. Worms, spiders, grubs . . . she'd eaten them all at some point.

Not recently. Not since moving in with the grandmother. But up on the mountain, if a plump worm wriggled out of the damp soil—why wouldn't she eat it if she was hungry?

Evie kept talking, going on about the cold, cruel winter and the famine and the Hard Times that followed, and how things were so much better now that mortals and faeries had parted ways.

Blue half-listened, barely able to tolerate Evie's pretty lies. There had been no "parting of ways"—not in the polite and civilized "it's for the best" sort of way that Evie was portraying.

She doesn't know, she doesn't know, she just doesn't know, Blue chanted in her head, desperate to drown out Evie's drivel.

Maybe Blue was equally blind, equally ignorant, but she didn't think so. She'd been brought up by Margie to believe that fae and mortals weren't so different as people thought.

The shape of an ear meant nothing. The argument that faeries were magical—and therefore dangerous—was as preposterous as saying that good swimmers probably had mermaid blood and shouldn't be allowed near sailors, or that farmers whose crops were consistently abundant were part dryad and no doubt practiced secret pagan rituals under the cloak of night.

The fae, unlike the mortals, had maintained their connection to the natural world. That was the only significant difference between fae and mortals. Some faeries, like Blue, could play with the energy that thrummed beneath the earth. Some, possibly, could do more than play. So?

The worms, though. The spiders.

Blue closed her eyes, clasping her hands around the back of her skull and pulling her elbows forward like blinders. Up on the mountain, she'd never been ashamed of who she was. Here, with Evie—and the book with the awful pictures, the book Blue herself had pulled out from beneath Evie's bed—her stomach churned with something that felt suspiciously like self-disgust.

A sense of time and reality came fuzzily back to her, and she realized that Evie had stopped talking. There was a furrow of concern in Evie's brow, and her lips were pressed together in a troubled frown.

"Are you all right?" she asked. She reached out and placed her cool fingers gently against Blue's cheek. "Blue?"

The tumult in Blue's chest quieted, replaced by an ache both painful and sweet.

Evie liked her. Maybe even loved her. Unlike those foolish illustrations, what existed between them *was* real.

Wasn't that enough?

"I'm fine," she said shakily. "A little lightheaded, that's all."

"Well, let's get you some food, you goose!" said Evie, uncrossing her legs and rising from the bed. She extended her hand to Blue, and Blue took it.

The world could go on as it pleased. The falsehoods of the town were simply that.

Blue and Evie, Evie and Blue—their truth was forged from unbreakable steel.

Chapter Thirteen

"The spot I want to show you is just over there," Blue told Evie. But Blue had been saying that for ages, and Evie no longer believed her.

"My legs," she groaned.

"There's only one last steep part left," Blue said.

"One *last* steep part? This whole hike has been a steep part!"

Blue shot her a grin. "Do you remember when you could barely go a mile?"

"I could go more than a mile."

"Now you can, sure. Maybe one day, you'll even be able to keep pace with me."

"Ha, ha," said Evie. She closed the distance between them and shoved Blue's shoulder. Blue stumbled back, but it was only for show, and Evie knew it. Blue moved through the forest like a creature born to do just that. Evie, despite her newfound muscles, would always be catching up.

They pushed on. Several minutes later, from high above the valley, Evie heard the rush of water, deep and powerful.

"Told you!" Blue called over her shoulder.

Evie smiled at seeing Blue so happy. Then her eyes

snagged on something else. In the distance, just beyond a thick line of trees, stood a row of squat stone buildings, half swallowed by vines.

She slowed. "Blue, wait."

"Evie, the waterfall is so close. I promise."

"I still want to see it." She pointed. "But look—that's got to be Graveyard Fields. Don't you think?"

Blue squinted toward the buildings.

"Do you know the story?" Evie asked.

"I know the river is strong here. Margie's told me to never swim this stretch."

"But do you know about . . . the rest?"

Blue shook her head, and something uneasy passed across her face.

Evie's heart ached. There was so much Blue didn't know —about Hemridge, about its quiet cruelties. Sometimes Evie wondered if Margie had kept her in the dark on purpose.

But Blue lived here now, just like the rest of them. And the history of a place mattered.

She led Blue to a fallen log, bleached pale by sun and rain, and they sat down like girls in church, their knees touching.

"It used to be a treatment center," Evie said. "A place for moral rebalancing."

Blue looked perplexed.

"They brought the fae here, after the Hard Times. The ones who were caught."

"Caught? Doing what?"

"You know what? I'm not sure anyone ever said. Too much magic? Not enough civic pride? Faeries weren't exactly known for attending town halls. Although, to be fair, those meetings do drag on."

She gave a small shrug. "If a fae got white-carded too many times, they were sent up here for virtue realignment, where they were given treatments that helped them assimilate. They were taught how to behave and blend in so that things would be smoother for everyone."

Her voice thinned. "But the fae who came back . . . if they came back . . . according to rumors, they weren't the same."

Blue's jaw went tight.

"When the treatment center was shut down, no one said why. It just . . . closed." Evie frowned. "I guess, at some point, there weren't enough fae left to justify the cost."

Blue grunted.

"Some of the fae returned, though," Evie said. She gestured. "Here. To the treatment center. After it was shut down."

"Why?"

"Because they'd memorized the woods around this area? That's what some people say—that when things got bad, and the faeries had to escape, this was where they hid out." She glanced toward the vine-choked ruins. "Others say that what happened here left a mark. That the faeries' pain soaked into the soil and . . . I don't know. Changed it. Made it sacred. And that's why the faeries chose this spot to build the bridge."

Blue glanced around. "What bridge?"

"Well, it's a little farther up," Evie allowed. She pointed. "Up there is a ravine. Past the ravine is Overlook Rock. From Overlook Rock, supposedly, the horizon stretches on forever."

"I know the spot," Blue said curtly. "There's no bridge."

"Because it's *invisible*, silly. It leads to a different world. A magical world." She bumped Blue's shoulder. "The river is rough, like Margie said. But every so often, someone tries to cross it—only to drown. Because mortals *can't* cross it. Only the Fair Folk can."

"On the invisible bridge," Blue stated.

"I know, I know. I'm not saying it actually exists." She rolled her eyes in an exaggerated fashion. "But wouldn't it be nice if it did?"

Blue turned and stared at the abandoned treatment center. Her mouth was set. Her eyebrows were downward slashes. "You bet. It'd be great."

There was ice in her voice. Evie flinched.

"I *like* the idea of an invisible bridge," she said, not understanding what she'd done to provoke Blue's sudden shift in mood.

Blue swung her head back and stared at her. "Of course you do. What's not to like?"

Evie's heart beat faster. Hadn't it been Blue who'd wondered out loud about invisible things, that day with the spiderweb? Hadn't it been Blue who'd thrown out the idea that people only saw what they were expecting to see? Something like that, anyway.

"I'm not saying *you* have to like it," she said. There was an edge to her voice now, too. "And, again, I do understand that it's not real. I'm not an idiot."

"No?" Blue said.

A gust rattled the trees, and spiders ran up and down Evie's spine.

No, not spiders. Anything but spiders.

She stood up and rubbed her bare arms. In her best *I don't give a damn* tone, she said, "Do you want to keep going, or should we just turn back?"

"Keep going," Blue said gruffly, pushing herself to standing and striding straight to the trail.

Blue hiked the last stretch to Overlook Rock at an angry pace, spine straight and shoulders squared. If Evie's mother were here, she'd be justified in saying, *Do you see, Evie? Tromping. Your friend is a tromper.*

Evie considered tugging Blue back to walk alongside her. Asking if she was all right.

Some instinct stopped her, or maybe it was just selfishness. The subject of faeries made Blue prickly, and when Blue was prickly, the energy she gave off felt . . . oppressive. Complicated. Evie didn't always want to take it on.

Eventually, Blue shook off her black mood. She went from tromping furiously to walking briskly to slowing down enough for Evie to catch up. When Evie did, Blue shot her a sheepish smile. *Sorry I got grumpy,* her smile said.

Everyone does, replied Evie with her own smile, which was mainly genuine and only slightly forced. *Think nothing of it.*

Chapter Fourteen

At the end of the trail was a narrow pedestrian bridge that was neither magical nor invisible. It was just a rotting wooden bridge suspended over a creek that fed the raging river. It had no railing, missing planks, and an alarming tendency to sway.

Evie drew up short, because there was no way she was setting foot on that thing.

"It looks scary, but it's not," Blue assured her.

"It looks scary because it *is*. Blue, that thing is a death trap."

Blue walked out onto it and bounced. "It's fine. See?"

Evie shielded her eyes. "Please stop."

"Do you trust me?"

"Not in the slightest. Not anymore."

Blue chuckled. "Take your hand away from your eyes and look at me. Good. Now, keep your eyes on me and walk forward. Just pretend you're on regular ground."

"The regular ground doesn't sway."

"It does if there's an earthquake."

"Not helping."

From the middle of the rickety bridge, Blue gazed at Evie

in a way that no one else ever had or ever would, Evie was sure of it. It was a look straight from Blue to Evie, heart to heart and soul to soul, and it made the last of Evie's uncertainty fall away. Not her uncertainty about the bridge. She remained extremely uncertain about the bridge. But she no longer felt wary of Blue, or annoyed at her, even a little. She let go of any lingering worry that she might not be as important to Blue as Blue was to her.

"You can do this," Blue said. "You're *Evie*, remember?"

Evie stepped onto the bridge.

It moved beneath her, and her stomach lurched.

She focused on Blue's steady blue eyes and took another step. Then another. Ahead of her, Blue walked backward, feeling her way along the wobbly planks with her bare feet.

As soon as Blue reached the other side, she stepped clear of the bridge and extended her hand, which Evie gratefully grabbed. With a final shaky leap, she was back on solid ground.

"That wasn't so bad, was it?" Blue asked.

"Excuse me?" Evie exclaimed. She shoved Blue. Then she shoved her again, for good measure. "That was the scariest thing I've ever done in my entire life!"

"Okay, okay," Blue said, laughing. "You did it, though!"

But then—Overlook Rock. The forest fell away, and before them stretched the sky, the mountains, and far below, the river, white and churning. Beyond the ravine was untouched wilderness, and beyond the wilderness, rising into the clouds, was a jagged, snow-capped peak called Old Mother.

From town, Old Mother was a constant presence, beautiful and austere.

From Overlook Rock, Old Mother was still beautiful—even more so—but savagely so, cutting so steeply into the sky that Evie had to crane her head all the way back to see the top.

"Wow," she murmured.

Blue stood beside her, her black hair rippling in the breeze. "No bridge," she said, but her voice was no longer laced with contempt. Just sadness.

Evie knew she should let Blue's remark go unanswered. She *knew* it. Still, she said, "Unless it's like the spiderweb you showed me, made of something so fine that you can only see it when the light's just right."

"It's not," Blue stated. "It's just a story someone made up, like Big Rock Candy Mountain."

"Big Rock Candy Mountain?"

"Yeah, from a song Margie used to sing." Blue lifted her eyes to Old Mother and sang, *"In the Big Rock Candy Mountains, there's a land that's fair and bright, where cookies grow on bushes, and you sleep out every night . . ."*

"That's sweet," Evie said. "A kid's idea of heaven, pretty much."

"And just like heaven, it's make-believe."

Evie hesitated. They'd never talked much about religion, she and Blue. "You think heaven is made up?"

Blue checked in with her with her eyes. "I don't know whether it's real or not. No one does."

"Plenty of people think they do."

"Well, and I understand why they'd want to," Blue said carefully. "If your life was hard and full of sorrow, wouldn't you want to believe in a better world?"

"Everyone's life is hard and full of sorrow. Not every

minute of every day, necessarily, but no one goes through life unscathed."

"Exactly."

"Yes, but believing in heaven isn't just ... it's not ..." Evie pushed her hand through her curls. "You don't have to be a child to believe in God and heaven and all the rest of it."

"If you say so," Blue said.

"As for the bridge ..." Evie chose her words carefully. She chose her tone carefully, too. She had the oddest feeling that something big was at stake, though she couldn't for the life of her put a name to it. "Dozens of faeries up and disappeared, and that was in Hemridge alone. After the Hard Times. They slipped away in the dead of night—do you really not know this story?"

Blue arched her eyebrows. "*Story* being the pivotal word."

"People saw them, though. From town. They saw a long line of tiny bobbing lanterns ascending up the mountain. The Fair Folk hiked all the way to Overlook Rock, and then ... poof. They were never seen again."

Blue glanced at the cliff's edge, then back at Evie. Her eyes were deep pools with depths that Evie couldn't reach.

"I'm just saying that maybe there *was* a bridge," Evie pressed. "Maybe."

"All right," Blue said.

Evie could hardly believe it. She rarely won arguments with Blue. "As for it being magical, who knows? Maybe it was a pathway you could only see at a certain time, and only if you knew where to look."

"Maybe so," Blue murmured. She stepped forward and

peered over the rocky outcropping. "Still, the water's awfully high."

"Where you're standing is awfully high," Evie said, trying to keep her voice from hitching. "Blue? Please step back from the edge."

To Evie's surprise, Blue did.

"Let's head back," she said, not meeting Evie's eyes. "Are you ready to head back?"

"Yeah. Sure."

Blue nodded. "Good. Me, too."

~

Storm clouds gathered as they made their way down the mountain, and it was drizzling by the time they reached the outskirts of town. They hurried into the grandmother's house and then from the foyer into the kitchen, where Blue tossed Evie a dish towel to dry off with. With another towel, she dabbed at her face and squeezed the water from her long, dark hair.

"Thirsty?" Blue asked.

"Very," Evie said.

Blue tossed her towel over her shoulder and poured two glasses of lemonade. Mrs. Freeman in her invalid chair rolled into the room as Blue handed Evie hers, and Evie startled.

"Oh!" she exclaimed as lemonade sloshed from her glass.

"I'll get it," Blue said, pulling the towel back off her shoulder and dropping to the floor.

"Clumsy girl," the grandmother scolded. She scowled at Blue, and her wrinkles jumped together and made her look like a dried apple.

"We hiked to Overlook Rock," Evie blurted, wanting to

divert the old lady's attention. "I told Blue about the bridge, but she thinks it's made up. Do you? Anyway, *I* spilled the lemonade, not Blue."

Blue rose and balled up the damp rag. "Let's go upstairs," she said to Evie.

"Wait," commanded old Mrs. Freeman. She grasped the wheels of her chair and thrust herself one inch forward, then one inch back. "The bridge isn't *made up*. What rubbish."

Evie blinked. She felt Blue stiffen beside her.

"How do you know?"

"Because I saw it, foolish girl. I saw it with my own two eyes."

Chapter Fifteen

Blue wasn't sure she wanted to hear the grandmother's story. But she knew she would listen, regardless. How could she not?

She helped the old woman to the toilet, prepared her a snack of cheese and crackers, and placed the plate on a tray, along with a china mug of tea. Only then did the old lady speak.

"I was sixteen," the grandmother began. She fixed her pale, sunken eyes on Blue and Evie, who sat stiffly at the kitchen table. "Just a little younger than the two of you. I was on horseback, riding with a neighbor boy. I carried myself well, I'll have you know. I was a fine equestrian in my day."

Blue pictured the grandmother as a girl, young and proud atop a horse. It should have been laughable, but a haughty, whip-wielding version of the grandmother as a girl was all too easy to imagine.

"We found them in a thicket of laurel," the grandmother continued. "An adult male and two young ones. Huddled together, pitiful things. The little ones looked barely weaned."

Blue clutched her hands and breathed. One breath in. One breath out. One breath in. One breath out.

"They'd been hiding for days, from the looks of it. Filthy. Gaunt. The man tried to shield them. Held out his hands like that would stop us." She sneered. "He should've known better. We chased them all the way to Overlook Rock, the little ones sobbing, the man trying to help them along. And then, at the ravine . . ."

She let the sentence hang.

"What happened?" Evie said. "At the ravine?"

"He had a ring," the grandmother said. "That's how he summoned the bridge. Gold band, engraved on the inside. 'Love thy neighbor.'" She chuckled. "As if that ever meant them."

Blue felt Evie glance at her. She kept her face a mask.

"They say the ring was made by one of their metal smiths, way back when. Only a few existed. They let you cross over to a wondrous land, but only if you had bog blood."

"And it worked?" Evie asked. "The bridge appeared, and they crossed to the other side?"

The grandmother lifted her bony shoulders, then lowered them with a sigh. "I saw it. I did. It was beautiful, too good for the likes of them."

Outside, the rain came down, drumming against the windows. Blue could hear her own breath, unsteady despite her efforts to control it. She felt her need to know like static in the air.

"The little ones crossed first," the grandmother said. "The man stayed back, just long enough to see them safe." Her voice dropped. "But the neighbor boy had a pistol."

She smiled, exposing brown bits where her teeth met her gums. "*Bang!*"

Evie flinched. Blue held herself so tightly her bones ached.

"Did he . . .die?" Evie whispered.

"Of course," the grandmother said. "Even magic can't stop a bullet."

"That's awful," Evie said.

The grandmother sipped her tea, unmoved.

"And you just watched all of this?" Blue said. She tried, for Evie's sake, not to growl. "You sat high on your horse and did nothing?"

"I most certainly did not!" the grandmother retorted. "What a question!"

"What did you do?" Evie asked.

"What do you think? I hopped off my horse, climbed down the ravine, and took the ring. Slipped it right off his finger."

Blue wanted to slap her. Kick her. Put her hands around her wrinkled neck and squeeze the life out of her.

"It was a foul, wicked thing," the grandmother went on, her voice souring. "Made me *feel* things. It didn't keep the bridge in place, though. Oh, no. Not for me."

"Where is it now?" Evie asked.

"The ring?"

"Yes. Do you still have it?"

"You think I'd keep a thing like that?" The grandmother scoffed. "I flung it into the river. Gone, just like the man the neighbor boy shot."

The rain lashed harder. Evie glanced toward the window.

"You should go," the grandmother told her.

Evie returned her attention to the old lady. "But—is there more? To the story?"

The grandmother tapped her nails against the armrest of her chair. "There's always more."

"Then—"

"You should go," she repeated, voice firmer. "This is my house. Do as you're told."

Evie stood up, shooting Blue a troubled look. "See you tomorrow?"

Blue nodded. Evie slipped out, and a moment later came the soft bang of the screen door.

The grandmother pinned her eyes on Blue. Her gaze wasn't soft and worried, like Evie's, but sharp. Knowing. "Most of the uglier conflicts in Hemridge took place years ago, during the purges. The Hard Times, as sentimental folks like to say." Her voice lowered. "We won, by the way. And by 'we,' I mean the God-fearing folk."

Blue kept her expression blank and gave up nothing. This was nothing new.

"For a long stretch, there was quiet. Not peace, exactly, but quiet. Then something happened about thirteen years ago. Right around the time you landed on Margie's porch." She smiled, slow and toothy. "Curious, isn't it?"

Blue's heart was a wild thing, and her ribs a cage.

"A Hemridge boy was killed. Ben Bratton was his name. He was a friend of the family next door." She tilted her head toward Evie's house. "You've grown quite close, you and the girl. Decided you like her after all?"

"What does a dead boy have to do with me?" Blue asked.

"She only puts up with you for lack of better options. The other girls want nothing to do with her."

"That's not true."

"Would she still choose you if she knew what you really are?"

Blue's pulse thudded. She wanted to walk away—wanted to be stronger than her own curiosity—but she stayed frozen in place.

The grandmother saw it and smiled. "The boy's mother was already dead. Cancer, which I suppose was a mercy. Better to die of that than a broken heart."

"How would you know? You don't have one," Blue said.

The grandmother's laugh sounded genuine. She eyed Blue and bobbed her head from side to side, as if gauging the quality of a cut of meat. "Well, well."

Blue started to rise.

"Sit back down," the grandmother commanded.

The sharpness of her tone dug right back into Blue's curiosity, burrowing fast and deep like a tick.

Slowly, and all the while insisting to herself that it was because she wanted to, Blue did as she was told.

Chapter Sixteen

"When they found Ben's body, it was white as snow," the grandmother said. "Every drop of blood drained out of him. Murdered by a fae boy. That's what they said. They knew it because of the prints he left behind—long bony feet. Barefoot, of course. Who but your kind would run barefoot through the woods?"

"Footprints don't prove anything," Blue said.

"Mmm," the grandmother mused. "They caught him, though. The fae boy who murdered Ben Bratton. Just a teenager. Thin as kindling. Black hair and ears like yours."

A memory stirred in Blue's mind. A name. A face. Not quite reachable.

"Hideous, those ears," the grandmother said. "If I were cursed with such ears, I doubt I could bear my own reflection."

She was trying to goad Blue. Blue barely heard her.

"What would Evie think of your ears, I wonder?"

Blue snapped back. "Where is he, the boy they caught? Is he alive? Did he confess?"

"No trial. No paper trail," the grandmother said. "The good folk of Hemridge prefer to clean up their messes quickly and quietly." With her bony hand, she formed a gun, pressing her finger to her temple. "Pow," she whispered and gave a small jerk of her head.

Blue was on her feet before she realized she'd moved. "No! That didn't happen!"

The grandmother rang her bell frenetically. *Ding ding ding!*

"Don't tell me what did or didn't happen," she snapped, clamping the bell to silence it.

Blue's head felt far away, like a balloon on a string.

The grandmother studied her. "You knew him," she said.

Blue's balloon head turned from side to side. No.

"You did. I saw it on your face." She began to count out facts on her fingers. "A mortal boy dies. A fae boy disappears. And just like that, my Margie finds a little one on her porch. A strange child with strange eyes and stranger ears, no name, no story." She curled all but one finger back and pointed it straight at Blue. "You."

Blue felt the terrifying prickle of tears behind her eyes. "Why are you so awful?"

"Awful?" The grandmother's voice was mild. "Is it *awful* to tell the truth?"

She wheeled herself forward in her monstrous chair, peering down the hall as if checking for Margie. Then she reversed, slow and smooth. She fixed Blue with her stare.

"He was your brother. Or a cousin. Family, at any rate."

The word hit Blue like a slap.

"And he died," the grandmother said. "He died and left you behind. How does it feel to be the last one left?"

~

Rain lashed the windows deep into the night. Thunder

rolled across the mountains. Blue tossed and turned, her dreams filled with a silver bridge shimmering in the moonlight, whispering, *Come, come.* Every time she reached for it, it slipped through her fingers like smoke.

At breakfast, she stabbed at her French toast and tried to tell herself she hated it. A lie. Blue loved French toast. She loved anything sweet.

Did all faeries crave sugar? Had her brother—*if* she'd had one—liked syrup-drenched toast, too? Or had the grandmother made him up just to kill him in that awful, rattling voice of hers?

If Blue did once have a brother, what had he looked like? What was his name? What kind of sister couldn't remember her brother's name? The questions looped in her head like the scrape of metal.

When Margie suggested she stop playing with her food and eat it, Blue glared.

"Yeah, great idea, only I—" She wanted to say, *Only I hate French toast.* Those were the words lined up in her head, but they refused to come out. She tried again and got no farther than the "I" before her vocal cords tightened and what came out sounded like the noise a cat made when coughing up a hairball.

Margie blinked. "Blue, good heavens. Are you okay?"

"I'm not hungry, okay?" she snapped. That "h-word" came out easily, no snags, maybe because it was true. She wasn't hungry. She let her fork clatter to her plate and added, "If you'd lay off with the nagging, I'd be just peachy."

Margie pulled back, surprised and hurt. "All right, Blue," she said quietly.

Shame burned Blue's skin. She forced herself to take a bite of the syrupy toast, which was warm and delicious, which only made her bad mood worse.

~

Blue found Margie later that morning, ironing one of the grandmother's house dresses in the laundry room.

"Need any help?" Blue asked, trying to ignore the strange beat of her heart.

Margie looked up. "Thanks, but ironing's a one-woman job." Then, in that mom way she had, she added, "You can keep me company, if you'd like."

Blue stepped fully into the room. She gathered her courage and said, "Margie, did I have a brother?"

The iron stopped mid-stroke. "Oh," said Margie softly. "Oh, honey."

Blue didn't want *oh, honey*. She wanted the truth. "Did I?"

Margie set the iron upright on its base. "Honestly? I don't know."

"Then tell me what you *do* know. All of it."

Margie studied her. "What brought this on?"

"Does it matter?"

"You know the story already. I have nothing new to add."

Blue pressed her palm to her chest. "Tell it anyway. Please."

Margie took a deep breath. "Well, as you know, I always wanted a little girl, but I knew I'd never have one. No partner, no baby. That's how it works."

Blue felt tight and heavy.

"And yet, every night, I prayed for a baby girl just like you."

108

"And then one day, I showed up," Blue filled in. She couldn't keep the sarcasm from creeping in. "Like magic."

"You did. Yes. I found you on the porch, wrapped in a gray blanket. Pinned to the blanket was a note. It said, 'Her name is Blue, and she is precious beyond measure. Please take care of her.'" Margie reached out as if to touch Blue, but let her hand fall back when Blue stiffened. "So I did."

"I wasn't a baby, though," Blue pointed out. "I was four when you found me on your porch. Didn't I *say* anything?"

Margie's expression took on shadows. "In the beginning, you called out for someone. 'Mumsy.' And you said another word. 'Digs.'"

Somewhere, far back in her mind, Blue saw a mug of milk tumble onto a dirt floor, the soil soaking up its contents. She heard a bang, and her chest clenched.

"I thought you liked to dig in the dirt, maybe." Margie laughed clumsily. "You were awfully dirty when I found you."

Blue frowned. Something wasn't right.

"Blue, if you'd just tell me what's wrong—"

"I want to know about my family," Blue said. "Who are they? *Where* are they? What happened to them?"

"I thought *I* was your family," said Margie.

Blue pressed her lips together, because that wasn't fair. Margie could tell her the truth, and Blue would still be hers.

Margie shut her eyes. When she opened them, she said, "Your people must have stayed in the mountains after most of the others left. Whoever they were, they would've been among the last faeries in Hemridge. Maybe the very last. I just don't know."

Blue looked at Margie beseechingly. She had to know something more. She *had* to.

Margie broke off eye contact. She said, reluctantly, "You had a twisted ankle."

"I did?"

"You could hobble, but you couldn't walk."

"Okay. I had a twisted ankle," Blue said slowly. "You think that means something. I can see it on your face."

"I don't, not really."

"You do. Tell me."

Margie sighed. "It just seems to be that whatever happened—and honey, this is all speculation. I don't *know* what happened. What I *do* know is that there was no way, with that twisted ankle of yours, that you could've kept up with . . . a group on the move."

"A group on the move," Blue repeated. Her stomach dipped. "So my family left me behind? Is that what you think?"

"No, Blue. I didn't say that."

"I was too much trouble. I couldn't keep up."

"I don't see the point in going down this road, and this is why," Margie said. "*We don't know what happened.* We probably never will. Don't let a hypothetical explanation—and that's all it is—take root inside you."

Too late. It already had. Blue's family had left her behind because she couldn't keep up. She'd been broken, so they'd deposited her on Margie's porch rather than take her with them.

Margie's eyes searched Blue's face. "If you tell me what you're thinking, or why you're having all these questions all of a sudden . . ." She oozed concern. "I might be able to help, you know."

"I'm not thinking anything," Blue said hollowly. When she'd been four, Margie's help had surely saved her. But she was seventeen now. She didn't want Margie's help. "Honestly, I'm fine."

Margie squeezed Blue's arm. "Well, I'm always here. I love you."

"I love you too," Blue said, and it was true. Just, sometimes it wasn't enough.

Chapter Seventeen

Evie, at twelve years old, had been told she was "a young twelve." Well, no. Evie had overheard her mother calling her that, to one of her mother's friends. The context had involved Evie being more interested in books than in boys, as she recalled.

Evie, at seventeen, supposed her mother would consider her "a young seventeen," and not just because of the books versus boys thing. It was also that she was flat-chested, not interested in lipstick or curling her hair, and didn't choose to spend her time with Trink and the other neighborhood girls giggling over bridal magazines.

Evie wasn't sure if she was a "young" seventeen or not, but she suspected she was—just not for the reasons her mother might cite. Evie wasn't brave. Evie *hated* conflict. Those weren't the qualities of a mature young adult, were they? And yet . . . here she was, stuck with herself. The story Blue's grandmother told yesterday had been horrific, and Evie suspected she should acknowledge the horror of it, if nothing else. Mrs. Freeman—old, wrinkled Mrs. Freeman with her glinting eyes—had practically gloated as she'd told it.

Mrs. Freeman's neighbor friend had shot a faerie. Shot him and killed him. "Even magic can't stop a bullet," the old lady had boasted.

Mrs. Freeman had then hopped off her horse, ran to the dead faerie, and stolen his ring right off his finger. She'd called it a foul, wicked thing, but there'd been something in her eyes when she'd mentioned it. A grudging acknowledgment, perhaps, of its fine craftsmanship. As for the bridge Blue had scoffed at, old Mrs. Freeman said she'd seen it, and that it had been "beautiful." She'd used that word exactly.

Evie had so many questions. Questions for Mrs. Freeman, and questions for Blue, as well. Because Blue, she'd gone so very still during the recounting of the tale. Still in a bad way. A scary way.

And then Mrs. Freeman had shooed Evie off, and Evie had fled like a good little Evie. Not brave. Not mature. She'd peeked back into the kitchen, though—once she was outside the Freeman's house, and even as the rain came down hard and drenched her—and she'd seen old Mrs. Freeman and Blue still at it. They'd remained at the kitchen table, exchanging . . .what? Not pleasantries, that was for sure. Not barbs, either, though.

Something powerful. Something that mattered. Whatever Mrs. Freeman had said, it had made the color drain from Blue's face. She'd pushed back from the table, Blue had, and left the room with the rigid posture of a soldier, her spine ramrod straight and her jaw so tight it could've shattered.

Mrs. Freeman had looked haunted, afterward. Not at first. At first, she'd looked gleeful. *You see? I win*, her expression had said. *I always do.* But then, when Blue was no longer in the room, all that smugness had fallen away, and she'd just looked old and sad. Very, very sad.

Evie wished she hadn't seen Mrs. Freeman's sadness, as strange as that sounded. It was easier to despise the old biddy before she'd gone and revealed herself to still possess a shred of decency, however feeble it was.

For that reason, and any number of others Evie couldn't find the courage to name, she avoided the topic of Blue's grandmother entirely the next day. When Blue showed up at her house midmorning, she simply said, "It's too muddy to hike into the forest. Want to walk into town and get a cinnamon roll?"

"A cinnamon roll sounds good," said Blue. "Anything but French toast."

Evie looked at her strangely, then said, "Right. No French toast."

As they ambled along the sidewalk, coins winked up at Blue the way they always did—coins Evie would have never noticed on her own. Blue crouched and picked up a copper penny, tilting it so that it glinted in the rain-washed light.

"How do you do that?" Evie asked.

"Do what?"

She gestured at the penny. "With . . . you know."

"You can have it," Blue said, tossing it to her without ceremony.

As they passed the filling station, Evie slowed down and then abruptly sped up. "Hurry!" she said.

"Why? What's wrong?"

"*Trink*," Evie said, tugging Blue along. "I don't want her to see us."

"Evie! Wait!" cried a girl's voice.

"Too late," Blue said.

Evie grimaced.

"Are you embarrassed of me?" Blue asked.

"What? No!" Evie exclaimed.

Blue looked skeptical—and a little angry. Tight, wound up, like she'd been with her grandmother.

Evie touched Blue's forearm. "Blue? Look at me," she said. She heard herself, and it made her heart ache, the echo of Blue's words from the day before, when Evie had been afraid to cross the bridge.

"I am not embarrassed of you," she told Blue. She looked hard at Blue and used her soul to push the words from her heart into Blue's. *I would never be,* she added silently. *I love you. Don't you know?*

Blue resisted. Soldier Blue, straight-spined Blue.

Footsteps scuffed the sidewalk behind them, quick and overlapping, and Blue's eyes flicked past Evie's shoulder to what was surely the gaggle of approaching girls. Blue braced as if for a blow, and Evie felt her stomach drop out of her.

Blue was afraid. *Blue.* Not of a rotting deathtrap of a bridge, but of girls who giggled and squealed and wore swishing skirts. Girls who cried, "Evie! Wait!"

"Hey," Evie said, centering herself on the sidewalk so that Blue was forced to look again at her. "You can do this. You're Blue, remember?"

Chapter Eighteen

"Evie!" Trink said breathlessly, joining them from behind. She beamed. "And Blue! Hi!" Trink was flanked by Marisol and Cookie. Trink's sister, Bronwyn, trailed behind, flipping through a magazine.

"Hi," Blue said, a touch too formally.

While both girls surely knew of the other's existence, this was the first time the two had officially met, Evie realized. Trink, who was tall and pale with a round, moonish face, made introductions all around, and Blue nodded *hello* to each girl. Evie detested the awkwardness of it all. She'd have rather kept Blue to herself.

"I am just so happy to finally *meet* you," Trink gushed. "Also? Your hair is to die for. It's so shiny! Do you use a tonic? What kind of brush do you use?"

"Um. Just a brush?"

Trink extended a hand as if to touch Blue's hair for herself. Blue stepped backward onto Evie's toe, and Evie pressed her lips together to keep from saying *ow*.

"I give my hair the full hundred strokes every night," Marisol chimed in. Marisol was short and chubby, with frizzy red hair. She gestured at her head. "And still it looks like this!"

"Rose petals are good for shine," Blue said hesitantly. "Boil them and rinse your hair with the water."

"Roses? I don't have any roses," Marisol said.

Blue looked at Evie, then back at Marisol. "You could pick some? In the meadow?"

Trink led the group to a grassy spot where they could all sit down, then passed a paper sack to Evie. Inside were pretzels, chips, and a selection of penny candies she'd no doubt purchased from the filling station .

"Help yourself," she said. "You, too, Blue."

Evie selected a pixie stick. Blue chose a chocolate chew.

"Did y'all hear?" Cookie asked through a mouthful of sunflower seeds. She spat a shell into the grass. "Over in Rosmond, folks are marching again. There's been rumors of bogglin sightings, and now everyone's all stirred up."

"Faeries," Evie corrected, throwing a glance at Blue.

"Whatever you say, Evie, but a skunk in a church house is still a skunk," Cookie said.

Trink and Marisol laughed. Evie's face burned.

Bronwyn reached over and gave Evie's leg a little pat, which made things worse. It was like she was saying, *Aren't you sweet, trying to be broadminded.*

The girls kept gossiping, but Blue didn't join in. Instead, she lay back in the grass and closed her eyes.

"I don't care what happens over in Rosmond," Trink said. "I just hope they don't start creeping into Hemridge."

"Look around," Cookie said. "Do you see any faeries here? No. And you know why? Because Hemridge isn't Rosmond. In Rosmond, they let the fae roam around, thanks to those . . . programs. That's the problem.

Harmony Hall trains them up and gives them job placements, like everything's normal. But it's not. It's creepy."

"My mom saw a faerie work crew once," Marisol said. "She said if it weren't for the ears, you'd think they were just regular folks."

"Really?" said Trink.

"She said some were actually handsome. And friendly! They *waved* at her."

"That's going too far."

Cookie hmmphed. "You got that right. If they think it's fine to wave at townsfolk, what's next?"

Evie glanced at Blue, who hadn't moved, hadn't reacted. She just lay there with her eyes closed. Was she asleep or just pretending?

"I have a joke," Bronwyn announced, setting her magazine aside.

"Okay, let's hear it," Cookie said.

"A mortal asks a faerie, 'Who's to blame for all the world's troubles?'" Bronwyn looked from girl to girl. "Now the faerie, he knows the answer he's supposed to give, so he says, 'The fae. And also the bicycle riders.'"

Evie saw Blue crack open one eye.

Bronwyn grinned. "'Why the bicycle riders?' the mortal asks. 'Why the faeries?' says the faerie."

Blue laughed.

Trink frowned.

Cookie scowled and said, "How is that a *joke*? Jokes are supposed to be funny."

Bronwyn shrugged, seemingly pleased despite the joke's mixed reaction. "Blue thought it was funny. Didn't you,

Blue?"

"I did, too," Evie offered, though she wasn't sure she did.

"I don't get it," Marisol complained.

Cookie looked to Evie. Evie looked to Blue.

"Just . . . the bicycle riders didn't do anything," Blue said.

Cookie's brows pulled together. "Okaaay. And?"

"Neither did the fae," said Blue. "That's the point. That's why it's funny."

"Only it isn't," Cookie muttered. "And I sure wouldn't let Silas hear you say that."

"Who's Silas?" Blue asked.

The girls turned toward the filling station where, behind the counter, a boy leaned against the cash register. He was tall and solid, with short brown hair and broad shoulders.

"His brother, Ben, was murdered by the fae," Cookie said, lowering her voice. "Ben was out in the forest one night, and a faerie boy killed him in cold blood."

"It might not have been a faerie," Bronwyn pointed out. "Nobody knows for sure how Ben died. It might have been a bear."

"Either way, it was bad," Trink said.

"I had nightmares for weeks," Marisol murmured.

"It was almost definitely a bear," Evie said, who'd heard her father say as much. "Either way, it was a long time ago." She was having a hard time reading Blue's expression.

"Might have been a bear. Might have been a faerie," Cookie said staunchly. "Or might have been a faerie who sicced the bear on Ben. Did you ever think of that?"

"How?" Evie said.

"Ben *died*, all right?" Cookie said. "And after that, his dad

—old Mr. Bratton—turned into a drunk. Right, girls?"

Marisol and Trink nodded.

"He is one mean, mean man," Bronwyn said, shaking her head. "I feel bad for Silas."

"Plus his mom is dead," Bronwyn told Blue. "It's just Silas and his dad."

"He's training to be in Corrections," Cookie said. "My mom says Harmony Hall's always hiring."

"Who will he correct?" Blue asked.

Cookie blinked. "What?"

Blue pushed herself to sitting. "If he's training to be in Corrections, who is he supposed to correct?"

"The residents," Cookie said.

"The *fae* residents?" Blue said, stressing the word "fae" in a way that made Evie nervous.

"It'll be his job to make sure they stick to the rules," Cookie said. She tilted her head at Blue. "How do you not know this?"

"She's homeschooled," Evie blurted. "And Margie—her mom—doesn't really . . . listen to the radio."

"Harmony House is an integration community," Bronwyn explained. "Most of the residents are ancient, but there are a few mixed-race couples, some kids."

"The Correction officers are guards, basically," Trink added.

"Guards," Blue repeated. "Because they need to be guarded, these ancient faeries and the little kids."

The shift in the group was subtle but sharp.

"Fae of all ages live there," Bronwyn said defensively. "And some of them—the ones with kids—*aren't* fae. There are mixed-race couples, like I said."

"Are the rules different for the mortals who live there?" Blue inquired.

Cookie scoffed. "The mortals are treated like everyone else, obviously."

"So, the same as the other residents," said Blue.

"The same as other *mortals*," Cookie said, shooting Blue the sort of look that said, *Did you get dropped on your head when you were a baby?*

"It's just the way things are, Blue," Evie said. Her heart was pounding really hard. Why was her heart pounding so hard? "I wish things were different. You know I do. I wish mortals and fae could just get along."

"Would you want to live next door to one?" Cookie asked.

"A faerie?" Evie said. Sweat pricked beneath her armpits, and she wished she hadn't eaten that pixie stick, because now all that sugar was roiling around in her stomach. This was why she hated conflict!

"What would be so bad about living next door to a faerie?" Blue asked.

"Um, everything?" Cookie said. "My great-grandmother was alive during the Hard Times. She grew up around faeries. They were a bad lot, she says, with no understanding of right versus wrong."

Bronwyn nodded as if to acknowledge Cookie's point.

"They stirred up trouble just for spite," Cookie went on. "Anytime a faerie was around, something bad was bound to happen."

"Did she explain how that worked, exactly?" Blue asked.
Cookie blinked.

"Because bad things *do* happen. They *still* happen." Blue waved a hand through the air. "Does your great-grandmother have an explanation for that?" Blue snapped. "Oh, wait, maybe she believes in *invisible* faeries. That way she still has someone to blame every time a cow dies."

"You're twisting my words," Cookie said.

"Am I?"

Bronwyn shifted closer to Cookie, protective now. To Blue, she said, "You've only been here a few weeks. You don't understand."

"Will I understand if I stay longer?"

"I'm sure you will," Bronwyn said.

Blue stood, adjusting the knot of her bandana. "Then I'll leave."

Chapter Nineteen

Blue heard the slap of shoes on the sidewalk and knew Evie was hurrying after her.

"Blue," she called, "hold up!"

Blue didn't. It wasn't fair, maybe, but she wasn't just mad at that fool Cookie. She was mad at all the girls in their little clique, Evie included.

"What's wrong?" Evie said. "Are you mad?"

Blue rolled her eyes, not that Evie could see her do it. She took long, angry strides, her fists clenched at her sides. She kept her distance from sweet, harmless Evie, whose face was surely etched with sweet, harmless concern. "Me? Mad? Why would I be mad?"

"Because . . . you know . . ." Evie struggled with her breath. "You seem a little upset, that's all."

"Ah," Blue said. So clever, that one. So spot on with her insights into Blue's moods. And Blue was a faerie! And Evie a mortal! And Evie was still able to divine that Blue was "a little upset." Amazing, really. Evie should probably be awarded a medal.

"Could you slow down?" Evie pleaded.

Nope, she could not. Blue picked up her pace.

Evie tugged on Blue's shirtsleeve. Blue shook her off.

"Blue? I'm not the enemy, you know."

Did she? Did Blue know that?

Blue kept moving forward, charging down the sidewalk like a bull in search of a china shop. Then she forced herself to slow down. To stop. She bowed her head and closed her eyes and told her muscles to unclench—her hands, her neck, her jaw. She tried to drop her shoulders, but they hiked right back up again.

She inhaled to the count of four, held her breath for another four, and exhaled slowly: *one, two, three, four*. She breathed the way Margie taught her to when she was younger and hadn't had a clue how to manage her emotions.

Thunk! as a cup of milk hit Margie's wall and spilled its contents. *Bang!* as the oil lamp shattered.

"Emotions come and emotions go," Margie had said repeatedly over the years. "There's nothing we can do to control them—and that's true for fae and mortals alike. But we *can* control how we respond to our emotions. We can decide to lash out . . .or not. We can say hurtful things, or we can decide to go for a walk instead. Sometimes a very, very long walk. And if nothing else, we can stop and breathe. That's it, Blue. Just breathe."

In for four. Hold for four. Out for four.

In for four. Hold for four. Out for four.

Her shoulders dropped of their own accord. She opened her eyes. There were her bare feet on the sidewalk. They were solid and real, and she knew she could rely on them, just as she knew she could rely on Evie. Because she *did* know that Evie wasn't the enemy, for the most part.

Usually.

Ninety-nine days out of a hundred, Blue knew that Evie wasn't the enemy.

Cookie, on the other hand . . .

Blue turned around and was surprised to see that Evie was still several paces behind. She'd stopped, too. She'd stopped chasing after Blue and was standing with her arms folded over her chest and one foot cocked on her heel, the toe of her Mary Jane pointing at the sky.

Evie arched her eyebrows. "Are you done with your hissy fit?"

Blue huffed a laugh. This was a side of Evie she hadn't seen. Would it be wrong to tell her how adorable she was?

Yes. Telling Evie how adorable she was when she was mad was a terrible idea.

Her adorableness softened Blue's heart, though, and *whoosh*, just like that, the fury flew out of her. Not all of it, but enough.

"Your friend, Cookie, is a bigoted cow," she remarked. She said it without rancor as she closed the distance between herself and Evie. When she was two feet away, she stopped. It was Evie's move.

"She's not my friend," Evie countered. "And yes, she is." She took a step forward. "But when someone's as dumb as a box of rocks with the lid nailed shut, I've found it's best not to engage."

Blue nodded. She knew this was Evie's way of declaring whose side she was on, and she appreciated it.

At the same time . . .wasn't it necessary to engage at some point? Could anyone, mortal or fae, run away from conflict forever?

Evie took another step forward. They could have kissed, they were that close. Two more inches and their lips would meet.

"Yes, sure," she began. "But . . ."

Evie waited, but Blue couldn't remember what she'd set out to say. She shrugged and gave Evie a helpless smile.

Evie smiled back. "I'm not Cookie," she said. She took both of Blue's hands. "I'm me."

"Yes," Blue said. That part, she could wrap her head around. Evie, Evie, Evie.

"And I'm still hungry for a cinnamon roll," Evie continued. "You?"

"Yes. Definitely."

~

At Anton's, the scent of butter and warm dough wrapped around them. Blue picked off doughy bites of pastry, letting the icing melt on her tongue. She and Evie chatted with Anton, and when he asked if they wanted to meet a kitten he'd found, both girls nodded. He led them to the back of the bakery, where the tiniest kitten Blue had ever seen sat in a cardboard box. Too tiny.

"She can't be more than a few weeks old," she murmured, crouching to graze the kitten's fuzzy cheek with her knuckle. "She's too young to be on her own."

"Found her in the culvert yesterday, just a sodden ball of fur," Anton said. "Spent half an hour searching for her mama, even a littermate, but no luck. They must've been washed away in the storm."

He handed Blue a small jar of mashed turkey. "See if you can get her to take a little," he said. "She needs the nourishment, but I've had no luck."

126

Blue settled onto the floor and lifted the kitten carefully from the box. Cradling the creature to her chest, she dipped her finger into the jar of mash and offered it to the kitten. The kitten turned away, but Blue was patient. Soon, her tiny tongue flicked out, tasting the food.

"That's a sight for sore eyes," Anton said, his voice loosening with relief.

"Hey, little girl," Blue whispered. She held the kitten close, stroking her fragile back. *You're safe, little one. And you need to eat. Can you eat a little more?*

She scooped up more of the mashed turkey with her finger. The kitten feebly licked it off.

Good! Blue encouraged.

Another lick. Then another. The kitten's eyelids blinked open to reveal soft green eyes.

"She's precious," Evie said.

"You have a way with her," Anton told Blue.

Blue kept stroking the kitten, feeling her purr against her palm as Anton spoke of other rescued animals he'd helped over the years.

"Toby, he's been with me for four years," Anton said of the sleek russet fox Blue had noticed at Anton's before. He nodded toward the kitten. "I can't let him meet this one, not yet. He's tame, but he's still a fox."

He told them how he'd found Toby crying in a den, his mother caught in a nearby trap. "She died trying to reach him. The steel teeth had cut clear to the bone."

Evie cringed.

"Any hunter who sets those traps ought to get caught in one himself," Anton said. "See how he likes it."

Blue pressed her cheek to the kitten's fur. *No traps for*

you, little one.

"I once found a rabbit in a trap, but the dogs got to it before I could free it," Anton went on. "Screamed so loud it made my hair stand up. You ever heard a rabbit scream?"

Blue shot him a look.

He caught himself, perhaps realizing he ought to mind his tongue. "You're Margie's girl," he said to Blue.

"That's right," she replied.

"You're better with that kitten than I am, and that's the truth. Think Margie would let you keep her?"

Blue knew she would. Margie was a sucker for wounded creatures of all stripes and colors. She looked down at the kitten, who'd fallen asleep but was still purring away, the softest, sweetest purr in the world.

"I'll call her Star," Blue said, the name bubbling up from somewhere deep.

"Star," Evie repeated, running a gentle finger down the kitten's head. "It's perfect. It suits her."

"Take this, and this," Anton said, placing several jars of mashed food into a box and handing it to Evie. "Now that she's got you girls, I think she'll be just fine."

Blue touched her nose to Star's. "Come on. Let's get you home."

Chapter Twenty

"She looks better already," Evie said of Star the next day, settling onto the overstuffed sofa beside Blue. Star was curled in Blue's lap, paws tucked neatly beneath her. "Her fur is shinier."

Mrs. Freeman, ensconced in her chair on the other side of the room, snorted, and Evie felt herself stiffen. She didn't know how to act around the old lady, and that was the truth. She wished she'd just wheel herself out of the room and give her and Blue some space. But no. Mrs. Freeman lived to plague Blue, it seemed. Wherever Blue went, Mrs. Freeman went, too.

"I think she's even put on weight," Evie pronounced, determined not to let the old lady shut her down.

"I doubt it," Blue said. "Not in the twelve hours I've had her." Still, she looked pleased.

Evie took the kitten's paw and shook it. "Hi, Star. How's it going?"

She released Star's paw, and Star promptly placed it back on top of Evie's hand.

"Aw!" she exclaimed. As a rule, she preferred dogs to cats, but Star was a cutie. Not as cute as her beloved old hound who died when Evie was a girl, but Evie could hardly hold that against her.

"You are a darling!" she told Star, widening her eyes and switching to the voice she used to use with Windsor. "Oh yes, you are!"

Star blinked and neatly reclaimed her paw.

"She doesn't appreciate being compared to a dog," Blue said.

Evie laughed. Then she crinkled her brow. "Wait. Just now, just this very second, I was thinking about Windsor, the dog I had as a kid. How did you know?"

Blue's eyes darted from Evie to Star to Evie again. "Cats don't like dogs, as a rule."

"I'm aware."

Blue fidgeted. "Well, there you have it."

So Blue was being Blue again. Cryptic. Cagey. But Evie hadn't meant to make her feel uncomfortable, and at any rate, this wasn't a conversation to have in front of Mrs. Freeman.

"Whatever you say, Blue," she said, only pretending to be exasperated. She knocked her shoulder against Blue's. "I'm just glad Anton found her."

"Me, too," Blue said. She scratched behind Star's ears. Star gazed up at her adoringly. "He saved you, didn't he, little Starshine? Anton saved your life!"

"Anton the baker?" interjected Mrs. Freeman. "Anton is no savior, I'll have you know."

Evie shot Blue a look.

The look Blue shot back said, *Don't even bother*. Her jaw tightened in that way of hers, and Evie wondered again what the old lady had said to Blue the day they'd hiked to

Overlook Rock. Not the story about the faerie man and the ring, which was bad enough, but afterward. She'd shooed Evie off, but she'd kept Blue pinned in place with her hard pebble eyes, saying things that had made Blue flinch.

How often did Mrs. Freeman say things that made Blue flinch? How long would it be before Blue decided she'd had enough?

Maybe Evie could stand up to Mrs. Freeman on Blue's behalf. Maybe even a small show of resistance would make it easier for Blue to stay, like a pressure valve on a steam engine—just enough to keep the whole thing from blowing.

"Anton's not a savior the way Jesus was," Evie said. "I'm not saying that. But he saves loads of animals. That counts for something."

"Oh, does it?" Mrs. Freeman said. She cranked her invalid chair forward until she was just shy of the sofa Blue and Evie sat on. She plunged her hand into her carryall bag, pulled out her wooden-handled bell, and rapped Blue's knee with it, the clapper chiming sharply.

Blue took pains not to react, or that's how Evie read it. Even though kneecaps were tender and bruisable, and metal bells were not.

"I'm talking to you, girl," the old lady commanded. "Do you hear me, or have you gone deaf?"

"I can hear you just fine," Blue said, scratching Star's cheek.

"Anton and I were neighbors when I was a girl," Mrs. Freeman said. "Lived right next door to each other, just like you two. Spent plenty of time together, too. Just like you two."

"If you were friends, then you know for yourself what

he's like," Evie said, lifting her chin.

"People change over time," Mrs. Freeman said. Since Blue refused to meet her gaze, Evie was the recipient of the old lady's creepy, cryptic smile. "Even a friend can let you down."

Evie rose from the sofa. She'd shown enough resistance for one day, she decided. "I'm going to go," she told Blue.

"I don't blame you," Blue muttered.

"Anton was the neighbor boy I told you girls about," Mrs. Freeman said, projecting her voice. "The one who went horseback riding with me."

Evie, who had almost made it to the front door, paused and turned around. Her heart was a floppy thing, a cold, wet frog.

"That's right," Mrs. Freeman said sweetly. "It was Anton who shot that faerie man."

Evie felt lightheaded—because, no. Not Anton. She looked to Blue for salvation, but Blue's attention had locked onto the grandmother. Only moments before, she'd refused to meet the old lady's eyes, but now she stared the old woman down.

"*Ohhh*," she said, as if she'd been given the solution to a great mystery. "So what you're telling us is that Anton changed for the better over the years, whereas you remained as hateful and ignorant as ever." She raised her eyebrows. "Is that how he let you down, by developing a conscience?"

The bell came down hard on Blue's knee, the same knee as before. *Ding!*

"Impertinent girl!" the old lady exclaimed sharply.

Evie heard Blue's quick intake of breath, but Blue neither

flinched nor looked away.

Then the old lady cackled, and in her cackle—it was the strangest thing—Evie heard amusement and what almost sounded like a dash of pride.

"So. Is he Anton the baker, murderer of fae?" Mrs. Freeman said. She rolled her chair backward and forward in that repetitive way of hers, a bad habit she couldn't conquer. "Or is he Anton the baker, savior of small creatures? Does one negate the other? Are his sins to be forgiven?"

"You're the one who said he'd changed," Blue retorted.

"Did I?"

"Do you remember—or have you gone senile?"

"I said *people* change over time," Mrs. Freeman said. "People. People!"

Blue turned to Evie. "Escape while you can," she said. "I'll come find you after Margie gets home and I'm done babysitting."

"Yes. Okay." Evie nodded foolishly. "Bye!"

Chapter Twenty-One

Once home, Evie retreated to the backyard and scaled the ladder of her childhood fort. She sat there, hugging her knees to her chest and fluffing her skirt out around them. From inside the house, her mother's piano students banged out "Für Elise" and "Jesu, Joy of Man's Desiring."

Evie reminded herself that the Hard Times had happened long ago. That things were different now, and that yes, some people *had* changed. Not everyone. There were still the Cookie Gardners of the world. There was still sour, bitter, dried-up Mrs. Freeman.

Every so often, Evie looked over toward Mrs. Freeman's house, wondering if Blue might emerge. When she didn't, part of Evie was relieved. It felt like a reprieve, but from what? From Blue?

After supper, she helped her mother with the dishes. When the kitchen was spick-and-span, she dried her hands and asked, "May I call Dad?"

"We'll talk to him on Saturday like always," her mother said. "Long-distance costs money."

"I won't talk long."

Her mother set down her dishcloth. "He's been gone a

long time, hasn't he?" She exhaled. "Go on, but no longer than three minutes. And pass him to me when you're done."

Evie lifted the receiver from the wall phone and cranked the handle. When the operator came on, she gave the name and waited for the clicks and hums to settle.

"Dad? Hi!"

"Evie, my sweet girl," her father said. "Now this is a surprise. Everything all right?"

She reassured him that yes, everything was as it should be. She was fine, Jax was fine, her mother was fine. Then she got to the point.

"Dad, were our ancestors cruel to the fae?"

Her father hesitated. "What a question. Why do you ask?"

"I don't know," Evie said. "Yesterday, some of us girls got together. We were just talking, and Cookie—you know Cookie—she said that her great-grandmother used to say the fae gave her the creeps. Said that the air felt wrong when they were nearby."

Her father exhaled. "Honey, that kind of talk's been around a long time. Forest legends, mostly. Superstitions dressed up as wisdom and passed down like a casserole recipe."

Evie gripped the receiver. "But Granny and Papa never talked like that, right?"

"Not that I recall," her father said, his voice as steady as ever. "But Evie, I grew up poor. You know that."

Evie cradled the heavy receiver against her ear. "What's that got to do with the fae?"

There was a pause, just long enough for the line to

crackle.

"My dad worked a patch of clay that barely grew turnips," her father said. "We didn't have shoes half the year. Ate whatever we could trap or trade. And still—still—my father would look at the fae working in the holler and say at least we were better than them."

"Why?" Evie asked.

"Because we didn't have pointed ears. Because we're mortals."

Evie's chest tightened.

"I hated the way folks treated the fae sometimes," he said. "The way they'd leave scraps at the tree line and call it kindness, but never once let a faerie step across their porch."

There was a faint, hollow sound, like he was shifting the phone from one hand to the other.

"I should've done more," he said, his voice roughening. "Should've spoken up. Should've been braver. But I was a boy, Evie. And boys . . . well, boys learn too much from the men around them."

Evie squeezed her eyes shut.

"That's why I raised you the way I did. Hoped you'd come out better. Braver."

Evie stayed silent, afraid her voice would break if she spoke.

Her mother appeared and gestured for the phone.

"Mom wants to talk," Evie managed.

"All right, sweetheart. I love you—and I'll be home soon."

Later, in her room, she reminded herself that technically, and as far as she knew, her dad had done nothing wrong. He wished he'd done more, but who didn't? Evie sure did, almost daily. She told herself that it spoke to his character that he'd answered her questions honestly and without shying away. Not all men would, especially when speaking to their teenage daughters.

Still, she struggled to make her new knowledge sit right. Until tonight, she'd considered her father the bravest man she knew. It hurt to let that go, like unclasping a medal from around her neck and dropping it into a river. Like watching it sink and disappear.

Chapter Twenty-Two

The next day, after an interminable morning spent with the grandmother—how did the old woman time her bodily functions with such precision, always waiting until it was Blue and only Blue who was present to aid her?—Blue escaped and clambered over the fence into Evie's yard.

"There's a raccoon up in the woods that should have just given birth, if my timeline's right," Blue said. "Want to go see the babies?"

"Raccoon babies?" Evie said. A smile played around her lips. "Yes, please."

It was July, humid and thick, and sweat trickled down Blue's spine as they hiked. Evie lagged behind, and Blue had to remind herself to stop every so often to let Evie catch her breath. The trail leveled out under the evergreens and made conversation possible.

"The mama raccoon—how do you know about her?" Evie asked.

Blue shrugged. "I don't know. I just do."

"And yesterday, when I was thinking about my dog, Windsor. I didn't say a word about him, not out loud, but somehow you knew. How?"

"How do you know how to make pie?"

"My mother taught me. But that's different. Blue, the things you know—"

Evie tripped on a root. Blue's hands flew out to steady her—one to Evie's forearm, the other to her lower back—before Evie's own muscles had time to react. Surprise flashed across Evie's face, followed by confusion.

"See?" Evie exclaimed. "Like that! You know things before they happen, practically."

"Or I'm just observant," Blue countered.

Evie shook her head. "It's more than just that. I swear, Blue, sometimes I feel like we live in two different worlds."

Blue didn't like the direction this conversation was heading. "Nope. Same ground, same trees, same roots to trip on."

"You have never tripped in your life," Evie said. "You spot invisible spiderwebs, and you can walk right up to a deer without startling it away."

"You were there, too, with the deer. They didn't run from you, either."

"Do you know why? Because I was with you."

Blue kicked a rock.

"I'm not. . . it's not. . . I think it's really neat, the things you know and the things you can do," Evie said. "I wish I could understand, that's all."

Evie couldn't, though. That was the problem. Whereas Evie saw the trees, Blue felt them. She understood the whispers of their leaves and pull of their roots, especially when it had been too long since the last rain. Whereas Evie listened to the weatherman on the radio, Blue sensed a coming storm in her bones. She felt the shift in the air before a heat spell, and she smelled a sweet tickling breeze when ripe blueberries were around the corner. The earth spoke to her of ancient ways and the deep groan of mountains being born. The soil itself breathed beneath her feet.

Blue's experience of the world was infinitely richer than Evie's, which seemed terribly unfair. It was as if Evie was color blind and didn't even know it. (Or perhaps she did, given her line of questioning.)

Then again, Blue had been Evie-blind until this summer. Evie was the real miracle. She made everything brighter and better.

Blue hopped onto a fallen log, then crouched and peered beneath a rocky overhang. "This is where her den is, the mama raccoon."

But when Evie stepped forward, Blue threw out her arm.

"Wait," she said, under her breath.

A low growl rumbled from the den. The hairs on Blue's arms prickled.

"Back up," she murmured to Evie. "Slowly."

The growl rose like the twang of a rusted wire, and from out of the darkness came a snarling, drooling beast, all claws and fur and ringed raccoon eyes.

"Blue?" Evie said, her voice quivering as well. "There's something wrong with it. What's wrong with it?"

It's sick, Blue thought but didn't say. It was sick, and the sickness had infected its mind, just like a bat that had flown straight at Margie's cabin one time. The bat had flown into a wooden beam and dropped hard, one wing crushed and the other flapping like a wet towel. It had hopped in frantic circles, baring its tiny teeth and emitting

140

a deranged skittering sound.

"Rabies," Margie had said grimly before banging the bat with a shovel.

The snarling, drooling raccoon had rabies, too. But Blue had no shovel.

"Stay back," she said sharply, driving forward and sinking her hands into coarse fur. The raccoon thrashed and snapped. Blue gritted her teeth, searching and searching—

There. With a twist, she wrenched the spinal column from the skull. The raccoon shuddered and went limp.

Blue flung the body down. She looked at her hands. Blood. She looked at Evie. Tears.

"What about the babies?" Evie asked. "Are they all right?"

Blue didn't tell Evie that the babies had died in their mother's womb, and that it was just as well they had. If they'd been born, the raccoon mother would have eaten them alive.

"There aren't any babies," Blue said roughly. "Sorry."

"It's not your fault," Evie whispered.

Blue squinted into the distance. "Listen, there's stuff I need to do. With the carcass."

"Oh," Evie said. She swallowed audibly. "Do you need help?"

"No. Will you be all right, heading back on your own?"

"Of course. But, Blue. . . can I ask you something?"

Blue pulled herself back and met Evie's soft brown eyes, which were full of questions. Big questions. Scary questions. Blue's pulse accelerated, and she curled her hands into fists. When she felt the slickness of blood, she shoved them behind her back.

"Sure," she said, her insides tightening.

Evie's chest rose and fell. Her lips parted, then came back together. She folded them inwards and held them there, as if the wrong thing might spill out if she wasn't careful.

"Will *you* be all right?" she finally blurted.

Blue exhaled, dizzy with relief. "Yeah. Yeah, I'll be fine."

"Okay. Good." Evie managed a weak smile and started down the trail.

Blue waited until she was out of sight, then knelt beside the dead raccoon and got to work.

Chapter Twenty-Three

After dinner, Blue went straight to her room, waving off Margie's concerns and avoiding the grandmother's prying eyes. She drew the blinds, curled up on her bed, and willed herself to sleep.

Sleep refused to come.

Star, warm and tiny, tucked herself against Blue's side, purring a whispery hum. Blue let the sound wash over her, let her body sink deeper into the mattress. Still, sleep stayed out of reach.

Near midnight, exhaustion finally won, and Blue slipped under, only to find herself facing a great and terrible deer. It was massive, its liquid-black eyes shining with timeless sorrow. *Is she with you? Is she safe?* the deer asked wordlessly.

Blue gasped and bolted upright.

Star looked at her reproachfully.

Sorry, Blue told her. *It's all right. Everything's all right.*

But was it?

~

Evie also lay awake deep into the night. She stared at the ceiling, thoughts churning.

Faeries. Blue.

How horrible—how absolutely horrible—it would be if Blue was fae and had to keep her identity secret, afraid to even tell her.

All the fae left Hemridge decades ago. Everyone knew that. But then there was Silas Bratton's brother, Ben. Cookie was wrong about how he died. A fae boy hadn't murdered him. He'd been killed by a bear—Evie's dad swore to it up and down.

But a faerie *had* been involved. Evie wasn't sure of the details, just that the boy hadn't been much older than Ben himself.

Afterward, Ben's father and some other men from town had tracked him down and dragged him out of his cave, kicking and screaming. He'd fought back hard—howling, biting, and shifting through a dozen wild shapes as he tried to get free. A bobcat. A fish. A slithering snake.

And then Bob Bratton shot him dead.

"Which he shouldn't have done," Evie's father had said heavily. "He needed someone to blame, that's all. He was out of his mind with grief."

"The fae boy, did he really change into all those animals?" Evie had asked. Goodness, but she'd been young. Only four years old, but the story had burrowed deep and stayed.

"Of course not," her father had said.

"You don't know if he did or didn't," her mother had countered. "The fae are tricky. Don't say they're not."

Evie felt sick at the thought of a boy being hunted like that—mortal or fae. Hunted down, dragged from his home, shot in the aftermath of a tragedy he may or may not have had anything to do with.

She imagined Blue in the fae boy's place. Scared. Alone. A gang of men crashing through the trees, closing in.

Evie's gut twisted, and she curled sideways into a fetal position, clutching her stomach. She couldn't go on like this, not when it came to Blue.

She needed to ask. It was as simple as that.

Then that's what I'll do, she vowed.

She pictured herself saying it—just casually, like it wasn't a big deal. *Blue, I was wondering . . . are you a faerie?* If Blue said yes, Evie would tell her it was fine. More than fine. Blue was Blue. Who cared about labels?

"It changes nothing," she whispered, practicing the words.

~

One house over, Blue stroked Star's cheek, then traced a finger down the fuzz between Star's eyes, lulling the kitten back to sleep. Then she slipped out of bed, crept down the stairs, and stepped barefoot into the backyard.

Above her, the night stretched wide. A full moon rose over the curves of the mountains. A shimmering mist stirred something restless in Blue's soul.

A breeze rustled the pines, sending needles drifting toward the ground.

Blue lifted her hands and kept them aloft. They hung there, twisting and turning in the silvery light.

She sighed, and the needles fell. *Plimp, plimp, plimp.*

She gazed at the mountains and felt sorry for herself, and alone.

But she *wasn't* alone, was she? She had Evie, and Evie was the most important thing in the world, aside from

Margie. Anyway, Margie didn't count, not in the same way. Margie was a given, like breath, like gravity.

Evie was different. Evie was a gift.

Blue had seen Evie's face, though, after the raccoon. She'd felt Evie's hesitation. She'd sensed the fear behind Evie's unfinished question.

Blue . . . can I ask you something?

Best friends with secrets didn't work.

She climbed the fence and hopped into Evie's yard, crossing silently to the back of the house. The gutter was cold under her hands, slick with dew. She moved carefully, silently, hauling herself up to the second floor. When she reached the overhang above the back porch, she inched sideways along the narrow strip of roof. One misstep would send her clattering down, but her feet were sure and certain.

She reached Evie's window and tapped lightly at the screen.

Inside, the room was dark except for a strip of moonlight pooling across the floor. Evie was awake. Blue could see the faint gleam of her eyes as she scrambled out of bed and across the floor.

Evie unlatched the screen and pushed it open.

Blue scrambled inside.

They stood there for a moment, neither speaking. One side of Evie's hair was mashed flat from sleep. The other side stuck out wildly, like she'd been struck by lightning. In the half-light, with her nightgown wrinkled and her face still sweet with dreams, she looked so beautiful, Blue could hardly stand it.

Her stomach flipped. Sweat dampened the back of her

neck, and not from the climb.

She was in Evie's room, safe and sound, and all she could think about was how much she wanted this to last—the lovely routine of their days together, just the two of them. Hopping the fence and hiking through the woods, gorging on blueberries until their fingers were stained purple. Splashing in the creek where the water ran cold. Floating side by side in one of the many swimming holes, nestled among the reflected clouds.

Sky above, earth below, and Blue and Evie drifting in the endless in-between.

She could still have all that. She could. Just . . .after.

Evie's hands found hers, warm and a little clumsy with sleep. She had a crust of dream dust in the corner of her eye.

"Blue . . ." Evie began.

Blue squeezed her hands. "Evie, listen . . ."

They both let out nervous laughs, breathless in the hush.

"You first," Evie said.

Blue's vision tunneled, the whole world blurring out except for Evie. Only Evie, perfect in the moonlight.

"The thing is . . ." she began. "The thing you should know . . ."

She looked at Evie and let the truth fall between them.

"I'm a faerie."

Chapter Twenty-Four

"Can you talk to animals?" Evie asked Blue the following day, once morning came and they'd reunited and dashed off into the woods. "Did you with the deer? And Star? Is that why she trusted you right away?"

Blue was relieved. The hard part was over. Evie hadn't gone pale at the news or fainted dead away. The two had met up after breakfast as always, and Evie had jerked her head toward the forest and said, "Let's go!"

But the answer to all of Evie's questions was "no."

No, she couldn't predict the future.

No, she couldn't turn invisible.

No, she couldn't fly.

As for shape-shifting? Good heavens.

"I absolutely cannot shape-shift," she said grouchily. They'd taken a break at the creek, sitting on the bank and submerging their feet in the rushing water. "Can *you*?"

Evie laughed. "Okay. Fair. So . . . what can you do?"

Blue was glad she'd shared her secret with Evie. And she was *very* glad Evie hadn't asked to see her ears. That would have made her feel freakish.

Blue didn't want Evie to think she was a freak. But

sheesh, she didn't want Evie to think she was boring, either.

She rose abruptly. "Follow me."

Evie scrambled to pull on her shoes and hurried after her.

In a clearing, Blue paced in a small circle, her head bowed and her hands clasped behind her back.

"Here," she declared.

Blue sank cross-legged on the forest floor and gestured for Evie to do the same. When Evie sat, Blue held out her hands, and Evie placed her palms in Blue's.

Straightaway, Blue felt a thrumming energy bloom inside her, as luminous and bright as the moon. A great rushing filled her head, and there was an eerie, blank moment when she forgot how to exist.

She lifted her face to the sky. Energy surged into her, wild and free.

She lowered her gaze.

"Watch," she murmured.

The dirt between them began to stir. Slowly at first, then faster, spiraling into a twisting funnel of twigs, pine needles, and crumbling leaves. A miniature storm, spinning, hissing, spitting earth.

Evie stared at the whirlwind.

Blue stared at Evie.

Then Evie gasped and yanked away her hands.

One moment, everything was flying.

Then, as if a switch had been flipped, everything dropped to the ground.

Blue sat blinking, dazed, coming back to herself. The trees stretched high around them, making Evie look small in comparison. Blue and Evie were both so small! And yet, in that moment, Blue felt big. Vast.

"I'm sorry I pulled away," Evie said. She looked abashed. "That was wonderful. *You're* wonderful."

A lump rose in Blue's throat, and she fought not to cry.

"Hey, hey," Evie said. She scooched closer and stroked Blue's hair. "Don't worry, Blue. I won't ever tell."

Evie had it wrong. Blue wasn't teary out of fear. But how could she explain the true source of her sadness? She couldn't. The well was too deep.

She rested her head on Evie's shoulder and let Evie keep stroking her hair.

~

At Evie's request, Blue made more stick and leaf tornadoes, each one bigger and wilder than the last. Evie loved them all and learned quickly not to resist or pull away. When Evie asked, Blue showed her other things, too, like how she could sing to trout and lull them into hazy bliss. They'd flip onto their backs in the cold mountain water and wiggle with pleasure, allowing even Evie to stroke their bellies. Blue chittered with the squirrels—a high, fast click of her tongue—and one leapt confidently onto Blue's shoulders, which made Evie laugh.

Blue passed on a message—maybe in her head?—and the squirrel craned forward to look Blue in the face. Blue nodded, and the squirrel turned around and sniffed at Evie.

"His claws are prickly little things. Be prepared," Blue said. "But he won't hurt you."

The squirrel put his front paw on Evie's shoulder, which was bare, as she was wearing a sundress flocked with tiny purple flowers.

"Eee!" Evie squeaked, but it was a controlled sort of "eee." Mainly.

The squirrel wiggled its hindquarters, then pushed off Blue and landed on Evie, all four paws finding purchase on her skin. His claws were prickly, all right, like sharp little needles. He sniffed Evie's ear, which tickled. He pushed his head into Evie's blond curls, exploring and sniffing all around, and when he lashed his fluffy white tail, it hit Evie squarely on her face.

She laughed and got squirrel fur in her mouth. Blue grinned.

"Give him this," she said, handing Evie an acorn she'd already uncapped.

Evie offered up the acorn on a flat palm, and it was enough to lure him from her hair. He sat on Evie's shoulder and held the acorn in his quick, clever toes. Fingers? He turned it this way and that, inspecting it, then drew it to his mouth and munched away.

"I love him so much," Evie told Blue, tearing up from how wondrous it was and how honored she felt by the trust this little guy was showing her.

"Do you think they bring good luck after all?" Blue asked.

"Hmm?"

Blue arched an eyebrow.

Evie's brow furrowed, then cleared, remembering that morning way back at the beginning of the summer when Blue had given her quite a lecture on squirrels, all lofty and superior. When Evie had shared her own squirrel knowledge—that white squirrels were special to their neck of the woods—Blue had scoffed as if she didn't believe her.

She gave Blue a look that said, *Hardy har har.* It seemed

so silly now, bickering about squirrels. Bickering *like* squirrels!

"I think they bring *some* good luck," she said, twisting her neck and rubbing her cheek against her squirrel friend's soft chest. She gave Blue a smile. "I think you bring more."

Chapter Twenty-Five

Another day, while cooling off in the shallows at the base of the waterfall, Blue knelt and thrust her arms into the creek bed. She stood up with a glob of mud cupped in her hands. Silt oozed from between her fingers, gloopy and thick, as she pressed her palms together. When all the mud had fallen free, she opened her hands like a book. Or, no. Like a seed pod unfolding after an afternoon shower.

In her palms waited a ring, wet and glinting.

"Go on," Blue said. "See if it fits."

Evie's heart swelled nearly to bursting as she lifted the ring and slid it onto her finger. It fit perfectly, because of course it did.

"But ... how?" Evie marveled, flexing her hand and admiring the shiny circlet.

"There's iron in the soil," Blue said with a shrug. "And mica, and quartz. They're part of the world, too. They listen."

That evening, she and Blue watched the sun set from the meadow of the golden roses. Dinner time was fast approaching. Evie's mother would be wondering where she was. But love tugged harder at Evie's soul than hot buttered biscuits ever could, and stolen moments of beauty were well worth the price of a reprimand.

Evie toed off her shoes and peeled off her socks as soon as they sat down. *You're becoming more of a heathen every day!* she imagined her mother scolding. She smiled and wiggled her toes in the grass.

Blue lay flat on her back, and Evie leaned back and positioned herself alongside her. Blue's hand found Evie's. Evie's foot found Blue's, their big toes pressing together. Above them, a hum of fireflies formed a flickering heart in the inky sky.

"Oh, Blue," Evie murmured. She started to say that she wished she, too, were magic. That sometimes she felt jealous. She thought better of it, because after all, being magic hadn't helped the fae in the end, had it? Being magic made the fae "other," or so went the logic. But there was no logic to it. Just fear. Fear and possibly jealousy, come to think of it. A potent mix, that.

"Thank you," she said instead.

"For what?" Blue asked.

The fireflies rearranged themselves into the shape of a star, and Evie squeezed Blue's hand. "For this. For everything. For sharing your magic with me."

"It's not *magic*," Blue said defensively.

"No?" Evie said. She turned her head sideways, one cheek pressed against the cool grass. Blue did the same, her blue eyes finding Evie's brown ones. "What is it, then, if it's not magic?"

Shadows flitted across Blue's irises, as dark as sorrow. Her lips parted as if she were about to speak. She pressed them back together. She kept her gaze locked on Evie's, though, and so Evie didn't retract the question, despite her pounding heart.

"What if it's just . . . me?" Blue finally whispered.

Then you are made of magic, Evie wanted to say. To her, it felt so right. So lovely and true. But Blue wouldn't hear it like that. Blue would hear, *Then we are different and always will be.* She would imagine a bridge between them that could never be crossed, and she would feel herself at fault.

Evie's throat tightened, because now *she* was imagining a bridge between them that could never be crossed—and she felt *herself* to be at fault. She knew, rationally, that neither she nor Blue was to blame for the differences that hung between them, uncrossable. She knew that their differences should be celebrated, not hidden or left unspoken. Not swept beneath the rug, even if the rug was made of golden roses.

Evie sat up.

Puzzled, Blue sat up, too. The sun formed a halo around Blue as it sank behind the mountains, dipping her long black hair in gold.

Evie stretched forward and picked one of the wild yellow roses that carpeted the meadow. Its stem was dense with sharp and grabby thorns. She poked one deep into the pad of her index finger. Then she took hold of Blue's hand and repeated the action.

Blue watched as a bead of blood bloomed on her finger, twin to the droplet on Evie's. She lifted her gaze, and Evie saw hope in those remarkable eyes of hers. Not sorrow. Not shame. But a flickering hope that made the lump in Evie's throat grow painfully thick.

She pressed her finger to Blue's, curling her free hand around them to bind them fast. Their blood met and mixed, and Evie felt a surge of joy. It was an ember igniting, a shooting star, the pulse of a million fireflies illuminating the heavens.

Did Blue feel it, too?

When she released Blue's hand, she felt lightheaded.

Blue gaped at her, then gathered herself with a shake.

"Evie," she said.

"Blue," Evie replied. She couldn't articulate what she wanted to say, so she pushed the thought at her as best she could: *You are not "tainted." You are not "other." Or if you are? Then I am, too.*

A smile spread across Blue's face, as clear and pure as the chime of a celestial bell.

Chapter Twenty-Six

The next day, Blue led Evie back to the meadow where the yellow roses grew. Once they were seated, Blue nudged Evie's knee and pointed. "See that blade of grass?"

"There's a lot of grass, Blue."

"The one with three dewdrops in a line."

Evie spotted it—three perfect, trembling spheres.

"Okay, found it."

"Watch."

The lowest drop quivered, then rolled up, swallowing the next. The two combined, swelling, absorbing the third. Then, impossibly, the dewdrop kept going, climbing the blade of grass until its weight bowed the stem.

With a sudden snap, the blade catapulted the dewdrop into the air.

Evie expected it to fall.

It didn't.

Instead, it *hovered*—suspended, shimmering—a tiny liquid lens. Inside it, her own face rippled, then Blue's, their reflections passing upside down between them.

When the dewdrop burst, a feathered thing flapped in Evie's chest, soft and grateful. Blue might not want to talk about her magic, but she shared it with Evie freely. If she could tap Evie with a wand and make Evie magic, too—if only there was such a way!—she would in a heartbeat. Evie knew it.

Another day, Blue tossed an apple into the air and kept it there, bobbing just out of reach until Evie jumped up and snatched it.

"Ha!" Evie crowed. "Last Halloween, we bobbed for apples in class. Kid stuff, I know. Anyway, I was terrible. The worst. But *jumping* for apples? I'm a natural!"

Blue pulled her eyebrows together. They were spiky and black and reminded Evie of caterpillars. "What does that mean, bobbing for apples?"

Oh. Right. Blue didn't do Halloween. No school, no class parties, no dunking your face into a tub of water for the privilege of biting a piece of waxy fruit.

There were certain things Blue didn't like to acknowledge. Well, there were other truths—hard ones—that Evie would just as soon leave unspoken. At the end of the summer, school would start back up, for example. No more long lazy days with Blue. No more wandering the woods until dusk.

How would she manage without Blue?

How would Blue manage without her?

Could Evie convince Blue to stay in town, even though Blue hated the grandmother?

"Not everything about living in town is bad, you know," she said.

"True," Blue agreed. "It means living next to you."

But eventually she would leave. Blue and Margie would go back up to their far-away cabin, and Evie would be left behind. Did this thought not trouble Blue the way it troubled Evie?

"What?" Blue said, searching her face.

"Nothing," Evie said.

Blue's eyebrows rose into peaks. They really were like caterpillars, if caterpillars came in black.

"Do caterpillars come in black?" Evie asked, knowing she was doing that Evie-thing of avoiding facing things head on.

"Yeah, sure," Blue said.

"Do they turn into black butterflies?"

Blue didn't answer. Instead, she stood, lifted her arms, and let them fall outward, fingers spread.

The wind shifted.

A whisper. Then a sigh. Then a steady exhalation.

The sky darkened—not with clouds but with movement.

Evie's breath hitched as from the trees, a tide of black wings surged toward them, swirling like ink in water.

Is this real? Evie thought, her gaze flying to Blue.

Blue turned to her, eyes glowing. *This is everything,* she seemed to reply.

The butterflies poured toward them, dark ribbons unfurling through the air.

"Stand up," Blue instructed. "Hold out your arms."

Evie obeyed.

A butterfly landed on her forearm. Then another. More followed, choosing first her fingers and wrists, then drifting higher—her shoulders, her collarbone, the curve of her cheek.

Evie marveled at the butterflies' ebony wings. She marveled at Blue, who, like her, was draped in a rustling midnight quilt.

Thank you, she sensed Blue silently telling them.

Yes, why not? Goodbye! the butterflies seemed to reply. They rose as one, a flurry of obsidian wings.

Evie dropped back down, the weight of the moment pressing into her. She plucked at the grass, grounding herself.

"With the deer," she murmured, "and just now, the butterflies, and all of it . . ."

Blue cocked her head.

"We don't have to talk about it. You don't have to tell me."

"Evie?" Blue said.

Evie felt silly. Her cheeks grew warm.

"I'll tell you anything," Blue said. "You know that. What do you want to know?"

"Just . . . what does it feel like, being you?" Evie asked. "I don't mean to make a big deal out of it. I don't want to make you feel uncomfortable, or odd. You're *not* odd."

Blue gave a wry smile. "I'm probably a little odd."

"Okay. Yes. But in a good way." Evie scrunched her nose, mad at herself for saying anything at all. "But, please. Forget I asked. It doesn't matter."

Blue dropped her gaze. Her eyelashes cast shadows on her sharp cheekbones. "Sometimes I hear hooves," she whispered. "A great stampede, thundering closer. Other times, it's like a million birds—flapping their wings all at once."

Evie wanted to understand. She wanted it more than anything. But hooves? In Blue's head?

Blue must have seen her confusion, because she tried

again. "Everything is connected, Evie. That's the first thing you need to know. You, me, the butterflies. All of it."

"Okay," Evie said.

Blue's expression grew serious. "Imagine... imagine a net stretched over everything. The whole world. But not a normal net. A net that's lighter than gossamer and softer than moonlight. It stretches but never breaks, and when one thread stirs, all the others sing in reply."

She checked Evie's expression. "I sometimes wonder if that's what it is. If being magic just means knowing that nothing lives alone. We're all part of the same miracle."

Evie felt a pressure building inside her. If she didn't speak, she'd burst. But what was she supposed to say? What *could* she say?

"You asked what it feels like," Blue said.

Evie nodded.

"It feels amazing, like touching the heart of the universe." Something—maybe a spark—shot through Blue and made her black hair crackle, creating hard geometries around her face. "But there's something else, too. A shadow. A whisper."

"Of what?"

"I have so many questions, Evie. About my family. My mom." Blue's eyes were fierce and searching. "What happened to her? Where did she go?"

"Margie?" Evie said, bewildered. Margie hadn't gone anywhere as far as Evie knew.

"Margie adopted me," Blue said. "She's not... " She smiled painfully.

Evie felt *so* dumb. *Wow.*

But this wasn't about her.

"Doesn't Margie know who she adopted you from?" she asked.

"My birth mother left me on Margie's porch, but Margie never met her. Never even saw her."

Evie scooted closer and put her arm around Blue's shoulders, and now the spark she'd seen shoot through Blue shot through her as well, though for different reasons. Or . . . maybe not? Love was magic too, wasn't it?

She felt the heat of Blue's body and shivered. She felt the power of Blue's stillness and trembled. She loved Blue—and the knowledge made her heart kick. Evie loved Blue in *all* the ways. She did.

"Are you all right?" Blue asked, regarding her strangely.

"I'm fine. Yes. Please, tell me more."

Blue did, and Evie drank it in: the soft gray blanket, the note, Blue as a toddler uttering "digs" and "Mumsy."

As Blue spoke, her eyes shone with wondrous things: fireflies and darkest night and the hot breath of a lumbering bear. Evie's heart hurt, knowing there was so much about Blue that she didn't know and never would.

"I'm sorry," she said inadequately. "That sounds . . . it sounds awful, all that not-knowing."

Blue sighed. "If I knew about my past and who I came from, well . . . it would help. It would be something"

"And Margie can't tell you?"

"She's told me all she can. Also, I don't know, but I get the sense she doesn't like it when I bring that stuff up."

Evie caught her lower lip between her teeth, because she could see how that could be true. Maybe Margie, like Evie, felt inadequate sometimes, as if the gap between her and Blue was too much to bridge. It wasn't—was it?

"There *is* a way, though. To learn more." Blue held Evie in her gaze.

Evie's pulse accelerated. "Oh? How?"

"There's a potion I read about in one of Margie's notebooks. A memory magnet. It requires special plants, but they're all ones I know how to find."

"Are they safe?"

"Sure. Mainly. If you know what you're doing."

Evie tried to keep her tone neutral. "And . . .do you?"

Blue nodded, and her excitement spilled into her expression. "I think so. I'm pretty sure. I'd like to try, but I need someone to watch over me." She twisted toward Evie and took her hands. "Evie . . . will you be my watcher?"

Chapter Twenty-Seven

"I'm nervous," said Blue. She ran her fingers over the pine needles that cover the forest floor where she and Evie sat. "But excited."

"I'm just nervous," said Evie. "Blue . . . I'm not so sure about this."

Blue was. She was absolutely sure. She'd gathered all the ingredients. She'd found a tucked-away clearing where no one would disturb them. She'd painstakingly copied the ritual's instructions, including Margie's margin notes, and she and Evie had gone over them step-by-step.

Evie had been supportive of Blue's plan until now, when Blue confessed that one of the plants they'd be using was angel's breath, a plant known for driving people mad.

"Evie, I'm young and strong," Blue told her. "Other people might break under it, but not me."

"And you know that how?"

"Plenty of people—mortals—have used this potion and come out the other side. I'll be fine. And the recipe's from Margie's notebook. She wouldn't let anyone do anything dangerous."

"And yet you didn't ask Margie to be your watcher," Evie

pointed out. "You asked me."

"Because you're my Evie," Blue said, widening her eyes.

Evie's slant-eyed scowl told Blue she wasn't so easily fooled. "Yes. And you're my Blue, and I love you." She arched her brows. "You know who else loves you? Margie."

"I know. I do. But I can't ask her for this. I don't want to ask her for this."

"Because she'd say 'no,'" Evie said.

Yes. True. But it was more complicated than that.

"Margie loves me the way a mother would," Blue said slowly. "As she should, because she's my mom. She is. And I love her—so much. As her daughter." She nodded as if to convince herself. "But she still thinks of me as a kid, which I'm not."

"Has Margie ever performed the memory magnet ritual on anyone? Did it work?"

Blue bit her lip.

Evie frowned. "Blue, you know that book of mine? The one under my bed with all the gruesome pictures?"

"*A Factual (and Fearsome) History of Faeries?*" Blue snorted "You understand now why I hate that book, right?"

"I got rid of it."

"You did?"

"Yes, obviously. Because of course I understand why you hated it. I hate it now, too."

"Oh," Blue said. "Thanks?"

"The thing is, I've read other books about faeries. Library books. They were more like fairytales than books about actual faeries, but still."

"Huh," said Blue. She wasn't sure she liked where this was going.

"More than one of the books said that faeries can't lie," Evie said. "Is that true?"

A laugh burst out of Blue. "What?" She tilted her head and scrunched her nose. "Evie. That's bananas."

"Sure," Evie said, nodding. Then she tilted *her* head. She scrunched *her* nose. "But I'm still wondering. This memory magnet potion, the one that involves angel's breath. Has Margie done it before?"

Blue took in a deep breath of air. She blew it out in a whoosh. Could she lie to Evie? Definitely. Probably. But did she want to lie to Evie?

She smiled tightly and said, "According to her notes . . . no. But that doesn't bother me. I'm not worried."

"It bothers *me!*" Evie said. "*I'm* worried!" She grew serious. "I don't want anything to happen to you, Blue. Can you imagine how awful that would be, if something bad happened, and it was my fault?"

"But it wouldn't be—and anyway, it won't."

"I'd feel a lot better if Margie were here. A whole lot better."

Blue bowed her head. She twisted a lock of her bone-straight hair around and around her finger. Evie wasn't wrong to be concerned. It would be far wiser to have an experienced herbalist here, watching over things and making sure nothing went wrong. But Blue didn't have the luxury of proceeding with caution. It was either proceed with Evie or not at all.

"You're right. Margie would say no," she admitted. "And not just because she thinks I'm too young."

Evie's eyebrows came together, pushing worry lines into her forehead.

166

"She would say no because there are things she doesn't want me to know," Blue said. "That's what I think. Not because she knows some deep dark truth. I don't think she does. But because she's afraid of losing me."

Evie opened her mouth as if to speak.

Blue held up her hand. "If you can't do it, then okay." She nodded, trying to come to terms with this reality. If Blue was asked to do something that might put Evie in danger, would she? Even if Evie did the asking?

"What I haven't told Margie—and I guess this is on me. Maybe I'm afraid, too. Some things are really hard to say." She tapped her chest. "But there's a hole, right here. A gap. An ache. Sometimes it's so huge, I feel like I might fall into it and never find my way out."

Evie's energy changed. Loosened. She placed her hand on Blue's knee.

"I can't make you do this with me, Evie," Blue went on. "I don't *want* to make you. That's not us. That's not how we work." Her throat tightened. "But—"

"If it's important, I will," Evie said.

Blue blinked back a sudden rush of tears. "Yeah?"

"Yes. But if something goes wrong," she warned, "or seems off in any way. . ."

"We'll stop. Yes. I agree. I promise." Blue bobbed her head a bit foolishly. She still felt teary and raw. "Thank you, Evie."

Evie hinged forward, uncrossing her legs and shifting up and onto her knees. She leaned in and enveloped Blue in her arms, her cheek grazing lightly against Blue's. So soft. So warm. Then closer still, hugging Blue tight, her chin hooked over Blue's shoulder as Blue burrowed her face into

Evie's curls. Blue thought of the snow white squirrel who'd hopped onto Evie's shoulders and done exactly this, and she understood the squirrel's motivation completely. Who wouldn't want to be as close as possible to this wonderful being who was Evie?

She gave a burbly sort of laugh that might have been part sob.

"What?" Evie said anxiously. She moved to draw back.

Blue clung all the more tightly. "Nothing," she said. Only it wasn't nothing. It was everything. She felt the whorls of Evie's shell-like ear against her lips as she whispered, "Thank you."

Chapter Twenty-Eight

Blue unscrewed the top of a Mason jar. "The first step is for me to drink this tea. It's brewed from mountain rose. It's meant to loosen my spirit for flight."

Blue raised the jar in a toast, then took a long swig. It tasted slightly of roses, but also of rain and soil and newness. She wiped her mouth on the back of her hand.

"Now what?" Evie asked.

Together, they leaned over Blue's notes.

"Now we burn the blackberry twigs on a flat rock," Blue said. She struck a match, and the twigs she'd gathered caught quickly, crackling.

"'Inhale its scent,'" Evie read. "'Lose yourself in its rising smoke, for where does smoke go but upward toward the boundary between this world and all others?'"

Blue closed her eyes and breathed in deep. She opened them just a peek. "You're doing great, by the way. You're a natural."

"I've found my calling. Hurray!" Evie grumbled. "I'm a hedge witch."

"An herbalist," Blue corrected.

Evie blew out the small fire, then ground her thumb into

the ashes and smeared a dusky streak across Blue's forehead.

"To open your inner eye," she said.

"To open my inner eye," Blue repeated. She strained to feel something, anything. *Inner eye? Open!* she commanded.

Evie handed Blue the dandelions they'd picked. "'Dandelions grant wishes,'" she read aloud. "'The roots open the passageway to long-buried memories. They are in this way a great help when setting out on an ancestral journey.'"

She lowered the paper. "I think whoever wrote this was touched in the head."

"Aren't we all?" Blue said. "At least a little?"

"You?" Evie said. "Definitely." She sucked in her lower lip, then released it. "But me?"

Blue grinned. "Definitely."

She separated the dandelions' tough roots from their more pliable stems, peeling off strips of dark fiber and placing them in her mouth. Bitter.

"You're supposed to chew the roots till they're pulpy, but don't swallow them," Evie said.

"Chewing!" Blue said with her mouth full.

"How do they taste?"

"Like the bottom of a boot."

"Keep at it for half a minute more."

When the time was up, Blue spat the masticated pulp into the dirt and buried it.

"'The final ingredient is angel's breath, also known as the whisper of remembrance,'" Evie read. She sighed. "Also known as the plant that can kill you."

Nervous tingles ran up and down Blue's spine, made their way into her lungs, and prodded at the hollows of her ribcage.

Evie lifted the paper. "'Angel's breath is critical for a successful psychic journey. It grants safe passage from one bank to another . . . but be forewarned: It can also take that passage away.'" She lowered the paper. She looked at Blue hard. "*Blue.*"

"We've started. Let's finish."

Evie handed her a speckled tin cup. "'In a chalice, blend one part mugwort with two parts honey.'" She waited while Blue measured and mixed. "'Press and gently squeeze the angel's breath leaves over the cup, then drop them in.'"

Blue stirred. Her eyes burned from the fumes.

"'The elixir should start off black and gluey,'" Evie read. "'When it's pink, it's ready.'"

Soon, the substance within turned a pearly pink. Blue tilted the cup to show Evie, who grimaced.

"It's going to taste awful," she warned. "Even worse than the dandelion roots. Margie's notes say that people often spit it out. If that happens, the whole spell is ruined."

"I won't spit it out."

"You can, though. If you need to spit it out, spit it out."

"Do I swish it around in my mouth, or am I supposed to swallow it?"

"You're supposed to swallow it," Evie said reluctantly.

It was slimy and clotted and made Blue gag. She dug in deep and forced it down. Then she thunked down the cup, slapped the soil, and shook her head violently. She smacked her lips, trying to get rid of the vile taste. "And you'll be here when I . . . when I . . ." Reality started untethering.

"Blue?" she heard Evie say from somewhere far away. "I think you better . . ."

Whatever Evie said next, Blue didn't hear it. She lay prone on the blanket, which became a flying carpet. Colors blurred. Worlds streaked by. It was too much—dizzying, dark, oppressive—until a perfect circle of a rainbow formed in the distance. A. . .window? A door?

Blue rolled off the carpet and swam toward it. The portal pulsed, dewy and shimmering. Blue thrust her hands over her head, cupped her palms, and pulled out and down, propelling herself through the shimmering opening.

And then—she fell.

She was tiny, an atom, a building block of the cosmos.

Dirt everywhere. But familiar. Known. And . . . arms? Strong arms holding her close. Rocking her. Singing.

Sweet little Blue-girl, fall asleep. Mumsy and Pups will keep you safe.

She was a baby. Life was a daffodil, sunshine, and soft butter.

Then she was two, toddling on wobbly legs toward the kind-faced man who knelt before her with wide arms. *You did it!* he cried, scooping her into a hug. *Digs, get your ma! Our Blue-girl took her first steps!*

She was four, foraging for berries. She slipped and tumbled, her ankle buckling beneath her.

The crack of bone. Blinding pain. Her parents' worried voices: *What will we do? What can we do?*

Something more. Something about Mumsy. But it hurt *so much*, remembering. Blue shook her head, and resistance slammed down, shattered her memories and sending them

172

flying.

But no, please wait, she hadn't meant—

Her body, if she had a body, flew backward. The portal receded, and Blue's head spun as she was plunged into a new reality, green and pulsing, living tendrils wrapping around her lungs. She was within the stem of a great tubular dandelion. It squeezed and squeezed until Blue couldn't breathe. It squeezed harder still, her skin tingling as if fire ants were biting her everywhere, until at last she was spat back into the present.

Her eyes flew open. She sucked in air.

"Blue?" Evie's hands were on her shoulders, shaking her. "Are you all right?"

She fell forward on her hands and knees and vomited. She heaved and heaved until nothing was left.

"Blue . . . please," Evie said. "You're scaring me."

Evie opened her arms, and Blue fell into them. She rocked Blue like Mumsy once had. Like Pups. Like Digs.

"I broke my foot," Blue choked. "We were leaving. Our whole family was going to leave. But—oh, Evie—I broke my foot!" Tears turned her words thick and clumsy. "I ruined everything!"

"No," Evie murmured. "Blue, no. You ruined nothing."

"Digs had to stay back. The rest of my family went on. But he and I—we were supposed to catch up. Only we didn't." Tears streamed down her face. "It was because of me, Evie."

"How old were you? Four?"

"Yes. Four."

"You're seventeen now," Evie said gently. "Do you think it's fair to blame your four-year-old self for breaking her foot?"

Blue hiccuped. She shrugged.

Evie released Blue, drawing back and looking her in the eyes. "Also, I think maybe there's something you're not seeing."

"Tell me."

"You think it was Digs at the end, taking care of you. Is that right?"

Blue took a shuddering breath. She nodded and said, "Yes. It was Digs, definitely."

"Then it couldn't have been your mother who left you on Margie's porch," Evie said. "It had to have been him."

Blue frowned.

"And do you know what I think?"

"What?"

"I don't know, of course, but what if Digs left you with Margie because he knew she could fix your foot?"

Blue tried the idea out. Margie *was* sympathetic to the fae. She always had been. And, Margie fixed all kinds of small and wounded creatures.

"I think he left you with Margie temporarily, but the plan was always to come back for you," Evie said.

A fluttering thing rose in Blue's chest. Then it sank down. "But he didn't. He never did come back."

"I know," said Evie. "And . . . that's not good." She scooted close and rubbed circles on Blue's back. "On the other hand, it suggests that your parents made it across the bridge—and that *is* good."

"Why do you say that?" Blue asked.

"Because your last memories of them are good. Happy. Or rather, *sad*, but happy-sad. Not tragedy sad."

Blue wasn't following.

"You don't remember anything terrible happening to them," Evie explained.

"True," Blue said.

"So let's say they went first, expecting you and Digs to join them. That's what you think happened, right?"

Blue felt trembly inside. Emptied out.

"I think so, but I don't know for sure."

"I know. But still." Evie's hand stayed on Blue's back, circling. Comforting. "If they hadn't made it to the other side of the bridge, Digs would have known. You would have known."

Blue poked at her theory for holes. There were many. Even so, it wasn't entirely nonsensical, Evie's logic.

"There's one more thing," Evie said. "There had to have been a reason your parents went first. Something urgent. Something they couldn't ignore. Don't you think?"

The fluttering thing—the small persistent promise of something beautiful—announced itself in Blue's chest again, and suddenly, she understood. She saw the final image the memory potion had offered her: Mumsy, her expression radiant as she murmured endearments into a blanketed bundle cradled in her arms.

"Oh," Blue murmured. Every cell tingled not with fire ants, but with awe. "Oh, *Evie.*"

"What?" Evie said, newly concerned. "Blue, you've gone all pale. What is it?"

"I have a baby sister," Blue told her. Her lower lip trembled. "Her name is Star."

Chapter Twenty-Nine

Blue turned the memories she'd unearthed—with Evie's help—over and over. She strained to remember more details, any little thing. But nothing rose to the surface.

She'd hoped the ritual would give her something to hold onto, something to make things better. And, it had . . . to a degree. But something felt wrong.

Not with the memories. They had been real.

What felt wrong was the ritual. Or rather, how abruptly it had ended.

She'd ended it prematurely, out of cowardice. She had wrenched herself free before reaching whatever truth waited for her at the other end.

At first, the memories had been warm. Mumsy's arms, Pups's laughter, Digs's easy confidence. Baby Star, bound tight against Mumsy's chest. (*Star*! That was why, when Anton asked Blue to care for the orphaned kitten, the name had risen in her mind. Star, her sister. *Blue had a sister.*)

But then, after the happy memories, came the loss. The loneliness. The grief.

Those suffocating emotions had risen like floodwaters, and Blue had panicked, flailing for the surface, flinging herself back into the present before she could drown.

She had turned away from the truth—*her* truth—just when she'd been closest to it.

Which meant she had to go back.

She awoke the next day with fire in her belly. She'd go over to Evie's after breakfast and tell her they needed to do the ritual again, and as soon as possible. Immediately, even. But Evie surprised Blue, bursting into the grandmother's kitchen while Blue was still eating the eggs she'd fried up. Evie was practically vibrating with excitement, words bubbling out of her so rapidly that Blue couldn't get a word in edgewise.

"My dad's on his way home," she told Blue. "He arrives tonight—and, Blue, he's bringing a *puppy*. A hound dog, just like the dog we had when I was a kid. My dad said I could name him. Jax has to agree, but that's fine. He will."

"Oh," Blue managed. She set down her fork. The bits of yolk clinging to the tines looked oily all of a sudden. Slippery. She found she was no longer hungry.

"We'll train him to be good with Star, don't worry," Evie babbled on. She swiveled her head. "Where is Star? Never mind. Doesn't matter. But Blue, I'm going to be awfully busy today. That's what I came by to tell you."

"Oh," Blue repeated. "Awfully busy as in...during the afternoon?"

Evie grinned. "As in the whole day long, most likely. I'll clean the house while she teaches her morning lessons— she couldn't cancel them; it was already too late—and then afterward, I'll help her cook a big welcome-home dinner."

Evie rolled her eyes if to say, *Chores—blech!* But she had yet to stop smiling.

Margie entered the kitchen, arms full of clothes. "All of the socks and sweaters need darning," she told Blue. "That's how I'll be spending the day. I know it's hard to believe, but winter will be here before we know it." She spotted Evie. "Oh, hello, Evie. You look happy."

Evie bounced on her toes. "My dad's coming home. Finally!"

Margie went still. "Is he?"

"And Blue, gosh, you haven't even met him!" Evie exclaimed. "Tonight will be family only, if I know my mother—which I do." Again, she rolled her eyes. Again, she didn't actually seem bothered in the slightest. "But tomorrow, okay? I'll introduce you to him tomorrow."

Margie deposited the clothes on the table, stepped behind Blue, and placed her hands on Blue's shoulders. "Blue might be busy tomorrow."

"I might?" Blue said.

"I thought I'd take you into Brevard to do some shopping," Margie said.

Blue craned her neck to look back at her. When had Margie ever wanted to take her shopping?

"Oh. Okay. That's fine," Evie said. She already had her fingers on the doorknob. "I'll pop by this afternoon if I can —although I wouldn't count on it." Her brow furrowed, then cleared. "Doesn't matter. We'll sort it out. Anyway, I've got to run. Bye!"

She dashed out of the kitchen, leaving Blue feeling forlorn and foolish. She longed to chase after her and say, *But what about* me?

She wouldn't, of course. Evie's day was full, and Blue wasn't in it.

She would do the ritual on her own, then. She had everything she needed. She knew the steps by heart. And if Evie wasn't bothered by spending the day without Blue, well, perhaps that was a bit of information worth noting. Blue was quite capable of spending the day without Evie, after all. If Evie *did* stop by later on, maybe it would be just as well if Blue wasn't here. Then Evie could think, *But. . . what about me?*

Oh, stop it, Blue scolded herself. She was behaving like a child.

Chapter Thirty

This time, the potion hit harder and faster, throwing Blue into her past so violently that it *wasn't* the past but the present, with no overlay of time to come.

Blue was four years old again.

Her seventeen-year-old self didn't yet exist.

It was early morning, and she was sitting with Digs in the cozy den where they lived. She was sipping a mug of cool milk—a rare treat—when the barking began. At first, she wasn't afraid. Why would she be? Dogs were witless creatures, puffed up with self-importance. They might chase a rabbit, sure—but could they track her? Or Digs?

Ha!

Then two of the dogs started pawing at the den's entrance, clawing madly at the soil and rocks to widen the opening.

They wanted to get into her home. Her *home*!

Fury rose in Blue's chest. She filled her lungs with air, ready to tell those dumb dogs to go away, but Digs clamped his hand around her arm and shook his head. His expression startled her so much that she dropped her milk.

Then came stomping, tromping footsteps, and dirt fell

from the ceiling, snuffing out their candle. Blue stood, wanting Digs, and pain shot through her bad ankle.

"Ow!" she yelped.

"*Shh*," said Digs.

A cold fingernail scraped up Blue's spine, because Digs was scared. Only, Digs was *never* scared.

When Mumsy and Pups had packed up most of their belongings and left with baby Star, Digs had squared his shoulders and told them not to worry. He'd look after Blue while her ankle healed, and then they'd all meet up "on the other side of the bridge." Blue didn't know what bridge they were talking about, or why they dropped their voices whenever they spoke of it, especially the "other side" part. This mysterious "other side" was a place Blue didn't understand the shape of.

She didn't let it bother her. Digs was her older brother and could do anything in the whole wide world.

"We'll come on the next full moon," he'd told their parents. "We'll be fine, I promise."

Mumsy had frowned and turned to Pups. "I don't know. Maybe we should wait?"

But Star was a baby, and babies cried. Crying babies made for easy targets.

Blue—bossy four-year-old Blue—had mimicked her big brother's stance, squaring her shoulders and tilting her chin.

"Mumsy, go. You have to, to take care of Star. You, too, Pups—to take care of Mumsy!" She'd glanced at Digs. "We'll come on the next full moon!"

Digs had grinned down at her and ruffled her hair. "Listen to Blue. She knows what's what."

Her parents had laughed, though anxiously. They'd allowed themselves to be persuaded.

Once when they were gone, Digs had made living on their own into a game.

"You stay here and guard the fort," he'd instructed her, "and I'll go forage for supplies. Got it, chief?"

"Got it," Blue had affirmed with a brisk nod.

He'd made it feel as if her task was an important one and not just code for, *Well, you can't do much on that foot of yours, now can you?*

Sometimes, he'd returned with berries and nuts. Once, with three rabbits he'd made into stew. On this day—the one seventeen-year-old Blue was reliving in her four-year-old's body—he'd returned home with pilfered milk in a cold glass jar.

"A man left it in a box, on the porch of another man," he'd explained when he produced it. He'd pulled a funny face. "What was I supposed to do? Leave it there?"

"No way, bluejay," Blue had said.

"Someone saw me, which wasn't great," Digs had admitted. He'd shrugged, like, *What can you do?* "A mortal boy. He ran out of the house and chased after me, just as fast as he could go. But guess what?"

Blue hadn't had to guess. She'd already known. "You were faster," she'd said.

"I was faster," Digs had agreed. A shadow had moved across his face, something that turned his tale from a *ha ha, mortals are stupid* story into something darker. "I lost him at the blueberry patch down by the creek. I knew the cut-through. He didn't."

"The blueberry patch the bear babies like?" Blue had

asked. That spring, a mama bear had given birth to two cubs. The blueberry patch by the creek was one of their favorite spots to play.

"The very one," Digs had said. "I might have woken the mama up. I hope not, but I might have."

Blue had shrugged. So what if he had? Bears were bears. Bears could always fall back asleep.

But Digs hadn't been scared when he'd returned with the milk. If he had been, Blue would have smelled it on him.

He was scared now, however.

Outside, a man's voice rose above the howling of the dogs.

"Git 'em, Casey! Git 'em, Windsor! Flush those rats out!"

Digs crouched and gripped Blue's shoulders. "Go below," he said urgently. "Townsfolk don't like the dark. But if you *are* found—"

"*I know.* Play dead."

It had been drilled into her since she'd been a baby. Mortals hated the fae. They hunted foxes for pelts and deer for meat, but they killed faeries just because.

"Play dead," Digs repeated. "Yes."

Feet thundered above. Soil fell away, and a dog's muzzle punched through, snapping wildly.

Digs shoved her toward the tunnels. "GO!"

She ran, doing her best to ignore her throbbing foot. She scrambled through narrow passageways, taking turns by memory as she burrowed deeper and deeper into the earth. Her heart was a trapped bird in her chest, then in her throat, fighting with thick wings to burst out. Her ankle screamed. Her lungs burned.

Where was Digs?

Why wasn't he behind her?

A dog forced its way into the den. Frenzied barks. A high-pitched squeal of pain.

Then—

A *gunshot*.

Blue's heart nearly exploded.

More voices.

"We got him!" someone shouted. "We got him, all right!"

Her whole body seized.

"Are there more?" another voice demanded. "Check every nook, every cranny!"

Careless boots sent loose dirt raining down. Men kicked and scraped at the upper chambers of the den. A man spat.

Blue curled into a ball, burying her face against her knees.

Digs was gone.

She knew it, she knew it.

"We're done here, Bob," someone finally announced. "It's time to go."

Heavy stomping. A sharp whistle. A dog whimpered, and the men cleared out.

Blue stayed curled where she was for minutes. Hours. Forever.

Then—

One man came back.

One man. One dog.

"All right, Windsor," the mortal man said. "Show me."

This man's scent wasn't the fury-stench of the others, but something more complicated. Could it be grief, like the time Blue came upon Digs crying behind the tangled roots of a fallen log?

184

No. Mortals weren't capable of grief.

The dog scratched at the soil.

Blue squeezed shut her eyes. *Play dead. Play dead. Play dead.*

The dirt wall gave way, and the dog was through, sliding and tumbling. With one great leap, he was *on her*, his chest vibrating with a low growl.

The man grunted, and soon he was through, too. Earth fell, and light illuminated the chamber even through her closed eyes.

"Ah, crap," the man muttered. "It's a kid. Just a little kid."

His hand reached toward her, and four-year-old Blue, small and terrified, failed to do what she'd been told to do. She didn't play dead. She flinched—

And snapped back into her young woman's body, gasping and choking and sobbing.

Chapter Thirty-One

Blue kicked dirt over her vomit, buried the remaining angel's breath, and made her way woozily out of the forest. The whole way back to grandmother's house, her body weaved and her mind did somersaults. Because, no. It couldn't be.

Windsor?

No. *No.* She'd heard wrong, or remembered wrong, or . . . or the memory spell had mixed things up.

Or maybe there were many, many dogs named Windsor. Was Blue an expert on what mortals named their dogs? No, she was not.

She slipped in through the back door, her only thought to reach her room. To sort out her thoughts. To nap. To nap first, then sort out her thoughts, because surely her thoughts would make more sense when her entire being felt less muzzy.

Raised voices stopped her cold.

Not Margie and the grandmother but Margie and a man. And not just any man, but. . .

Blue stumbled for the wall and slid down hard against the floor. The man Margie was talking to was the man from the den. The mortal who'd found her all those years ago.

The one with the dog.

The dog called Windsor.

Blue was shaking so badly she thought she might pass out.

The man who'd found her was Evie's father.

Through the wall, his voice rose, thick with anger. "Why did you bring her here? And why, for the love of God, did you allow her to become friends with my daughter?"

"You think I *allowed* it?" Margie replied. "You have kids, Abe. When has forbidding something ever worked? Believe me, I'm no happier about this than you are."

"You could have stopped it," he snapped. "You could have found a way."

"How?"

"I don't care how! She's *fae*, Margie. You know that."

There was a charged silence. Then Margie said, "Why yes, Abe." Her voice was furious, but controlled. "As a matter of fact, I do."

"Then you know that she doesn't belong here. And she sure as hell doesn't belong with my Evie!"

"Why? Is 'your Evie' too perfect to be friends with my Blue?"

Blue heard footsteps. Pacing. A heavy breath sucked in and exhaled hard. All of these sounds together, these male and mortal sounds, sent Blue straight back to her stolen childhood. She remembered wet soil, snapping teeth, the bang of a gun. *Digs.*

If Blue were any other girl, it would have been too much. But she wasn't any other girl. Her fear hardened into something sharp-edged and ho. She pushed herself to standing.

"Wait," came a rasp from the shadows.

Blue jerked around and saw the grandmother in her invalid chair. She was just down the hall, situated slightly beyond the spot where the living room light spilled out. "Leave Margie be," she said. "She deserves the chance to speak her mind."

Using her hands to roll the wheels, the grandmother propelled herself toward the kitchen and gestured for Blue to follow.

Blue stayed put.

"As you please," said the grandmother. "But you must have questions—and I'm the only one who will tell you the truth."

Blue gritted her jaw and set out after her.

In the kitchen, the grandmother maneuvered her chair to the table, and Blue, antsy and itchy, sat down across from her. From the living room, voices rose and dipped, too low for Blue to make out what was being said.

The grandmother rapped the table. "Abe asked a lot of my daughter when he brought you to her."

Blue's skin prickled. "When he . . . ? I'm sorry, what?" Evie's father was the man who had found her, yes. He'd found her in the den she'd shared with Digs and her family. Blue had grasped and accepted that ugly fact. But after finding her, he must have . . . he would have . . .

"He had some nerve, showing up and handing over a child."

Blue's mouth went dry. "Me? Are you saying I'm the child? No."

"You're not stupid. Don't start acting like it now."

Blue shook her head. "My mother left me on Margie's porch. Or maybe my brother. No one knows."

"Wrong," said the grandmother. "Three people know." She ticked off the names on gnarled fingers. "Margie, Abe Carpenter, and myself." She leaned forward, her eyes like splinters. "You were handed over to Margie like a wounded animal, and it was Abe Carpenter who did the handing. It was the only thing he could think to do, other than put you down."

"No," Blue insisted. "I was left on Margie's porch by someone from my family, because they knew Margie would take me in. It wasn't supposed to be forever."

"Is that the story Margie told you?"

"I was wrapped in a gray blanket. The softest thing in the world."

"Were you?"

"I was. Yes. Why do you even care either way? You weren't there for Margie when she needed you most. You've never cared a whit about her."

The grandmother's voice was flinty. "Margie is my daughter. Of course I care."

"You have a funny way of showing it. You visited *once* after she took me in."

The grandmother regarded her for a long moment, then said, "Come with me."

She turned her bulky chair and began down the hall.

From the living room, Margie and Abe's voices droned on. Her head spinning, Blue followed the grandmother into the old lady's musty bedroom. She gestured to a wooden hope chest and said, "Bring me the family album."

Blue found it buried beneath knitted blankets and brittle

letters tied with string. She handed it over, and the grandmother flipped through the stiff, yellowed pages, her fingers careful, until she came to the photograph she was looking for. It showed a younger Margie sitting stiffly on her worn sofa, the sofa in the cabin. Beside her, wrapped in a gray blanket clutched as tightly as a second skin, was a child. Blue. Her hair was snarled, and her jaw was set. Her eyes were wary and mistrustful.

"Do you see?" the grandmother said.

"That's me, with Margie. What of it?"

The grandmother flipped to the beginning of the album and tapped another photo. This one showed a different baby, but the baby was wrapped in the same gray blanket. Blue's stomach dropped.

"Margaret Eleanor," the grandmother murmured. "My Margie. I knitted her baby blanket myself."

No. It couldn't be.

"But . . . there was a note," Blue managed to say. "It was pinned to that blanket. *My* blanket. It said my name was Blue and that—"

Her throat closed. Her sentence was cut short.

Her name is Blue, and she is precious beyond measure. Please take care of her. That was what the note said. That was what Margie had always told her.

But if the blanket came from the grandmother. . .

Blue saw spots. Had there never been a note at all?

Chapter Thirty-Two

"So Margie *lied* to me?" Blue managed when her power of speech returned. "She lied to me then, and she's lying to me still?"

The grandmother closed the album, her hands trembling. "There are two sides to every story. Maybe Margie made up a story in order to protect you. Or maybe she wanted to protect herself, so she could continue to protect you."

Blue's nails bit into her palms. Her world was breaking apart.

"And maybe *I* wanted to protect Margie," the grandmother went on.

Blue laughed harshly. "How? By rejecting me?"

"By reminding her of the chasm between a mortal's life and the life of your kind. A chasm too deep to be crossed."

"You're a prejudiced old cow if that's what you believe."

"And you're a fool if you don't. When Margie took in Layla, how did that end?"

"Layla needed Margie's help. What else would you have had Margie do?" Blue said. "And guess what? They loved each other—yes, a mortal and a faerie—whether you want to believe it or not."

"Margie loved Layla," the grandmother allowed. "I do believe she did. But did Layla love Margie?"

"Of course she did! How could she not?"

"It was illegal, by then, for a faerie to assume the rights of a townsperson," the grandmother said. "Layla knew it, and yet she still stayed in Margie's home. Slept in her bed. Layla let Margie harbor her, risk her standing, risk everything."

"It was Margie's choice. Margie chose to protect her."

"Margie chose to *defile* herself, and all for a girl who folded the moment the truth came out. Layla handed Margie over in return for a lighter sentence, as you may recall."

"It wasn't Layla's fault she was born fae!" Blue's voice rose. She glanced toward the hall. She tried to rein herself in. "It was mortals who made it illegal for her to exist just for being the way she was. Mortals were in the wrong."

"All of them?" the grandmother asked.

"Except Margie, yes! And maybe a few others."

The grandmother tilted her head. "So . . . the faeries were innocent. All of them."

Blue paused. The grandmother had said *faeries*, not *bogglins*. It made Blue wary.

The grandmother leaned in. "Let's say you're right. What should be done now?"

"About what?"

"All those fae who disappeared over the years." Her tone was mild, but her eyes were sharp. "The ones who were questioned. Reassigned. Sent away. If mortals made that happen, don't they deserve to pay?"

"Yes! Obviously!" Blue faltered. "Well, not the ones who

weren't *there*—"

"Weren't where?"

"And not the ones who weren't born yet when that stuff was happening . . ."

"'When that stuff was happening,'" the grandmother echoed. She eyed Blue. She eyed the bandana covering her ears. "Is it not happening still?"

Blue's pulse raced, but she didn't answer. She knew what she knew.

"If you'd been in Layla's shoes—and yes, she did wear shoes—what would you have done?" the grandmother inquired. She tipped her chin toward Evie's house. "If your freedom were at risk, would you give it up to protect your little friend? Imagine it. No more fresh air. No more mountains. No more long barefoot walks with the wind in your hair. Just a shared dormitory room at Harmony Hall where your nails aren't the only things that get clipped. Where integration counselors watch what you eat and tell you which parts of yourself are allowed."

The grandmother arched her thin brows. "Would you stay quiet, if giving up Evie were the only way to avoid ending up at a place like that?"

Blue shook her head fiercely. "We're not talking about me and Evie. We're talking about Margie and Layla. If you'd been in Layla's place, what would *you* have done?"

The grandmother leaned back. "Exactly what Layla did," she said in a tone of satisfaction. "I would have saved myself, no matter the cost."

Blue hated how dizzy she felt. Tricked, almost. "Then how can you say she's evil if you'd have done the same thing?"

"All I said, Blue, is that we're not so very different, mortals and fae."

It was the first time the grandmother had called her by her name. Blue had never hated her more.

She ran out of the room, banged out of the house, and fled into the forest. Her lungs burned as she pushed herself, hiking higher and higher up the mountain, all the way to Overlook Rock. When she reached the summit, she bent forward at her waist and braced her weight on her thighs. She breathed hard. She hadn't set out to come here, but here she was, as if her internal compass had drawn her here.

She straightened and walked to the edge, where the land gave way to open air. Below, the river roared, swollen from summer rain. It tore over rock and root like a living thing. *Come to me,* it coaxed.

It was the nature of water to demand surrender, but Blue knew better than to listen to the river's call. Not here, where the current pulled strong.

Blue edged closer. A fine spray hit her face. She jerked herself back, knowing that to leap from the cliff would be suicide. But she'd made her decision. She would give it a shot and let fate decide.

She scrambled down the rocky slope, grabbing at branches to slow her descent. Stones dug into the soles of her feet, and a twig snagged in her tangled hair. She yanked it free.

That old photo of her as a four-year-old, with wild eyes and wicked tangles. *Feral*, the grandmother had said.

"I don't belong here," she whispered.

She went to the river's edge and dipped a toe in the

rushing water. The far bank was obscured by the frothing water, but it was there. And maybe—just maybe—passage across was possible.

Maybe her family was waiting.

Or maybe all that awaited was a watery grave.

Blue stripped off her clothes, leaving them in a neat pile on the bank. She pulled the bandana from her hair and placed it on top. Then she stepped into the current. Ice-cold water stole her breath, and the river yanked at her thighs, nearly knocking her over. She brought her arms up over her head, overlapped her hands, and pushed herself forward in a shallow dive.

Everything turned muted—a rushing, liquid tumble.

Sunlight shattered against the surface, blinding. The current sucked her back under. She was dragged along the riverbed, tossed up, pulled under, flipped, and swirled.

Blue was strong, but the river was stronger. When she finally wrenched herself free and clambered onto the bank, she was still on the same side but a mile downstream. She curled into a fetal position, her body shaking with sobs.

Later, as the sun sank below the mountains, Blue trudged back to the grandmother's house. Her knees were scraped raw, half a fingernail was gone, and her hair was a horror, like something fished from a clogged drain.

The grandmother looked her up and down and sniffed. "I told you. Crossing is impossible without the ring."

Blue wanted to slap her.

"Blue, is that you?" Margie called from the kitchen. Her voice was normal, and the sound of it sent Blue into a spiral of despair. This was how they would play it, then?

"Yes," she said, forcing the word past the knot in her

throat. "It's me."

"I could use a hand with dinner. Come help me shuck the corn?"

"Of course. Just let me wash up."

She paused on her way out of the room, glancing through the back window to see Evie with her family in their backyard. Her mom wore a gingham dress, and her hair was freshly done. Jax tossed a squeeze toy to a puppy, a clumsy, goofy creature who tripped over his own ears. Evie laughed, as did the man at the picnic table—broad shoulders, sun-streaked blond hair, crinkling eyes.

Tightness coiled in Blue's chest. She muttered, "Cats are better than dogs."

"Far more clever," the grandmother remarked.

Blue stiffened. She hadn't realized she'd spoken aloud.

"Your friend's having a fine time, isn't she?" the old woman went on. "Could've invited you if she wanted. Oh my, my. If she wanted you there, all she had to do was ask."

Chapter Thirty-Three

Evie neglected Blue those first few days after her dad returned. She could acknowledge that, and she could acknowledge that her behavior had hurt Blue's feelings. But her dad had been gone for so long, and now he was back. And Margie had taken Blue to Brevard on one of those days. Or somewhere. Margie had kept Blue busy with all sorts of things, it seemed. So it wasn't all on Evie, the days of little to no contact.

Plus, there was Dunbar to contend with, their new puppy. Dunbar was adorable and delightful and a *puppy*, and puppies required a lot of time and effort.

There was one last complicating factor as well, an uneasy sentiment Evie didn't quite know how to name. When she spoke of Blue to her father, her father's expression changed. Not much, but Evie saw the tic of his jaw, the slight tightening around his eyes. Only her father didn't know Blue, so the problem couldn't have been Blue. Which meant that the problem was Evie . . . and Evie's feelings. The ones she had for Blue.

When Evie spoke of Blue, her father's expression tightened. Why? What did her father see? Did he think Evie was hiding something? *Was* Evie hiding something?

Today, for the first time, Blue had hopped the fence to Evie's yard after breakfast. She was here at last, watching Evie attempt to teach Dunbar to obey commands, only instead of being happy to see her, Evie felt jumbled up inside. It didn't help that Blue clearly didn't like Dunbar and made no effort to hide it. It was as if Blue was jealous of Dunbar. Of a puppy! Which was ridiculous, especially since Dunbar was nothing if not puppy perfection.

"Aren't you?" Evie crooned, rubbing her cheek against Dunbar's floppy ears. "You're the most perfect boy ever! Oh yes, you are!"

Blue rolled her eyes—loudly. Evie didn't know how she pulled such a feat off, but she did.

She tried not to let Blue get under her skin. Training Dunbar was her job, and she was determined to make her dad proud. Jax helped when he could. So did their father. But Evie had the most time.

"I'm going to give Dunbar a scrap of bacon every time he ignores a squirrel," Evie said. Maybe if she could get Blue to participate, Blue would grow interested. "Want to help?"

"Sure," Blue said. She pointed at a fluffy white squirrel. "Look, Dunbar. A squirrel!"

Dunbar barked and galloped wildly after it.

"*Blue.*"

"What other animals are you going to teach him not to chase?" Blue asked.

"I won't let him chase Star, if that's what you're worried about," Evie said crossly.

"What about rabbits? What about foxes? Are you going to let him hunt foxes, like Toby?"

"For heaven's sake, Blue. He's a hunting dog."

"I'm on the fox's side," Blue said. "Sorry."

Before Evie could respond, Blue turned and hopped the far fence, disappearing into the trees.

~

The next day, Blue was less hostile. "Sorry I was cross," she said.

Evie wasn't ready to forgive her. "No harm done," she said frostily.

Dunbar, who couldn't keep still to save his life, barked and pawed at Blue's legs. When he shoved his nose where it didn't belong, Evie clapped a hand over her face. "Dunbar, down."

Dunbar didn't listen.

Blue pushed him away. She opened her mouth as if to say something, then changed her mind. Then tried again—and changed her mind again.

"What?" Evie said. "Just say it."

A cloud crossed over Blue's face. "I did the ritual again. To learn more about my past."

"You did? Blue, you shouldn't have. That was dangerous."

"And I learned some things," Blue said doggedly. "Hard things."

Evie threw Dunbar's bone as far as she could. "Fetch, Dunbar! Good boy!"

"Don't you want to know?" Blue asked.

"Of course I do. I assumed you'd tell me when you were ready."

"It wasn't Digs who left me on Margie's porch."

"No?" said Evie. Dunbar bounded back with the slobbery

bone. Evie scratched his head and threw it again.

"No, because he was murdered before he got the chance. By a mortal."

"That's terrible," Evie said. She knew, as she spoke, how inadequate the words were. But what if everything didn't have to be about mortals versus fae? What if, today, it was just about two girls and a puppy? Would that be so awful?

Blue gave Evie the strangest look, a blend of anger and pleading. "You don't believe me, do you?"

"I never said that."

"Townspeople do bad things, Evie."

"Sometimes, yes," Evie said carefully. "But, Blue. . . " She sighed. "Until a few days ago, you didn't even know Digs existed. These things you say you've remembered, how do you know they're real? They could be visions. Hallucinations."

Dunbar trotted over, tail wagging. He stuck his nose between Blue's legs again.

"Go away," Blue snapped, shoving him aside.

"Don't shove him!"

"Don't let him sniff me and get his slobber all over me!"

The back door banged. Both girls jumped.

Jax strode over, confident and grinning.

"Hey, Blue," he said easily. "How've you been?"

"Fine," Blue muttered. "You?"

"Couldn't be better." He squatted and tied a leash to Dunbar's collar.

"We're taking him to the woods," Evie told Blue. "He needs to get used to new sights and smells while we're there to keep him calm."

"Ah," Blue said. "I bet that'll be really effective."

Jax started off with Dunbar. "Evie? You coming?"

"One second!" She sidled up to Blue and dropped her voice. "You're punishing me for wanting to spend time with my dog—and my brother. Do you realize how immature that is? You can't make me choose between you and Jax."

"It hardly matters, does it?" Blue said.

"What? Why?"

"Evie, either come or don't. I'm not going to wait forever," Jax said.

"I said I'm coming!" Evie called crossly.

Blue stepped backward to let Evie pass, displaying her palms. "Because you already did."

Chapter Thirty-Four

Blue didn't set out to give Evie the silent treatment. It hadn't been planned. But Evie chose Jax over her, and yes, it hurt Blue's feelings. So Blue took a break from talking to her.

It only became official when Evie called her out on it. Once it was official, it was hard to take back.

"Blue. Just talk to me," Evie had begged the first day, after she got back from the woods and Jax had left to do his own thing.

By the second day, Evie's tone had sharpened. "Really?" she'd said, standing on the grandmother's porch and speaking through the wire screen of the window. "You're not going to invite me in? That's childish, Blue. So childish."

On the third day, Evie came and stood at the fence between the two yards. She said, "Blue, please," and her voice broke. "What did I do? Tell me so I can fix it."

Blue almost relented. She wanted nothing more than for their whole dumb fight to be over.

But then Jax came out with Dunbar, who barked and spun in giddy circles, making Evie smile through her tears.

Blue didn't hate Evie. But she glared at her as if she did, and Evie recoiled. Then Blue turned and went inside. She didn't look back, even when Evie called after her.

It was a horrible feeling, power.

On the fourth day, Evie fought back. Instead of pleading, she lavished attention on Dunbar, throwing sticks, wrestling in the grass, laughing as he tripped over his floppy paws. She shot Blue defiant glances instead of desperate ones.

The only time she didn't fawn over Dunbar was at meals, when he was crated in the laundry room or let outside.

Blue hated that stupid puppy.

No, she didn't. Not really. But she was dealing with a lot of emotions that felt a lot like hate—or could be pushed in that direction—and so lucky Dunbar got to bear the brunt of her anger, confusion, and despair.

She missed Evie—and felt betrayed by her, even though Evie had technically done nothing wrong.

She felt distant from Margie—and felt doubly betrayed by her adoptive mother, even though she wasn't sure if Margie had done something wrong or not. She felt tricked, regardless. Margie had withheld information from her for thirteen years. Thirteen *years*!

And the grandmother had known. All along, the grandmother had known more about Blue than Blue herself had known. The knowledge sickened her and made her feel foolish and fragile, like a helpless little kid.

But Blue wasn't a helpless little kid and refused to feel like one. Rather than examine her emotions, or breathe into them and through them, she balled them up into something tight and hard and sharp. She tried to swallow that sharp thing, but it cut too deep, so she flung it away instead—at Dunbar.

Here, you dumb dog. Go fetch.

That evening, Blue slipped into the backyard and watched through the slats of the side fence as Evie and her family ate, warm voices and yellow light spilling from their dining room. Evie wasn't thinking about Blue. She was too busy laughing and chatting and being part of her happy family.

She was on the inside.

Blue was on the outside. Always on the outside.

"Here, Dunbar," she called. She slapped her thighs. "C'mere, boy."

Dunbar perked up from the shadows of Evie's yard and lolloped over.

"Good boy," Blue murmured, scratching his ears through the fence. "Who's the stupidest, smelliest, most annoying dog ever? That's right, you are."

He panted happily, soaking in the attention.

Forest, Blue told him, directing his attention toward the open land beyond the long fence that marked the perimeter of both yards. On the near side of the perimeter, tame lawns and a play fort. On the far side, wild forest.

Rabbits and squirrels and foxes, Blue told Dunbar.

Dunbar followed Blue's gaze. He barked to say, *Yes, oh yes! Forest-forest-forest!*

"Shh," Blue said.

Dunbar turned to her with hopeful, liquid eyes. *Go! Chase! Run?* said the riot of his thoughts.

Blue moved to the corner of the grandmother's yard, where the side fence intersected with the longer exterior fence and made a T. The gap between the bottom rail of the fence and the ground was *almost* big enough for a puppy to slip beneath.

If the bottom rail was loose, and the puppy worked up, a bit of eager digging would be all it took. The hole would widen, the loose rail would hike up, and the puppy, belly low and paws scrabbling, would make it to the other side.

Blue stuck her leg through the slats of the side fence and hooked her toes under the bottom rail of the exterior fence. When she applied upward pressure, it rose.

If Blue could weaken the fence with her bare foot, could the fence really be expected to contain a puppy?

Careless, that's what Evie's father was. He'd been away so long, he'd let things slip.

Dunbar stuck his nose through the widening gap, ears perked.

Blue thought of Star and how she curled up next to Blue when Blue was in bed. The way she purred against Blue's ribs.

She let the rail drop into place, and Dunbar jumped back, startled.

Blue dropped to her haunches and reached through the fence, rubbing Dunbar's head with her knuckles. "Go," she commanded, pointing toward the safety of Evie's back porch.

Dunbar wagged his tail and licked Blue's hand before bounding off, his floppy paws kicking up dirt.

Chapter Thirty-Five

Late into the night, Blue heard Evie and Jax calling for Dunbar. She rolled over and clamped her pillow over her head. She'd dropped the rail back into place. She had.

"That puppy of theirs must have wiggled through the fence," Margie said the next morning. She cradled a cup of coffee and gazed out the window at the connected backyards. Evie's whole family was outside, searching for Dunbar. Her father examined the split-rail fence while her mother rapped a spoon against an open can of dog food. Jax kicked at the tall grass on the other side, presumably looking for paw prints. Evie stood on top of the play structure's fort, her hands cupped around her mouth as she called, "Dunbar! *Dun*bar!"

"Blue, you're Evie's friend," Margie said. "Why don't you pop over and help?"

"You're Evie's father's friend," Blue said. "Why don't you?"

The grandmother arched an eyebrow.

Margie looked flustered.

Everyone stayed exactly where they were.

~

Half an hour later, Evie knocked on the grandmother's front door. Her eyes were big and worried, dark smudges beneath them attesting to her exhaustion. Behind her stood Jax, his hair sticking up in tufts.

Evie abandoned her standoff with Blue without preamble. "Dunbar's missing. We let him into the yard last night, and he escaped."

Blue considered her choice of words. *Escaped.* It brought to mind other words, like trapped, caught, hunted down and killed.

"Oh no," she said tonelessly.

Hurt flashed across Evie's face. Blue bowed her head, toying with the metal strip on the doorsill with her bare foot.

"Jax and I are heading into the forest," Evie said. "Will you come with us and help?" She crossed the threshold and lightly touched Blue's shoulder. "Please?"

Blue lifted her head and met Evie's gaze. "Fine," she muttered.

For what felt like hours, they plodded in widening circles through the woods.

"Here, Dunbar!" Jax called.

"C'mere, boy!" Evie wheedled. "Where are you, bud?"

Blue knew exactly where Dunbar was. She just wasn't ready to say. Anyway, it wasn't as if Evie had flat out asked her where Dunbar was. Keeping the information to herself wasn't the same as lying.

Evie tripped over a rotting log and went down hard, her ankle twisting beneath her. "Ow!"

"Stay put," Jax said. "Let me see." He knelt, frowning as he tested the mobility of her foot. "Push against my hand.

Does that hurt? What about now?"

He was gentle with her, Blue noted grudgingly.

Evie rotated her ankle. She winced, but Blue could see that the pain was already fading.

Jax met Blue's eyes, and she joined them, positioning herself on Evie's other side. Together, she and Jax helped steady Evie as she tested her weight.

"I'm fine," she said. She shook them off and strode forward—in the wrong direction completely. "Come on. We have to find Dunbar."

Blue fought an inward battle with herself. "We should try Graveyard Fields," she said grouchily.

"There's no way he could have gotten that far," Jax said.

"He's a dog. Dogs get around."

"It can't hurt to look," Evie said.

Blue led them up the narrow path, which wound through the abandoned treatment center for moral rebalancing. The crumbling buildings sagged into themselves. A rusted gate leaned open like a broken jaw.

Jax threw a glance at the ruins and said, "If Mom and Dad knew I was here, they'd kill me. If they knew I let you two come with me, they'd kill me twice." He craned his neck to look at a skeletal roof. "This whole thing could come down on our heads."

A high-pitched yip pierced the air.

"Dunbar!" Evie cried, scrambling forward. "Buddy, where are you?"

"Careful, Evie," Jax warned.

Dunbar burst up from below, tail wagging furiously.

Evie dropped to her knees, and Dunbar launched himself into her arms, covering her in mud and slobber.

"You silly boy!" she said, laughing as she held him close. "You live with us, mister. You don't belong out here." She touched her nose to his. "Let's get you home. What do you say?"

"Yes. Let's go," Blue said stiffly. She hadn't expected a parade in her honor, but it wouldn't have killed Evie to give her a simple thank-you.

Jax, meanwhile, had wandered deeper into the ruins.

"Jax, come back," Evie said. "You just said we shouldn't be here."

He ignored her, poking his head into what was once a public bathhouse. He grimaced. "God, I can still smell them."

"Jax, stop," Evie snapped.

"There's dung everywhere." He kicked at a patch of dried dirt, and a foul puff rose into the air. "Guess that's what happens when you coop them up together."

Evie shot a worried look at Blue, who was already feeling the hot fizz of fury travel up her body.

"Maybe the facilities weren't properly maintained," Evie told Jax. "Or, more likely, whatever you're kicking around wasn't left by the fae at all. The treatment center's been closed for decades."

"Sheesh, are you a sympathizer now?" Jax chuckled. "Aw, Evie, going soft and mushy over those pointed ears."

"What do pointed ears have to do with anything?" Blue asked.

"It's proof that they're not like us," Jax said. "Anyone who says otherwise is just deluded."

Blue's eyes narrowed. Like father, like son.

"You girls have never met a faerie," he went on. "That's

why you romanticize them. But fae don't care about morals, not like we do. All they care about is tempting humans into sinful alliances."

"That's the dumbest thing I've ever heard," Blue said.

"Mortals tried to integrate with fae. It didn't work. Do you remember that from fifth-grade history, or have they gone and changed the textbooks?"

Blue stepped toward him.

Evie grabbed her arm. "This is all Silas," she whispered. "He's been brainwashed by Silas Bratton."

"Even the Bible warns about unnatural unions," Jax said. "There's a reason they were banished, after all."

Blue's breath sharpened. Just past him, near the spot where he'd kicked at the dirt, was a snake's nest containing a tangle of timber rattlesnakes. Babies. They were slender and disoriented, tiny coils of death.

"Jax? Look behind you," Blue said.

Jax turned—and went rigid.

More earth crumbled. More rattlers tumbled loose, eight in total. One slithered onto Jax's sneaker. A second ventured higher, drawn by the warmth of Jax's skin.

"They like you," Blue noted.

Dunbar whined and pressed up next to Evie.

The mother snake slithered into view, four feet long and thicker than Jax's arm. She lifted her tail and set it thrumming: *chkk-chkk-chkk-chkk*. The dry clatter made the little hairs on the back of Blue's neck stand up.

Not me, Blue said. She flicked her eyes at Jax. *Him.*

The snake mother undulated as she approached him, the rattle of her tail sharp and rhythmic. Jax's chest rose and fell. A dark spot bloomed on the crotch of his jeans.

"Please, Blue," Evie whispered. She clung to Dunbar's collar. "He's my brother."

"Only if he takes back what he said."

"I take it back!" Jax said, his voice rising as the snake mother flicked her forked tongue. "Whatever got you riled up, I take it back!"

Blue closed her eyes and listened to the shush-shush inside her, the distant call of roots and soil and damp, dark nests. She heard the *cr-r-r-ick* of paper-thin eggshells and knew the joy of new life. Little tongues. Little bodies. A mother's cold, fierce pride.

She opened her eyes and saw nine bodies flatten and stretch as they shot across the undergrowth until, with one last tail flick, the timber rattlers were gone.

Chapter Thirty-Six

Evie's legs felt hollow, and beneath her ribcage was a gaping hole. This was how it felt, then. This was how it felt when the world cracked apart. Dunbar whined, and Evie let him go. He dashed to Jax, nosing him, licking his hands, then sniffing insistently at his jeans.

Jax shoved him away. "Get off," he snapped.

He turned to the girls, red splotches traveling up his neck and spreading over his face. "You better not tell."

Blue laughed, a light, sharp sound. "Tell what, and to whom? Bronwyn and Eliza?"

Jax stalked away from the barracks, practically jogging down the trail.

Life rushed back into Evie's legs. She shot Blue a furious look and ran after her brother, who had wet himself out of fear. In front of Evie. In front of Blue—who had laughed.

At home, Jax told their parents he'd come within an inch of death.

He didn't mention his jeans, which had dried out during the long hike back.

He *did* mention Blue.

"It was Evie's friend who sicced the snakes on me," he

ranted. "I don't know how. I don't know why. But if it wasn't for her . . ."

"I don't understand," said their mother. "Did she do something?"

"No. Yes. I did nothing to her, I swear, but for some reason, she hates me."

Their father's jaw tightened. "Margie's girl? Is that who you're talking about?"

"Yeah," Jax said. "*Blue*." He spat the name. "We hiked to Graveyard Fields to look for Dunbar—"

"Graveyard Fields?" their mother interrupted. "Jax, you know better. Someone could have been hurt!"

"Exactly!" Jax railed. "*Me*! There were these snakes, and —and I don't know. I don't know! But *Blue* made me look like a fool, and she did it on purpose."

Their father's gaze shifted to Evie. "This Blue. She's the new friend you've told me about?"

"She didn't mean for anyone to get hurt," Evie said. Her thumb went to her ring finger, where she'd normally find the ring Blue made her. The one that sparkled with mica and quartz. The one she twisted when she was nervous. "Anyway, she saved Jax in the end."

"Like hell she did!" Jax exclaimed.

"Language!" said their mother.

The ring must have slipped from her finger when she'd hurried after Jax, probably when she'd tripped and nearly fallen, managing to keep her balance only by grasping a handful of low pine branches. The needles were sharp and had caught on her skin—and no doubt the ring as well.

"Everyone, calm down," their father ordered. "Jax, take me through it from the beginning."

Jax told the story again, his voice rising as he struggled to name the unnameable. He searched for words that wouldn't deepen his shame—Evie watched the struggle play out across his face—but they didn't exist.

Evie's pulse was thick and heavy. Jax wasn't dead. He wasn't even hurt. But he'd been frightened.

Evie, too, had been frightened.

There'd been so many snakes.

And then there was the other thing, the most unnameable wrong.

She slipped from the den, leaving Jax alone with their parents. Outside, in Mrs. Freeman's backyard, she scooped up a handful of pebbles and tossed them against Blue's window until Blue appeared. Evie gestured for her to come down, and Blue nodded. They met in the far corner of the yard, away from watching eyes.

"Jax is really upset," Evie said. "You scared him nearly to death."

"*I* didn't," Blue said. "The snakes did. The snakes *he* disturbed."

"You could have stopped them sooner."

"You could have stopped *him* sooner," Blue retorted. "You heard what he said." She lowered her voice and made her eyes go dull. "'The fae are stupid, and they stink. It's not hate. It's facts.'"

Evie's cheeks burned.

"He needed to be taught a lesson," Blue said with a shrug. "You know it the same as I do."

Evie glared, and Blue's eyebrows drew together.

"Wait. Evie." She peered at Evie, then she shook her head as if to clear it. "Are you actually upset?"

"Actually, I am." Evie dug her fingernails into her palms. "What if he'd been bitten?"

"He wasn't."

"What if he had been?"

"Pff," said Blue. Evie could see that she'd gone from confused to annoyed. "Why are you on his side? Why aren't you worried about me?"

"*You!*" Evie exclaimed. "You don't need my worry. You don't need anyone's worry."

"But Jax does? Jax, who's a mortal—and a male. Jax, who's . . ." Blue made a scoffing sound. "Remind me, how old is he again? Your big brother with the boots and the gun and the best friend who's itching to get a job at Harmony Hall?"

Evie pressed her lips together, furious at Blue for making it seem as if things were black-and-white, mortal and fae, right and wrong. Furious at Blue for being so sure of herself all the time.

If Jax had died—he *hadn't*, but *if*—what would people say?

She thought about Ben Bratton, Silas's brother, who'd been either killed by a bear or murdered by a faerie, depending on who you asked. If Jax had died, would they blame the rattler that bit him, or would they blame the fae girl with wildness in her eyes?

Evie's heart thumped sickly. "With the snakes. I know you . . . talked to them, or whatever. Did you tell them to crawl all over him?"

Blue shrugged.

"Did you know he'd wet himself?"

A grin tugged at Blue's mouth, though she wrestled it

back down. "I didn't. But that was great, you've got to admit."

"No, Blue, it wasn't." Heat climbed up Evie's neck. She lifted her hair off her neck, then let it fall. Her emotions were all over the place. "I think you should go home."

Blue frowned and gestured around them, spreading her arms. "I *am* home." She pulled back. "Unless you mean the cabin? You think I should go back to the cabin?"

"No. I said it wrong." Evie sighed. "I meant *I* should go home."

Uncertainty flickered across Blue's face. "Okay. Whatever. But Evie . . .you're acting like this is my fault."

Wasn't it?

Evie drove the toe of her shoe into the grass, twisting it back and forth.

"You asked me to help find Dunbar," Blue said. "And I did."

"I asked you to help Jax."

"And—again—I did."

"But only on your terms!" Evie said. She couldn't shake the image of Jax and those snakes. Blue and those snakes. "Only after he said what you wanted to hear."

"You're made that I made him apologize?" Blue's eyebrows shot up. "What Jax said was hateful and disgusting."

"Of course it was! But Blue, he doesn't know better!"

"He does now."

"You think?" Evie spread her hands. "What, exactly, do you think he's learned?"

Blue faltered.

"The snakes," Evie said, her voice dropping. "You *talked*

to them. And they listened. And the look in your eyes when it was over . . ." She blinked. "You liked it, with the snakes. That's what it looked like."

Blue paled.

"And now everyone's mad at me, and I didn't even do anything."

"Evie, wait."

Evie looked back over her shoulder. She felt as if the world were zooming away from her. As if Blue were zooming away from her. "No, Blue," she said. "I just . . . I need to not see you for a while."

Blue's face crumpled. She stood slackly, arms loose at her sides. "How long is a while?"

"When I know, I'll tell you."

She turned her back on Blue and walked away.

Chapter Thirty-Seven

"Blue, my goodness," Margie said when Blue trudged into the house. "What happened?"

"Nothing," Blue said. She felt as hollow as a split seed pod, cracked and brittle. She headed for the staircase, but Margie stepped in front of her.

"You look like you're about to cry," she said, placing her hand on Blue's shoulder. "What's going on?"

Blue twitched away from Margie's touch. "Nothing. Don't worry about it."

"I am worried about it," Margie said. She furrowed her brow, only her concern did nothing but make things worse. "I'm worried about *you*."

"Well, don't," Blue said.

"Blue—"

"Did I ask you to worry about me? Have I ever asked you to worry about me? No, I haven't."

The grandmother must have heard the fuss, because she rolled her chair over to see what was going on.

"Oh my," she tutted, sounding more delighted than distressed. "Have I interrupted a mother-daughter squabble?"

Blue shot daggers at her through the film of her tears.

Margie gave her mother an equally sharp look. She touched Blue's elbow and said, "Come with me."

In the laundry room, the door shut for privacy, Margie folded her arms across her chest and lifted her eyebrows into peaks. "Was it Evie's father? Did he say something?"

Blue's gut tightened. "What? No." She wondered if they were finally going to have the conversation she wasn't at all sure she wanted to have. Her heart beat faster. "Why would he?"

"Then who did? Jax? Evie?"

Blue pressed her lips into a line.

"Something happened in the woods," Margie said, stating it as if it were fact and watching Blue like a hawk.

Blue blinked. *"You liked it, with the snakes,"* Evie had said. *"That's what it looked like."*

And, about Jax, *"Did you know he'd wet himself?"*

These were not things to be spoken of. Blue held her tongue.

Margie sighed. "I'm not asking for the fun of it, Blue. I need to know. Either you tell me, right now, or I'll go nextdoor and ask Evie's parents."

Blue saw spots. She backed dizzily into the wall, needing it for support.

"All right," Margie said. She stepped forward and reached for the doorknob.

"No!" Blue exclaimed.

"Then talk," Margie said.

So Blue did. She didn't share every last detail, but she told Margie roughly what had happened at Graveyard Fields. She included the part about Jax's jeans.

Margie's face drained of color. "Oh, Blue," she said, her voice barely a whisper. "This is bad. This is so, so bad."

"He disturbed the snakes," Blue muttered. "Not me."

Margie pressed her hands to her temples. "Does Abe know? Of course he does. What am I saying?" She paced in the cramped space. "And Nicole. Oh my Lord, Nicole. She'll blame you, I'm sure—when it's all the fault of that damn dog!"

Blue had never heard Margie curse before.

"But Jax is fine. Evie is fine. Even Dunbar is fine," she said.

Margie stepped close and grabbed Blue's shoulders. "Tell me exactly what Evie said, afterward."

Blue's throat contracted. "That . . . she needs to not see me for a while." The words felt like rocks. "But she'll change her mind."

"No, she won't," Margie said. She paused. "Or . . . maybe she will. I *do* think she cares about you." She pushed her fingers through her hair. "Regardless, no more contact with mortals, ever. Those days are over."

Blue gaped. "Margie, *you're* a mortal, or did you forget?"

"Of course not."

"Are you saying I can't have contact with you?"

"Don't be ridiculous. I'm your mother. Fae, mortal—I love you to the moon and back, and that will never change." Her expression changed. "But you can't see Evie again. I'm sorry, Blue."

Blue backed up, bumping hard against the door. She shook her head. "But . . ." She couldn't remember how to breathe. She saw not just spots, but stars. "I love *Evie* to the moon and back. That won't change, either."

"And yet she sent you away," Margie said.

Blue's eyes flared wide.

"We have to leave. That's the only answer."

"Margie. No."

Margie was no longer paying attention to Blue, but seemed rather to be talking to herself. "I'll tell Mother. She won't be happy, but she'll have to accept it."

"Evie will forgive me," Blue said. She blinked ferociously. "She'll realize none of this even matters."

That brought Margie back. "Maybe. Eventually." She huffed a bitter laugh. "But Jax? Oh, honey. Jax will never forgive you."

"So I'll stay out of his way," Blue said frantically. "He's a dumb mortal. If he tries to do anything, I'll outfox him."

"And if he brings a gun?"

Blue shook her head. This was happening so fast. Too fast. If she could just think things through . . . or go back in time . . .

Should *she* apologize to *Jax*? She blanched at the thought. But . . . would he listen? Would it help?

"Margie, I can fix this," she said desperately. "I know I can."

"Go to your room, Blue," Margie said. She returned to pacing back and forth in the small space, her face lined with worry. "Pack your things. I'll talk to Mother."

Blue's pulse roared in her ears. "No."

"Your best friend's brother wet his pants in front of his sister. In front of *you*."

"Yes, but—"

"He *peed* himself," Margie said. She stopped pacing and gave Blue the strangest look, as if Blue were a ghost. As if she already didn't exist. "There's no coming back from this, Blue. Not ever."

Blue's breath rushed out. "Margie," she said. Her chin trembled. "Are you mad at me, too?"

Margie shut her eyes and pressed both fists to her sternum, one on top of the other. When she opened her eyes, her expression was raw. "Blue, you publicly humiliated a teenage boy. I'm not mad. I'm terrified."

Chapter Thirty-Eight

Evie wasn't terrified, not yet. But she was getting there. Her parents forbade her from having anything to do with Blue ever again, and when she pushed back, Jax exploded.

"You were there! You saw what she did!" He glowered at her, and then his expression shifted, his features slackening for just a moment before resolving into even harder lines. "Jesus, Evie. How long have you known?"

Evie's stomach dropped.

"Known what?" her mother asked.

Jax strode out of the house and slammed the door behind him.

"Known *what*?" Evie's mother pressed, turning to Evie.

She spread her arms and showed her palms, knowing she couldn't let her rabbity heart get the best of her. "I don't know," she said. She widened her eyes and played into the role her mother had assigned her long ago. Timid Evie. Hunched-shouldered Evie. A "young" seventeen. "That he's scared of rattlesnakes?"

"Who isn't?" her mother said. She grew pale and sank into a chair.

"He's safe, Nicole," Evie's father said, going to her.

"That's what matters. Everyone's safe and sound."

"Jax was kicking up dirt, knocking things free," Evie offered.

Her father's expression looked an awful lot like Jax's.

She sidled toward the stairs. "The snakes wouldn't have bothered him if he hadn't bothered them first. That's all I'm saying."

"A nest of baby rattlers," Evie's mother murmured. "And the mother, dead set on protecting them." She fumbled for Evie's father's hand. "Oh, *Abe*."

Her father shifted his attention to her mother, and Evie took the opportunity to dash upstairs.

In her room, she fretted and paced, one hand wrapped around her ribs and the other hand up by her mouth. During the tense hike down the mountain—Jax stiff and furious, Evie a riot of conflicting emotions—she'd told herself that Jax didn't know Blue was fae. Not for sure. Maybe the thought hadn't even crossed his mind, consumed as he was by his own humiliation.

The thought certainly crossed his mind five minutes ago, right before he slammed out of the house. *Jesus, Evie. How long have you known?*

Jax knew, all right.

But would he tell?

Every two minutes, heart in her throat, Evie peeked out her bedroom window, hoping to see Blue's nimble figure hopping the fence that separated the two yards.

No. Blue respected Evie's wishes and stayed away.

Hours passed, and Evie's anxiety ratcheted higher and higher until she could no longer stand it. She tugged on her shoes and slipped out the door with neither parent the wiser. When she far enough from her house to not be spotted, she paused to think. She couldn't go to the meadow of golden roses, nor to the creek. She couldn't escape to the cool pool at the base of the waterfall. Those places were Blue, all Blue, and so . . . *no*. Not now. Not yet.

Anton's bakery. Maybe a brownie would help. Then she heard old Mrs. Freeman's words in her head: *Anton? He's no savior. He's the one who shot that faerie man.*

She wandered aimlessly until she reached the town center, where not so long ago she'd sat with Blue and listened to Cookie Gardner spew nonsense about faeries and what a bad lot they were, with no understanding of right or wrong. How they stirred up trouble just for spite.

She headed toward the filling station, thinking to get a Moon Pie, and drew up short at the sight of Jax. He was across the way from Evie and had his back to her, which was good. But he was talking to Silas Bratton, which wasn't. He gestured broadly as he spoke, emphasizing his words with angry movements.

Silas, by comparison, was the picture of self-control. He stood relaxed, thumbs hooked through his belt loops, nodding as he listened. When it was his turn to speak, he did so calmly. Then he looked past Jax and caught Evie's gaze. His chin jerked in acknowledgment.

Jax spun around, saw her, and glared. Silas said something that pulled Jax back. He pulled out his wallet, handed Jax a few bills, and clapped him on the shoulder.

Jax threw Evie another glare, then turned and strode into Taylor's Guns & Gear.

Silas strolled over to Evie, whose stomach was a knot of nerves.

"Hey, Evie," he said.

"Silas," Evie said, guarded.

"How ya doing?" he asked.

"Why are you here?" Evie demanded. "What's Jax buying?"

Silas ducked his head and chuckled. He looked up at her, placing his hand on the back of his neck, and said, "Nothing strange. Nothing to be alarmed by. Jax is buying supplies, that's all."

"What kind of supplies?"

"Crackers. Soda pop." He scanned the plaza, then returned his gaze to her. "Listen. I need to talk to you about something serious."

Evie's skin prickled.

"I know about your friend," he said gravely. He leaned in too close, making the moment feel intimate in the worst of all possible ways. "Jax told me all about her."

Evie's world tilted. She despised her brother. Detested him. She hated him, hated him, hated him.

"Hey," Silas soothed. "Don't worry. I haven't told anybody." He nodded toward the handful of townsfolk scattered about the square, all going about their business as if it were a perfectly ordinary day. "If I had, I reckon you'd know. Don't you?"

"What are you going to do?" Evie said.

"Do?" Silas said. He lifted his shoulders. "What would I *do*?"

"Then why are we talking about it? What do you want *me* to do?"

Silas propped a boot on a low stone wall. "Well, mainly I'm thinking about Jax. Concerned about him, because he's my friend. Something happened between him and your friend, though he won't give me any details. He's real upset about it."

Evie wrapped her arms around ribs. "Nothing happened. Jax is fine."

Silas looked at her with soft brown eyes. "You're not allowed to see her anymore. That's what Jax said."

"I'm seventeen," Evie said. "I'll see her if I want to."

Silas put his book back on the ground and straightened up. "Mortals are tribal, Evie. So are fae. We all are, when it comes down to it."

"Fine. Great. But Blue and I aren't 'tribal' against each other."

"Sure, sure. If you say so."

"She's not . . . there's nothing . . ." Evie made an exasperated noise. "You'd like her, Silas, if you got to know her."

"Huh," he said. He moved his mouth around as if tasting the idea, then let his expression smooth into something bland. "Would she like me?"

Evie's gaze dropped to his boots—scuffed and solid, the kind Corrections Officers probably wore at Harmony Hall. She dragged her eyes upward, past the set of his broad shoulders to the stubble shadowing his jaw.

"You're young," he said. "That's not your fault."

Evie gave him an indignant look. Silas Bratton was two years older than she was, tops.

"But you understand why Jax is riled up, don't you? It's his job to look after you."

"I beg your pardon?" she said.

Silas squinted at the jagged peaks of the mountains,

where the late afternoon light cast long, slanted shadows. "She won't stay here much longer, your friend. She and Margie must know it's only a matter of time before people start talking. You think they'll stick around and wait for the fallout?" He shook his head. "Nah. They'll run."

Evie's throat went dry. "Silas, don't say that," she managed. "Blue isn't running anywhere."

He gestured toward the craggy ridgeline, where mist curled at the highest points. "I hear Margie's got a cabin up there. You ever been?"

"I haven't. No."

"Keep it that way. Especially tonight." He gave her his easy smile. "It's a full moon. Strange things happen when there's a full moon."

"What do you mean? What kind of strange things?"

Jax emerged from Taylor's carrying a large paper bag.

"Silas, what do you mean?" Evie repeated. Her head felt foggy.

"Mission successful?" Silas asked Jax.

Jax opened the bag to let Silas peer inside. Evie craned to see, but couldn't.

"Nice," Silas said. "You did good, brother."

Jax rolled the top of the bag down to make a handle. "I won't be home till late," he muttered, addressing a hazy region above Evie's head. "I'll eat with Silas."

Evie tried to understand what was going on, because something clearly was. "Eat what? Crackers and pop?"

"Yes, Evie, crackers and pop," Jax said, his voice coiling and growing mean. "If we're feeling crazy, maybe even a Charleston Chew. Do you have a problem with that?"

"Aw, Jax, that's no way to talk to your sister," Silas said

mildly. "Evie doesn't have a problem with anything." He threw her a wink. "Do you, Evie?"

Chapter Thirty-Nine

That night, there was extra chili to go around. Extra cornbread, too. But Evie wasn't hungry.

"You've done some good stirring there," her dad remarked. "Why not throw caution to the wind and eat a bite?"

Evie stopped. Her spoon listed sideways in the bowl like a tiny abandoned oar.

"You can't forbid me from seeing Blue," she told him. She kept her voice steady, though it felt like all the air had left the room. "I'm not a child. I'm an adult."

"Not as long as you're living under this roof, you're not," her mother said. "You know better than to question your father."

"But she didn't do anything wrong," Evie said. "All she did was help us find Dunbar."

Her parents exchanged a look. Evie tried to decipher its meaning—What did they know? What were they thinking? —but they shuttered their expressions.

Her mother pushed back from the table and started collecting still-full dishes. "This is what happens when a child is allowed to run wild. That girl is Margie all over again. Completely lawless. Feral." She snatched Evie's bowl. "Didn't I tell you, Evie? Didn't I tell you that Margie's unconventional ways would come back to bite her?"

Okay, her mother still thought Blue was Margie's daughter. That was something.

"And to think there was a time when you took a shine to that woman, Abe Carpenter! You and Margie Freeman!"

Evie's father leaned back against his chair, his expression neutral. But there was something there, just below the surface. Evie saw it. A worm, or maybe a spider, wanting to crawl out.

"Just plain ludicrous," her mother said. She strode into the kitchen, turned on the faucet, and banged the dishes as she scrubbed them.

Evie's father lifted his glass of iced tea and took a sip. "What, exactly, happened at Graveyard Fields, Evie? I'd like the truth."

"Nothing. I told you."

"Have people been talking? Is there gossip going around?"

"No, Dad. No gossip."

He grunted, and Evie pushed back her chair and excused herself, preferring the quiet of her room to the company of her parents.

Half an hour later, the phone rang. Her mother answered pleasantly, but within seconds, her tone shifted and grew tense. Evie slipped out of her room and went to the top of the stairs. From there, she spotted her mother poised anxiously in the doorway between the kitchen and the sitting room.

"Bob Bratton's on the line," her mother told her father.

"He's going on about the boys, and he's in an awful state."

Her father rose and ducked into the kitchen. Evie crept halfway down the stairs, desperate to hear what was being said.

"Dang it, Bob!" her father exclaimed. "When did you notice they were gone?"

And that was it. That was all it took. Evie bolted back to her room, yanked open the window, and climbed out onto the roof. She edged sideways, refusing to give herself time to hesitate.

She should have been gone already.

She'd known it, and yet she'd pretended she hadn't.

As she shimmied down the gutter and hopped onto the grass, her mind flicked back to earlier, when she'd ran into Silas and Jax in the town square. When the boys had sauntered off, something in Jax's bag had made a clinking sound. But crackers didn't clink, and when soda cans bumped one another, they made a liquid *thunk*.

She cursed herself for wasting so much time, when the answers to all her questions had been in front of her all along. The racks at the front of Taylor's Guns & Gear were filled with snacks, candy, and Cherry ChapStick. In the back were rounds of ammunition in red and silver cardboard boxes, the kind her father used for his Winchester. She'd been with him a hundred times when he'd bought them.

The rounds, when loaded into paper bags, made a sound Evie knew well, stirring in their boxes like metal-plated snakes.

Chapter Forty

Blue leaned against the laundry room counter and gazed through the window, her elbows propped on the counter and her chin in her palms. The moon rose over the mountains, round and creamy, evoking the memory of a boy with a roguish grin. *Digs.*

She saw his hands cupped over hers as he taught her how to whistle using a blade of grass, the sound startling a robin into flight.

She remembered a bedtime story about a fox with three tails that could make fire with a flick.

She heard a soft tune amplified by close soil walls. "The earth likes it," he'd told her. "It hums back if you listen."

Then came all the rest. Clumsy footfalls. Dirt raining down. The candle flame jumping and dancing, and the terror in her brother's eyes. Spilled milk. The jostle of men.

Go, Blue. Go!

In the laundry room, Blue bowed her head. What was done was done—there was no going back—but the unfairness of it all cut through her like rough glass. Those with power sowed fear and division. Those without fought back and lost, or submitted and lost.

But the way Blue saw it, the winners lost, too. By creating division where there was none, they made themselves *less*. They hollowed themselves out. And Blue wanted to be *more*.

She wanted it for Evie. For Margie. For poor Ben Bratton, who was dead. She wanted it even for Jax, who wasn't.

Footsteps creaked behind her, and Margie's hands settled on Blue's shoulders. "I'll make Mother one last cup of tea, and then we'll go."

Blue raised her head and locked her eyes on the bone-white moon. As it swelled over the crags, it illuminated a fine silver mist, and within the mist, shapes formed and fell apart. A mother. A father. A baby girl. A serpent with glinting scales.

"Stay here," Margie murmured, squeezing Blue's shoulders. "I'll come for you."

Blue waited until she heard Margie moving about in the kitchen, then ducked out the back door and into the yard.

She took two steps toward Evie's fence—then stopped.

I need to not see you for a while.

How long is a while?

I'll let you know.

She pivoted, heading for the trees. She wasn't running away. Not yet. She'd do that with Margie soon enough. But the pulse of missing Evie throbbed inside her like an open wound. She *had* to move.

She hit the trail to Overlook Rock, slipping into the forest, welcoming the darkness that swallowed her. She hiked fast, her breaths growing heavier as the trail steepened. She hiked even faster, trying to outrace her thoughts. She collided with a pine tree and cried out, pain shooting up her hip.

"What was that?" a male voice called out.

Blue froze. She knew that voice.

"What was *what*? Where?" called a second voice, also male. The arc of a flashlight beam sliced through the trees.

Blue pressed her spine to the trunk, barely breathing.

"Told you she'd make a run for it," Jax said.

"So let's find her," said his companion. Silas?

The light passed over Blue's hiding spot and kept going.

"You think she heard us?" Jax asked.

"I think she heard *you*, yeah."

"Well, I hope she's scared out of her pants," Jax said. He huff-laughed. "Think we'll see her tail? You know, if she's scared *out of her pants*?"

"She doesn't have a tail," Jax's friend replied flatly.

"It was a joke, Silas. Geez."

Silas it was. Of course.

Silas swung his flashlight, and the beam traced a jagged *V* across the undergrowth. "Which way?"

Jax's beam joined with Silas's. "Keep going up. I'm pretty sure we can get to Margie's cabin if we hang a right at Overlook Rock."

Their footsteps receded, and Blue eased out from behind the tree. She needed to get back to Margie, let her know the boys were out here. Then what? If they were heading for Margie's cabin, she and Margie would have to go somewhere else. But where?

From up the mountain came the crack of branches, a tumbling thud, a high fearful cry. A girl's cry. *Evie.*

Blue's body reacted before her mind had a chance to

process what the cry meant. Adrenaline flooded her veins, and she took off toward the sound.

"Did you hear that?" Silas called.

"It's her! It's got to be!" Jax cried.

They crested the hill, silhouetted by moonlight: two young men, armed with rifles, their stocks jouncing as they blundered through the brush.

Urgency swelled in Blue like a storm-swollen river. She had to get to Evie before they did.

She caught a whiff of her scent in the mulch of a fallen tree, then again beneath a low-hanging bough. She followed the wisps like breadcrumbs, veering left as the boys continued straight. Even so, their routes ran parallel, too close for comfort.

She hopscotched across the loose shale where Jax had disturbed the copperheads. "Evie, where are you?" she called in a hushed voice. "Evie? Are you here?"

A faint reply: ". . . *Blue*?"

Blue ducked beneath a tangle of blueberry bushes—then stopped, body going rigid.

A wild, savage odor slammed into her, and every part of her went wobbly.

Bear.

A rustle in the undergrowth. A low guttural huff.

"Evie?" Blue whispered. She scanned the shadows.

"Blue?" Evie's voice floated back.

The rustling stopped. The bear had heard.

Blue's heart pounded as she moved carefully forward. "Evie, listen. Be very, very—"

Evie screamed.

Blue abandoned all caution and shoved through

brambles. She saw the bear, a hulking mass of muscle and matted fur. He pawed the ground, his black eyes gleaming. He swayed his head from side to side.

Several yards away, her pale hair a beacon, Evie inched backward.

"Be still," Blue hissed. "*Stop. Moving.*"

From the opposite edge of the clearing came the crashing of branches and the thud of boots. A sharp inhalation as someone skidded to a halt. Blue couldn't see them, but knew it had to be Jax and Silas.

"Oh, crap," she heard Jax say.

Then came a cry, raw and pained, paired with the thud of a body hitting the ground. Blue broke fully into the clearing and saw Jax sprawled on his back, his rifle knocked out of reach.

The bear curled his upper lip, baring huge teeth.

"Stay still," Blue called out to Jax as calmly as she could.

Jax scrabbled for his gun. A growl rumbled from the bear.

Behind Jax, Silas fired his rifle. *Bang!*

The bear flared its nostrils.

"Get up, Jax!" shouted Silas. He scrambled to reload.

Little bullet, big bear, Blue thought wildly.

"Don't shoot!" she cried. "It'll only make him madder!"

Bang!

Bellowing, the bear charged. A paw lashed out, and Silas went flying. His rifle soared through the air and clattered down a rocky ravine.

The bear turned back toward Jax, who'd risen to a squat and was backing away, one hand held out in supplication.

"N-no," he whimpered.

The bear reared to his full height, teeth bared and ears pressed back. His roar shook the mountain.

"Blue, do something!" begged Evie. "You have to save him!"

But I don't, Blue thought, even as her heart thumped and pushed blood into her willing limbs. *He came for me with a gun. Why would I risk my life for him?*

Evie turned away from Blue and lifted her arms, yelling and drawing attention to herself. "Over here!" she choked out. "This way, bear!"

Blue swore. Then, body tingling, she sprinted forward and flung herself into the air.

Chapter Forty-One

The bear's broad back rushed to greet her, and Blue smacked onto it with an *oomph*, limbs splayed wide. The bear bellowed and twisted, trying to shake her loose. Blue leaned forward and wrapped her arms around the bear's thick neck. *It's okay,* she told him. *I'm a friend.*

The bear galloped in a frenzied circle, its massive shoulders bucking beneath her. Blue clung tight, locking her fingers and toes into his coarse fur. From the corner of her eye, she saw Evie crouched beside Jax, urging him toward the edge of the field. Just past them, Silas was on his feet, limping toward Jax's abandoned rifle.

"No! No guns!" Blue shouted, sliding sideways as the bear pitched violently. She righted herself, surrendering to the rhythm of his ropy muscles.

Shh, she soothed, but the bear *knew* rifles. *Hated* rifles. Their bullets nipped like bee stings—hardly anything—but the noise and flare sent rage clawing through him.

Silas strained for Jax's firearm.

The bear reared onto his hind legs and roared.

"No guns!" Blue cried. "Tell him, Evie! No guns, or we're all dead!"

"Silas, listen to Blue!" Evie shouted. "You're scaring the bear!"

"*I'm* scaring the *bear*?" Silas let out a sharp, incredulous laugh.

Evie darted forward and kicked Jax's rifle out of his reach.

Blue sagged with relief. *Yes! Good! See?* she told the bear. *No more guns. All better.*

The bear's frantic loping slowed. He roared again, but his crazed rage was ebbing.

I know, I know, Blue murmured. *They're just silly boys. But you're a big strong bear.* She loosened her grip and scratched behind his stubby ears.

The bear stilled. With a snuffling huff, he stretched his neck and leaned into Blue's touch.

"The hell . . . ?" Silas managed.

"You scared him," Blue said. "But I told him it was a misunderstanding." She patted the bear's muscled shoulder. "Which it was, right? Or do you have a bone to pick with him?"

"Nope! No bones!" Silas said.

Jax sat slumped in the grass, blinking. His shirt was torn, a streak of dirt—or blood—smeared across his cheek. A bruise bloomed above his left eye.

"No bones," he said faintly.

Evie cleared her throat. "What about Blue? Do either of you have a bone to pick with *her*?"

Silas hesitated.

"She saved your life," Evie reminded him.

His lips parted, but he didn't speak.

Evie turned to Jax. "And you? What do you have to say to

her?"

Jax's gaze moved upward, and he looked at Blue as if she were some kind of hallucination. A girl astride a bear, speaking in a language no one else could hear.

The bear abruptly sat, and Blue tumbled off, laughing.

"Hey!" she protested. As she shoved herself upright, the grin slid from her face. Her head snapped toward the trees. "Someone's coming."

Silas and Evie turned toward the crunch of footfalls, heavy and fast.

Blue slapped the bear's rump. "Go!" she urged.

The bear hesitated for half a breath before padding toward the forest, then breaking into an easy lope. His parting roar sent the trees quivering as Abe Carpenter and Bob Bratton burst into the clearing.

"Jax! Evie!" Abe's voice was raw. He rushed forward, frantically scanning the shadows, then crouched by his children. "Are you hurt? Talk to me."

Bob Bratton braced the butt of his rifle against his shoulder and pointed the muzzle at Blue.

"Why lookie here," he sneered, and Blue felt the world slip away from her.

She *knew* that sneering voice.

She knew his scent, too: sharp, acrid, tinged with sweat and gunpowder.

It dragged her backward through time, to the damp walls of a den, to milk spilled over packed earth, to Digs's wide terrified eyes. To heavy boots kicking through leaves, to the *crack* of a rifle, to the sound of her own breathing as she fled, fled, fled—

"This your doing, Silas?" Mr. Bratton asked. "You capture

this dirty bogglin?"

Silas threw a glance at Blue. "Dad, she saved us. She's not
—"

"She sicced that bear on you? Worked her dirty magic?"

Silas's throat worked. "Dad, wait."

Mr. Bratton shoved him away. "No, sir, I will not. This girl is unclean. She will always be unclean."

He killed Digs, Blue thought, staring down the muzzle of Mr. Bratton's gun. *It was him. It was Silas's father.*

She raised despairing eyes to his trembling hands. The barrel wavered, but his hatred held steady.

The man who had killed her brother was going to kill her, too.

Chapter Forty-Two

Evie threw herself between Blue and Mr. Bratton, arms spread wide. "Didn't you hear what Silas said? She *saved* him! She saved your *son!*"

"Move," Mr. Bratton growled, lifting his rifle an inch.

"Now, Bob, hang on." Her father's voice was steady, almost conversational. He took a slow step forward. "This isn't the first time we've hunted her kind together. You know where I stand."

Evie's breath hitched. Her father—a faerie hunter?

"But that's my daughter there," her dad continued, nodding toward her. "And you've got your gun pointed straight at her."

"So tell her to move," Mr. Bratton snarled.

Her father sighed. "Evie . . ."

"No!" she shouted. She planted her feet and squared her shoulders. Her voice cracked as she said, "You'll have to shoot me first!"

Mr. Bratton's hands trembled around the stock. "I will if I have to."

"Bob," her father said, firmer now. "Take a breath." He glanced toward Blue, who sat motionless on the ground, her fingers clenched in the dirt, her eyes locked on the barrel of the gun. "I want the faerie dead as much as you do —"

"Dad!" Evie choked out.

"—but use your head. One this age, especially a girl, can't survive these mountains alone."

Mr. Bratton's grip tightened. "She's right here, ain't she? Alive and breathing."

"For now," her dad said evenly. "But winter's coming. Where's she going to sleep?"

In Margie's cabin! Evie almost yelled, the words bursting to be free. *She'll go away and never bother anyone again, okay?!*

Her father's eyes flicked toward her, just for a moment, and—oh, the relief she felt made her knees go weak. He was stalling. He wasn't here to hurt Blue. He was here to make sure that no one else did, either.

Mr. Bratton spat into the dirt. "Where's she going to sleep? On the cold, cold ground, where the wolves will find her carcass. Now, get your girl out of my sight so I can finish this."

"Walk away, Bob," her father said, closing the distance between them with painstaking slowness. "Take Silas. Go home."

The hammer of Mr. Bratton's rifle clicked into place.

Her father lunged, hands clamping onto it and wrenching it free.

"Silas, take it!" he barked.

"No!" Mr. Bratton roared.

Silas lunged forward and snatched the gun from Evie's father's grasp. He stumbled back, clutching it to his chest.

"We're letting her go, Dad. I'm sorry. But we are."

Evie's knees buckled. She pressed both hands to her mouth, her whole body shaking. *Thank you, thank you, thank you.*

Then—

CRACK.

Evie's father staggered from the kickback, his own rifle jolting high.

A muffled *thud*, as soft as a kitten pouncing on a leaf.

Evie twisted to see Blue—crumpled in the dirt. Evie let out a mewling cry. She, too, sank to the ground.

"Go on home, Bob," Evie's father said heavily. "I'll clean this up."

When Mr. Bratton didn't move, he cut a look at Silas. "Take your father home, Silas. Jax, go with them."

Silas hooked an arm around his father's shoulders. "Come on, Dad. We're going home."

Jax trailed behind them, his face blank. The three of them trudged off, and soon, the low rumble of a truck engine carried through the trees.

Evie's father crossed the clearing, knelt by Blue, and took her hand. "It's safe," he said gently. "They're gone."

Chapter Forty-Three

Blue opened her eyes to see Evie and her father looming over her. While Abe looked worried, Evie was absolutely wrecked—eyes red-rimmed, mouth a quivering line.

Blue shot up and hugged her ferociously. "Evie, it's all right. I'm all right, see?" For her to think, even for a moment . . . If their roles had been reversed . . .

No. The notion of Evie not being alive was too much to bear.

Blue pulled back and let Evie take her in.

Evie's breath was ragged, but color was returning to her cheeks. "But you were dead!"

"I wasn't."

"My father shot you!"

"He didn't."

"He did! I saw him!"

Abe shook his head. "No, honey."

Evie swiveled toward Blue. "You fell over. You died."

Blue looked to Abe, who gave a small nod.

"I *played* dead," she explained. "Your dad told me to."

"*What*?!" Evie's head snapped between them. "When?"

"I guess, gosh, about thirteen years ago?" Self-conscious,

she plucked a twig from her hair. "He's the one who gave me to Margie."

Evie's brow furrowed. "Daddy?"

"I didn't 'give' her to anyone," Abe corrected. "You give away old furniture, not children." He shifted his stance uncomfortably. "Blue was little. Alone. I entrusted her to someone who could keep her safe."

"Why was she little and alone?" asked Evie. She took Blue's hand. "Blue, why were you little and alone?"

Maybe, if they'd had more time, Blue could have told her. Maybe, in a different world, they could have rewritten the rules and shown everyone how things should be. A world where a girl like Blue didn't have to play dead just to stay alive.

But this wasn't that world.

"Blue?" Evie's voice wavered.

Abe exhaled. "We need to go."

"Where?" Evie asked.

"To the grandmother's," Blue said. She rose and swept her hair off her face, lifting and releasing the silky weight of it. Her bandana had fallen off when she'd keeled over—or maybe when she'd tumbled from the bear. She felt Evie's gaze as Evie saw, for the first time, the delicate points of her ears. Blue looked away, not wanting to see revulsion or shock or even awe on Evie's face.

"To the grandmother's? All right, then," Evie said, and she was by Blue's side. She smiled and reached up, tucking a stray lock behind Blue's ear as if it were the most natural thing in the world. "Let's go."

They climbed into Abe's truck. The night pressed against the windows, vast and moonlit. The engine rumbled. No one spoke. Abe kept his hands tight on the wheel, his eyes fixed on the road. Blue gazed out at the trees rushing past in dark blurs. Evie sat between them. Without looking at her, Blue found her hand and squeezed it.

"Dad, you should have seen her," Evie said. "Blue with the bear—she jumped right on top of him. Rode him like a horse!"

"Did she?" Abe said. He navigated the curvy mountain road with a tight jaw.

"I was scared out of my mind. But not Blue!" Evie's voice was far too bright, and Blue's heart hurt, knowing what all would come next.

"But everything worked out," Evie babbled on. "Thank goodness!"

"Mmm," said Blue. Mr. Bratton had pointed a rifle at her. He would have pulled the trigger if Abe hadn't stopped him.

Evie's forced cheer wavered. "Dad? Blue? Everyone's safe. Isn't that good news?"

"It is, honey," Abe said.

"Then why are you using that voice?"

"What voice?"

"*That* voice." Evie laughed, but it fell flat. "Honestly, both of you—why are you acting so strange?"

No one answered her question.

"We're taking you *home*, Blue," Evie said. "That's good. Isn't it?"

"He's taking me to the grandmother's house," Blue murmured.

"Yes, well, it's still where you live."

Blue turned and met her eyes. "Not after tonight. Not

anymore."

Chapter Forty-Four

In the living room, Abe and Margie murmured in hushed, grown-up voices. In the kitchen, Blue gave Star a final kiss on her damp pink nose, then lowered her carefully to the floor, where she twined lovingly around Blue's ankles. Blue moved gently so as not to step on her by accident. She shoved an apple and a wedge of cheese into her rucksack. She wrapped a knife in a handkerchief and added that, too.

"Blue, please," Evie whispered. "Margie has a plan. You said so. She knows what's best for you."

"Margie's plan is to hide. She thinks if we're quiet, the world will forget about me." She slid the rucksack over her shoulders. "But people like Bob Bratton don't forget. Tomorrow, or maybe tonight, he'll return to spit on my body—or worse. When he sees that there is no body . . ."

"You can't just leave," Evie protested. "Where would you even go?"

"To the place for people like me," she said. Heat rose on her cheeks. "Across the river."

"But Blue, no one's ever made it across."

Blue laughed ruefully. "Aren't you the one who told me differently? All those faeries, all those years ago . . .they didn't just disappear, you said." She hitched her shoulders. "Anything's better than waiting to get shot—or locked up in Harmony Hall."

"That's not going to happen. I won't let it."

"Oh, Evie," Blue said. She placed her hand on Evie's cheek. "This isn't something you can fix."

Blue knew it was time. Margie wouldn't hash things over with Abe forever. But pulling away from Evie felt impossible.

A familiar *shush-shush* cut through the air, and from the darkened hallway emerged the grandmother on her throne of steel. Blue dropped her hand from Evie's face, but not before the grandmother saw. She took in Evie, who stood taller and moved closer to Blue.

"Running away?" said the old lady, gesturing at Blue's rucksack. "How do you think that will play out?"

"It's better than staying here," Blue shot back.

The grandmother looked pointedly at Blue's bare feet. She dragged her gaze up, taking in Blue's overalls, her thin cotton shirt, the exposed tips of her ears. She tapped her bony fingers on the armrest of her wheelchair, a hair's breadth from the satchel that held her infernal bell.

"You're nothing but a rabbit," she said. "A foolish rabbit who thinks it can outpace the hounds. But you can't."

"She'll be fine," Evie said fiercely. "She always is."

The grandmother arched her brows.

"You never wanted her here anyway!" Evie went on. "Well, now she's leaving. You should be happy!"

"Should I?"

Evie lifted her chin. "At least she's not old and mean and hateful, like you!"

The grandmother thrust her hand into the satchel. "You, girl, need to respect your elders!"

The walls of the kitchen seemed to expand and contract, and Blue's vision tunneled, all the world depending on the satchel and its contents. Within it, the grandmother's fingers clutched and grabbed, the fabric squirming as if alive.

Then the fabric stilled, though the grandmother's hand stayed tucked within. "I didn't hate her," she pronounced. She turned to Blue. "I didn't *like* you—there's not much to like—and I certainly didn't want you here. But hate?"

The grandmother narrowed her eyes.

Blue's pulse pounded.

"Well. Perhaps I did hate you, after all. Perhaps I still do. Or perhaps I hate myself."

"What do you mean?" Blue asked.

The grandmother glanced toward the living room, her lips flattening at the sound of Abe and Margie's fretful murmurs. "I can't have you break my daughter's heart. I just can't have it."

Her glittering eyes locked on Blue, and she pulled out the bell.

Blue braced for the frenzy of chimes that would summon Margie and Abe, but the grandmother didn't ring it.

"Come closer," she said brusquely, motioning for the girls to approach.

Blue and Evie exchanged a glance, then inched forward.

The grandmother laid the bell sideways in her lap, her fingers knobby and wrinkled against its smooth wooden handle. She fumbled inside the brass dome, muttering about being "too damn old" and having "useless hands," before thrusting the bell at Blue. "Remove it."

"Remove what?" asked Blue.

"The clapper. The part that makes it ding."

Blue took the bell and worked by touch, prying at a twisted knot of wire until it straightened and the clapper slipped free.

It wasn't a lump of metal, as she'd expected, but a large gold ring, intricately carved, with a crystal set in its center. The sight of it made the little hairs on the back of her neck stand tall.

"Is that . . . *the* ring?" Evie asked. "You didn't throw it into the river after all?"

"Of course I didn't, silly girl."

Evie's voice swelled with hope. "And it'll let Blue cross to the other side of the river?"

"She's a faerie, isn't she? Well, the ring's chock-full of faerie magic, so I reckon so."

"But it's too big," Evie blurted. She plucked the ring from Blue's palm and slid it onto her index finger. It hung loosely. She lowered her hand, and the ring tumbled off, bouncing and hopping across the linoleum. Star pounced on it and swished her tail.

"Shh!" the grandmother hissed. She gestured at Blue. "Pick it up. Put it on. Hurry!"

Blue knelt and claimed the ring from the kitten.

"Put it *on*," the grandmother insisted.

Blue slid it onto her finger, and the gold band shrank to fit her, snug and sure. She held her hand out, marveling as she turned it this way and that.

Evie looked at Blue, then at the ring.

"I *told* you," the grandmother said querulously. "It only

works for someone with the old blood." She made a shooing motion. "Now, go. I'll hold off Margie as long as I can. Abe, too. I'll say you're upstairs bawling like babies, saying your goodbyes."

Blue crossed the room, Evie at her side. At the door, Blue turned back. She saw Star, sitting with tiny feline grace at the base of the grandmother's chair. She saw the grandmother blinking fiercely, helpless against the silver tears that streaked her weathered face.

Chapter Forty-Five

Blue and Evie's feet barely skimmed the ground as they dashed across the yard, scrambled over the fence, and darted into the forest. A storm was brewing, fog rolling in thick and heavy. It swallowed the trees and pressed against their skin like a living thing.

The trail narrowed and steepened, and the roar of the river grew louder. When they stepped out onto Overlook Rock, wind erupted from nowhere, shrieking through the trees, pushing against them like a force determined to tear them apart. Evie's curls streamed toward town. Blue's dark hair snapped in the opposite direction, a wild flag whipping toward the river far below.

Blue braced herself, bare feet digging into stone.

Evie tried to reach for her, but couldn't. Her limbs had grown heavier than gravity. Anguish built and swelled inside her until she feared she might burst. One *pop*, and she'd be gone, atoms shattering into stars.

Then Blue's hand found hers, and the world fell silent. Something ancient rippled through the air, a deep hum of energy.

A net that's lighter than gossamer and softer than

moonlight, thought Evie. *It stretches but never breaks, and when one thread stirs, all the others sing in reply.*

She had never in her wildest dreams imagined it would be so beautiful, this swirl of energy from an ancient realm. Fiery reds glittered and clashed with shards of icy blue. Streaks of gold flared and flickered and flared anew, always moving and never still. Greens sizzled and popped, and patches of sweet, soft yellow—more yielding than a buttercup—wafted and spun like a handful of scattered petals.

The veil hurtled toward Blue and Evie from across the ravine, then slammed to a stop. Then came the most beautiful singing Evie had ever heard. It filled her with an irresistible yearning, as if she would do anything not to disappoint someone whose opinion mattered more than anything. Tonight, right now, that someone was Blue.

Evie knew it was time.

She *knew.*

"This is it," she whispered. Her voice was barely a thread. "This is as far as I can go."

Blue's mouth tightened as if she was trying not to cry.

Evie glanced at Blue's ring, the gold gleaming in the moonlight. She looked at the invisible bridge made visible, but not for her. For Blue.

"You'll be okay," Evie said, willing herself to believe it, willing every ounce of her strength into Blue.

Blue didn't look convinced. "Will I? It feels . . . Oh, Evie, it feels like I'm heading off to die."

"No! You have to cross the bridge. That's all."

"Sure. That's all."

"Blue," Evie said fiercely. "*Blue.*" She squeezed until she felt Blue's bones grind beneath her skin, until Blue cried, "Ow!" and came back from wherever she'd gone.

"I believe in you," Evie said. "You can do this."

Blue's chin wobbled. "I don't know if I can. I don't think I can say goodbye."

Evie's tears spilled freely. *Then don't,* she wanted to say. *Just stay!*

But there would be dogs with sharp teeth and men with guns.

Evie reached up, trembling, and traced the tips of Blue's ears. With both hands, she cupped Blue's face and kissed her.

"Oh," Blue gasped, and she was kissing Evie back, and everything was warmth and love and salt. The softness of Blue's lips, the solidity of Blue's body pressed to hers. Evie's entire being lifted, and when at last she pulled away, she had to pant to find her breath.

Blue's eyes held the moon and the stars. They were vast pools of blue, and her long black hair rippled as if she were underwater.

"Go," Evie said.

The wind gusted, separating them, and Blue's hair flew every which way. She stepped out onto the silk-strung bridge, which hummed and bobbed but didn't break. She looked back, smiling through her tears, then turned and pressed onward, her slim figure disappearing into the moonlit mist.

~

Evie made her way down the trail in tripping, uneven steps. The fog was thicker now than ever, obscuring the moon and turning the trees against her. Their branches became ghostly limbs, clawing and scraping. Their bulbous roots bulged and flattened, eager to see her fall.

You can do this, she told herself. She had to—for Blue. She had to make her way back home—or to the grandmother's house if that was where Margie and her father still were—and tell them Blue was gone. That she'd crossed the river to be with others like her. That she was with her people now and safe, so there was no point in looking for her.

(But wasn't *Evie* Blue's person, just as Blue was hers?)

Evie paused and squeezed shut her eyes. *Please,* she prayed. *Just . . . please.*

When she opened them, she spotted the bouncing glow of flashlights.

"Evie?" her father called.

"Blue! Evie!" called Margie. "Girls, where are you?"

Evie cried out and ran toward them, barreling into her father's broad chest.

"Oh, thank God," he said raggedly. "Evie, you're safe, thank God."

"Where's Blue?" Margie said. She grabbed Evie's shoulder and spun her from her father. "Why isn't she with you?"

Evie answered as best she could. She told them about Blue and the river and the brave set of her jaw. She longed to tell them about the ring—that frightful, wonderful ring— but instinct warned her against it.

"But she's all right," she told Margie. "I promise."

Her father squinted up the mountain, perhaps envisioning the trail that twisted upward. The treacherous crevice at its peak. The river far below. He turned and looked back the way they'd come, where the path widened and the terrain leveled out.

His hand fell onto Evie's shoulder. "Well, let's head on back, then."

"Head back?" Margie exclaimed. "I'm not going back, not with Blue still out there. She's my girl, Abe. My daughter!"

Evie touched Margie's arm. "The bridge. It came. She's safe, Margie. She truly is."

Margie shook her off. "Maybe so. I'm going after her just the same."

Evie expected her father to argue, but he just nodded.

"Come along," he said to Evie. His boots crunched the undergrowth in steady, deliberate steps. "They're not so different, you know. Margie and Blue. I reckon they're both strong enough to get through pretty much anything. Don't you?"

Evie felt a great rush of love for him, first for saving Blue's life and now for acknowledging, in his gruff way, the truth of fairy tales, even for the mortals left behind.

I do, she tried to say, but the words got stuck. She burst into sobs, and her father held her tight.

Chapter Forty-Six

Word of Margie's missing daughter spread fast, and the townsfolk responded the way they always did—gathering, whispering, picking the story apart piece by piece.

From her window, Evie watched a slow, steady stream of neighbors climb the grandmother's walkway, arms weighed down with casseroles. They passed along their condolences, and when they weren't invited in, they hovered too long on the stoop, stretching out the moment, waiting for scraps of new information to fall into their laps. Every so often, the grandmother's strident voice broke through the murmurings—proof that she, at least, had no patience for these drawn-out performances.

Evie spotted Mrs. Langley and Mrs. Trask—two of her mother's church friends—leaning in close as Margie spoke from just within the house. Their heads tilted at just the right angles, their faces arranged in perfect masks of concern. But the second Margie closed the door, their postures straightened, their eyes went bright, and their mouths moved in quick, clipped pecks, picking the story apart and searching for every last crumb of drama.

Evie knew her mother would make a similar sympathy

visit soon. The scent of tomato sauce and warm, bubbling cheese wafted up from the kitchen. The lasagna she'd prepared was almost done. Evie's mother would deliver it across the street and tell Margie, in a tone that sounded generous but was anything but, *If there's anything I can do, anything at all . . .*

When she'd return, she'd hum and look pleased, and Evie would sense her unspoken judgments.

Well, Margie, are you honestly surprised by any of this? Letting that girl run wild, allowing her to put my boy at risk because of her foolish ways . . . None of this would have happened if that girl had been raised right!

Evie gripped the windowsill. Not Blue. Not Margie's daughter. Just *that girl*, a wild thing who'd never belonged here in the first place.

At noon, a sheriff's cruiser pulled onto their street.

Evie expected him to head straight for Margie's house, but Sheriff Boyde loped in long strides to Evie's house and rapped on their front door instead. His comb-over was already loosening from the heat of the day, and his uniform shirt hung loose on his scarecrow frame.

From upstairs, Evie heard the scuff of a chair on carpet and the rise and fall of polite conversation.

"Evie!" her mother called. "The sheriff's here. He's got some questions for you. Could you come downstairs?"

As she descended the stairs, she considered how best to handle the situation. She knew Blue was safe. She knew that Blue had gone to a place where no one would ever find her. But if anyone—the sheriff, Bob Bratton, even Anton the baker—suspected Evie of hiding anything, they'd hound her for details, maybe even try to figure out how to cross the river themselves.

If the townsfolk learned what was waiting on the other side—not just a faerie hideout but something better, something pure and good and untouched—they'd want it for themselves. They'd march in with their laws and their morals, their preaching and their plows, and they'd do whatever they wanted to do.

Mortals ruined almost everything. But Evie wouldn't be one of them. She'd keep Blue's secret.

She dropped into the chair farthest away from Sheriff Boyde, who peppered her with stupid questions:

"Why the woods?"

"Why did you go with her? Why did you turn back?"

"Was it her plan all along to run away?"

"I don't know," Evie said again and again. "Maybe."

Finally, Sheriff Boyde released a soft, resigned sigh. He stood, tucking away his notebook. "If you do think of anything, you know where to find me."

~

For days, the town buzzed. At first, it was more of the same—worried speculations, fretful declarations that little girls didn't belong alone in the woods. But by Wednesday, when Evie was sent to pick up a loaf of bread, she could tell something had shifted.

The whispers followed her as she walked past the café, the hardware store, the laundromat.

"It wasn't a *girl* who went missing," Evie heard Mrs. Cobaine tell Mrs. Evans. "It was a *faerie*!"

Evie whirled to face them, then turned away, her breath coming fast. She spotted Margie on the other side of the street, where people walked around her, giving her a wide berth. They were the same people who had clutched her hand and murmured sympathies three days earlier, but their pity had soured now that the "missing girl" was something else. Something other.

Evie crossed the street and joined her. "They're awful, every last one of them!"

"No, they're just people," Margie said. "Now that it's no longer a town girl who's missing, they'll call off the search." She nodded, as if trying to convince herself. "It's for the best."

She gave Evie a small smile and headed off.

Evie stayed put, mulling over Margie's statement. *It's for the best.*

For whom? The townsfolk, who could let their concern curdle into disgust and get on with their lives?

Evie's throat thickened, and hot tears pricked behind her eyes. One day, perhaps, Blue's absence would turn into something gentler, something she could carry. But she doubted it. Her chin wobbled, and she fast-walked, then ran, down the dusty dirt road that led out of town. The bread could wait.

She ran all the way to the meadow of the golden roses before collapsing onto the grass and crying for the girl she loved.

Chapter Forty-Seven

Sheriff Boyde returned the following day. Evie's father was at the hardware store, but Evie's mother was home, as was Evie.

"Yes, what is it?" Evie's mother said briskly.

"I need to file a formal report now that we know what we're dealing with," Sheriff Boyde said, stepping into the house. He sighed and turned to Evie. "Did you know?"

"Know what?"

"That Margie's girl wasn't . . . like the rest of us. Did she ever do anything strange? Say anything? Plant ideas in your head?"

Evie met his gaze squarely. "Blue was my friend. That's all."

"I see," said the sheriff. He scratched behind his ear. "You sure that's how you want to play it?"

"Play what? How am I *playing*?"

The sheriff flipped his notebook closed and tucked it away. "If I knew where she was, Evie, I could help her."

"She doesn't need your help."

"Evie!" her mother exclaimed.

"No, no, it's all right," the sheriff said, lifting his palms.

"Just hear me out. Margie's girl—she's just a kid."

Margie's *girl* had a name. Was the sheriff afraid to use it?

"She's probably alone. Probably scared."

Evie rolled her eyes. Had he met Blue?

"I'm on her side, is all," the sheriff finished. "If you find yourself in her vicinity . . . let her know."

Her mother stepped forward, planting her hands firmly on Evie's shoulders. "Evie made some bad decisions, Callum. Neither Abe nor I will argue with you there. But those days are over, and as for Margie's daughter . . ."

Evie twisted free. "If I find myself in Blue's vicinity, we'll have far more interesting things to discuss than you. Now, if you'll excuse me?"

Sheriff Boyde stared at her. So did her mother. Evie's cheeks went hot, and if she could rewind time, she'd have left that last bit off.

If she could rewind time . . .

Well.

She couldn't.

She hurried outside and walked downtown, just to have something to do. When she passed the filling station, Marisol whispered something to Cookie behind her palm. When she passed the bank, Mr. Evans tipped his hat stiffly, like he was no longer sure how to acknowledge her.

Mrs. Cobaine and Mrs. Whittaker gazed openly at Evie when she crossed in front of them. Mrs. Whittaker cleared her throat and took half a step forward.

"Now listen, everybody," Mrs. Whittaker said loudly. "Our Evie is confused—and can you blame her? She's been under that faerie's spell for months. They're devious like that."

Evie stopped short, slammed by the weight of a dozen pairs of eyes. Then she commanded her feet to start back up again, one step after the other. Her heart pounded as heads turned toward her, one after another. People were watching her, studying her, deciding what box she now belonged in.

And then there was Mr. Bratton, who was very clear on what box he'd like to put her in if he could. "Bogglin lover," he spat at her, his face twisting with hate.

Evie's hands curled into fists. She wanted to throw herself at him, to claw his face and scream until her throat gave out.

A bell jangled, and Jax dashed out of Taylor's Guns & Gear. He planted himself between the two of them and said, "Don't, Evie. Don't give him the satisfaction."

Evie stepped around Jax. "I'll never see her again, thanks to you. Are you satisfied?"

Mr. Bratton worked up a loogie and hocked it in her direction. It landed with a splat on the dusty sidewalk. "When all of the bog-bred are cold and dead, *that's* when I'll be satisfied."

Evie lunged.

Jax restrained her. "Let it go. He's not worth it."

By the time she got home, her limbs felt heavy, and her head felt thick. She passed her father, who was pulling weeds from the front flower bed. He grunted but didn't look up. Her mother, on the other hand, tracked Evie's movements like a hawk, pursing her lips as Evie poured a glass of water at the kitchen sink.

"All you all right, Evie?" she asked. "You look pale."

"I'm always pale."

"Paler than normal."

Normal? What did *normal* mean?

"I'm fine," Evie lied. "Just tired."

The landline rang, and her mother startled.

Evie stared at her mother.

Her mother stared at the phone.

It rang again. *Brrring!*

Evie didn't know much, but she knew that her mother's sudden reluctance to answer the phone, with its reliable feed of gossip, was far less *normal* than Evie's supposed pallor.

"Phone's ringing!" her father called from the back porch.

Yes, Dad, thanks, thought Evie.

When it rang for a third time, Evie's mother fixed Evie with haunted eyes. Her fingers found the collar of her dress and tugged at it.

"I can't," she whispered. "If one more busybody thinks it's their job to tell me how to raise my children . . ."

The back door squeaked open and banged shut behind Evie's father, who answered the phone mid-ring.

"Hello?" he said gruffly. "Yes, put him through." As he listened, his spine went rigid. "Is that so? Huh. Well, Callum, the problem with that—"

He broke off, his fingers tensing around the receiver.

"Understood," he said and hung up the phone.

"Dad?" Evie said.

"Was that the sheriff?" her mother asked. "What does he want now?"

Evie's father rubbed the back of his neck, gazing off at nothing. Then he grabbed his keys and jerked his chin at Evie.

"Hop in the truck, honey," he said wearily.

"Why?" her mother demanded. "Where are you taking her?" She crossed the room and clutched at her husband's shirtsleeve. "Who was that on the phone, Abe?"

"It was Callum Boyde, as you know full well. He's asked me to bring Evie to the station."

Chapter Forty-Eight

The floor of the police station was dirty. Evie stared at a smudge near the toe of her Mary Jane, a dark streak of something ground into the linoleum. Mud, maybe. Or oil. Something ugly that had been trampled over and left to harden.

She kept her eyes locked on it as Sheriff Boyde cleared his throat and rustled papers behind his desk. "Thanks for coming, Abe. I know this isn't easy."

Evie focused on the smudge.

"Evie," the sheriff said. She had no choice but to look up.

A pile of clothes lay on the desk—a pair of overalls and a thin white shirt. The shirt was dirtier than before, and there was a rip at the shoulder.

"You recognize these?"

"Yes. They're Blue's. Those overalls—she always wore them."

"They were found up near Graveyard Fields, near the river."

Evie's pulse fluttered, because she no longer knew the script. Why had Blue's shirt and overalls been found in the forest?

"According to Margie, she wasn't wearing shoes," the sheriff said.

"She always went barefoot," Evie replied automatically.

Her father and the sheriff talked above her, their voices a low drone. Words floated past: *size-eleven boot prints, dogs, forensics team. Unconfirmed. Margie will need to—*

Evie tuned them out. None of it mattered. Just a lot of noise.

She reached for Blue's shirt and draped it over her lap. The rip was more of a hole, really. A hole the size of a penny, like the one Blue had knelt beside and plucked from the sidewalk the day they'd gone to the bakery and found Anton trying unsuccessfully to feed Star.

There was a stain around the hole and a couple of smaller stains below. Blueberry juice, more red than blue, because that's what happened when the berries were overripe. If you pushed through dense clumps of them, they'd leave stains just like this—pulpy and bruised and red.

Rub with lemon. Dab with hot water. That was how to get berry juice out.

The sheriff's voice cut through her thoughts. "No body was found. No signs of struggle. No remains."

Well, of course not. What *remains* would there be?

He ran a hand over the cropped hair on the back of his head. "Just the bloodstain on the shirt. But that's enough."

Evie's head jerked up. "This isn't a bloodstain. It's blueberry juice." Her heart pounded loud and fast. "Why would it be blood?"

Sheriff Boyde shared a look with Evie's father, one that said he only believed a thing was true if he saw it with his own two eyes.

"Go on and take her home," he said. "Shouldn't have asked you to bring her here in the first place, I reckon. Certain truths . . . they're too hard for a girl."

"Her ring," Evie blurted. "When you found her clothes, did you find a ring?"

If Blue's ring was gone, then the hole in the shirt didn't matter. If Blue's ring was gone, then Blue was safe, and all of this was just a distraction. A glamour or some such. A reasonable explanation to settle the hearts and minds of the townsfolk, those who had forgotten how to believe in magic.

Sheriff Boyde dug his hand into his pocket, his fingers finding something and curling around it. Evie's chest contracted, and the dizzying wrongness of the world made her feel physically ill.

He opened his hand for her to see—and a whooshing filled her body.

It was a ring.

But it wasn't *Blue's* ring.

"Evie?" her father said.

She barely heard him. She hadn't realized, until now, just how frightened she had been.

Sheriff Boyde cleared his throat and said something to Evie's father about returning Blue's things to Margie.

"I'll do it," Evie rushed to say.

"Are you sure?" her father asked.

"Yes," she said. She felt clammy, covered with a layer of fear sweat, but her body was coming back to her. Blue was alive, and so Evie could keep on living, too. "It should be me."

Sheriff Boyde passed over Blue's clothing, as well as the

ring. *Evie's* ring, the one made of mica and iron and quartz. She slipped it on—a perfect fit.

Chapter Forty-Nine

Weeks passed. People settled. They still gossiped about Blue, Evie was sure, and she knew what they'd be saying, even if the words didn't reach her ears: a whole lot of bull. The world didn't care about right or wrong. Goodness wasn't rewarded, and cruelty wasn't punished. That was the way of things.

But one night, as Evie pushed her food around her plate, the front door banged open so hard it rattled the silverware. Trink stood in the doorway, breathless and wide-eyed.

"Bob Bratton's been arrested!" she blurted.

Evie's father set down his fork. Jax's hand froze mid-cut, knife wedged in a slice of ham.

Evie's mother's eyes flared wide. "Arrested? Good heavens! Why?"

"For killing a faerie!" Trink said. "He shot a fae boy years ago. I guess nobody knew, but . . ." She shrugged. "Now they do. There's evidence and everything."

"What kind of evidence?" Evie's mom asked.

"The kind that sticks," Trink answered. "I reckon it'll be in the paper tomorrow morning. But Evie, I just wanted to say . . . I'm real glad it wasn't Blue."

Evie met Trink's eyes and nodded.

"It's still sad. It's still awful."

"I know," said Evie. "Thanks, Trink."

"Yes, thank you, Trink," said Evie's mother, her voice like ice. "You can go now. Go on."

"Okay. Bye," said Trink, throwing Evie a final anxious smile.

As soon as the door clicked shut, Evie's mom threw up her hands. "What is this world coming to? Bob Bratton, jailed for killing a faerie?"

No one answered.

"It won't stick," she declared. "Someone will provide an alibi for him."

"You mean *lie* for him?" Evie said.

"Don't sass me, young lady." Her fingers tapped the table. "Someone will vouch for him because that's what we do. What we've always done. We take care of our own."

"Nicole, honey, times are changing," Evie's father said. "That's a good thing."

She faced him. "If Richard won't vouch for Bob, then you will, Abe. You can say—well, anything you want!"

He shook his head slowly. Firmly. "Bob's where he's meant to be."

Evie's mother's mouth twisted.

"Ten years ago—heck, maybe even five—someone might've gone to bat for him," Evie's father allowed. He glanced at Evie and dipped his chin. "Lied for him. But not anymore."

"But we're talking about Bob Bratton!" her mother cried. "One of our own!" She gasped and pressed a hand to her chest. "Silas! Goodness, of course. *Silas* will set this straight."

"No, Mom," Jax said.

"What do you mean, 'no'?"

"Silas is the one who turned him in."

Evie's mother went still.

"He got drunk and confessed," Jax said. "Told Silas he'd killed a fae boy, years ago. Thought the fae boy murdered Ben, and so he took it upon himself to get revenge." He paused. "Silas drove him down to the sheriff's office himself."

"Silas turned in his own father?" Evie's mother said.

"Hardest thing a son could do," Evie's father said. "And the most loving."

Evie's mother lost her steam. She pushed her hand through her hair and said, "But what will happen to Silas? He's barely older than you, Jax."

"There's a men's group in Asheville that'll help him out," Jax said. "Help him find housing, that sort of stuff."

Help him find housing, that sort of stuff.

The words sounded good at first. Then they slid sideways because what Silas needed—what everyone needed—wasn't just housing but a home. A family. A town. A world where everyone was accepted.

And there it was, the punch of helplessness that gutted Evie every time she was forced to face reality. When would she grow up and stop wishing for impossible things? There would never be a world in which everyone was accepted just as they were. It was too much to ask for.

No, came a voice. It rang as clear as a bell.

Evie glanced around. A tingling spread up her body and

made her lightheaded.

No, the voice insisted.

Evie let the realization envelop her. The world she and Blue had dreamed of remained dismally out of reach, and wishing people would just up and change was naive. That was true.

But wanting a better world wasn't childish. That was equally true—and putting in the work to *make* it better wasn't dumb at all.

Chapter Fifty

The ceremony was simple. No coffin, no grave, but that was fitting. Blue had never been the kind of person to be contained.

The townsfolk gathered in the clearing behind the church, where the land sloped gently downward. The sky stretched wide and cloudless, the air rich with the scent of pine. Evie wore the pale pink dress her mother had picked out for her and didn't complain. In exchange, her mother frowned when she saw Evie's ring but managed—just barely—to keep her opinion to herself.

Evie twisted the metal around her finger. It warmed to her touch.

Trink sang one of Margie's favorite songs, a plaintive ballad that posed impossible questions. *"When my body won't hold me anymore,"* Trink sang, *"where will I go?"*

Her voice was beautiful. Who knew? Clear and warm, it carried through the trees, and when the chorus came around, people joined her. Their voices rose together, low and solemn, filling the spaces between them.

Evie ached with how much she wanted Blue to be standing beside her, enjoying the song but feeling the pull of the mountains even so. Eager for the ceremony to end so that she could take Evie's hand and pull her away, both of them laughing as they ran for the woods.

Trink finished and stepped back, blushing and smiling shyly.

Then, the balloons.

Margie had come up with the idea, and to Evie's surprise, the townsfolk had embraced it. They were trying, in their own way, to help heal the wound they had helped create.

On Margie's signal, everyone lifted their hands. A rustling sigh accompanied the balloons, all of them blue, as they soared upward in the evening light.

One by one, they disappeared from sight. One by one, the people around Evie nodded and lowered their heads. Some turned and left. Others lingered, talking softly in small groups.

Only Evie kept looking, and so only Evie saw it. A wash of color, rushing in from the horizon and spreading everywhere. Fiery reds mingled with shards of icy blue. Streaks of gold flared and flickered. Greens popped, and patches of soft, buttery yellow wafted and spun like drifting petals.

The colors swirled and stretched, lighter than gossamer. Softer than moonlight.

After the play of lights had faded, Margie appeared by Evie's side.

"Oh, Evie," she said. "I miss her so. But I know she's still with us."

Evie nodded. The magic that was Blue would *always* been here—in the mountains, in the forest, in the river. In the way she taught Evie to see the world.

A branch of a nearby maple dipped as a white squirrel landed on it, tail flashing like a banner. It paused, then leapt again—down the limb, across the air, onto the next branch that called to it. Unbothered, as always, by county lines.

Evie felt a trembling in her soul. The ache wasn't gone. It would never be. It was one flick of a squirrel's tail lighter, however. A white squirrel, of course, because white squirrels brought good luck.

She found Margie's hand and held it tight. The grandmother, parked in her grass-flecked invalid chair, said nothing, but her eyes weren't as steely as they used to be.

The sky softened to a dusky violet. Evie helped the grandmother get her wheelchair back to more suitable terrain. Margie clasped her forearms behind her back and tilted her face toward the heavens.

That night, Evie lay on her bed and gazed out her window, the curtains left purposefully wide. She tracked the moon as it rose high in the velvet sky. Everywhere stars. Everywhere Blue.

She turned onto her side, blinking drowsily. Draped over her bedside table was a soft gray blanket, and on top of the blanket was a silver baby rattle. Margie had gifted both to Evie, insisting that Evie should have them.

"When Blue was little, she loved that blanket," Margie had explained. "The rattle, too." She'd smiled. "She used to hide under the blanket as if it made her invisible, my sweet, funny girl. She'd pull the rattle under there with her, clutching it tight and pouring into it all of her worries, her fears, her dreams."

"Blue had a baby blanket?" Evie had marveled. "And a *rattle*?"

"They hold a bit of her still. That's what I think," Margie had murmured, and when she'd passed the items to Evie, Evie had accepted them without protest. "I hope they'll bring you comfort."

Evie reached out and fingered the soft blanket. She grazed the handle of the rattle with her thumb. It shone in the moonlight, and Evie's heart filled to bursting with memories of Blue.

Tomorrow night, the moon would rise again, and again Evie would think of Blue. Every night, Evie would think of Blue. Some nights, she would remember today's balloons and Trink's singing and the great wash of color that had filled the sky. Other nights, she would gather her energy and send a piece of herself outward, stretching past the trees, past the river, past what was known.

Hi, Blue. Are you there? Can you hear me?

Evie wiggled deeper beneath her quilt. She yawned and thought about the bridge between her world and Blue's world.

Might she cross it herself one day? Not because of dying, but because . . . maybe the veil that obscured it would thin. Maybe the world *could* change, if Evie helped others be kinder and less inclined to judge?

Not if. When.

Evie rolled onto her side, tugging her quilt up under her chin as her eyelids fluttered shut. Her thoughts slipped to wriggling frogs and the liquid gaze of a baby deer. She saw Blue in the meadow, covered with butterflies. She saw her sitting among the golden roses, asking the fireflies to draw the letter *E* for *Evie*.

As Evie's memories melted into dreams, the fireflies traced a heart in a purpling sky—and Evie, deep in sleep, felt freshly born.

A Sneak Peek

of

The Queen's Box

Some boxes should never be opened. Some truths aren't meant for mortal hearts. And not everyone is who they say they are.

Willow Braselton has always believed in fairy tales. As a child, she glimpsed a magical world no one else could see. At thirteen, she dreamed of a fae prince. At nineteen, those dreams crystallized into certainty: her prince was real—and he needed her just as much as she needed him.

But no one believed her. Not when she spoke of the other world. Not when she told the truth about what happened her senior year, the night she was alone with her adored drama teacher. Not her sisters. Not her father. Not the polished world that told her to smile, look pretty, and stay quiet.

So when a renowned folklorist hints that the Old Blood might run in her veins, Willow bolts—trading pearls and parties in Atlanta for the watchful mountain town of Hemridge, North Carolina. There, she meets Cole, a quiet, sharp-eyed local who carries grief like a second skin. With his help, Willow uncovers a fabled relic: a coffin-shaped box said to open only for the right ones.

It opens for her.

And then it slams shut—locking her in the unseen seams between worlds, the cracks where lost things wait.

When the Box releases her, it's into the spun-sugar realm of Eryth, where Queen Severine welcomes her like kin. The queen's son, Serrin—the prince from Willow's dreams—is dying. Only Willow can save him.

Or so she's told.

But Eryth is built on secrets. Stolen children. Stunted dragons. Curdled blood rites. And all of it, somehow, leads back to Hemridge...

To Cole.

To Willow herself.

Because the Queen's Box isn't just a portal. It's a test.

And it doesn't just rewrite destiny—It rewrites you.

Prologue

Scilla slipped through the forest, a shadow among shadows, feet silent on the leaf-littered ground. Even in the hush of the late hour, she remained wary. Sentinels prowled these woods, and worse still, the Secret Sisters. To be caught meant conscription if she was lucky, death if she wasn't. Or perhaps it was the other way around. Wouldn't bleeding out beneath the trees be better than being forced to live and toil among the Blighted, shunned by the queen's courtiers if they were in a good mood, kicked and whipped if the courtiers were irritable—or simply bored?

What if Scilla was caught by a Secret Sister and imprisoned in their vast network of underground caves? The Sisters kept duskwyrms in those dark caves, if the rumors were true. Cages upon cages of them, their forked tongues flickering. Would a Secret Sister offer Scilla to one of the wyrms, even though she was no plump cheeked babe, but a gaunt and scrawny girl of thirteen? If so, and if the wyrm struck—and of course the wyrm would strike—then Scilla wouldn't just be thrown in among the Blighted. She would become blighted, burned from the inside out and deemed untouchable for the rest of her days.

But she was this year's messenger, and Scilla refused to shirk from her task. She would serve the True Guard with clear eyes and a fierce heart, honoring the work of all the girls and women who came before her. She'd made this journey twice already, after all, and no ill fortune had befallen her. Ten more times—nine after tonight—and her term would be served.

She broke into the clearing, heart hammering. There, at last, loomed the Seeing Tree, illuminated by the milk white belly of the pregnant moon. Its ancient trunk twisted upward. Its branches clawed at the inky sky. The skull for which the tree was named rose higher each year, impaled through the eye sockets by a prong of gnarled oak.

Scilla fell to her knees and lifted her face. Her ribs constricted, but she didn't look away. The Seeing Tree only answered those who were willing to be seen.

"She will come. She will," Scilla whispered. In her mind's eye, she saw the elderwomen of the Guard, voices hushed but insistent. "A savior," they whispered. "A girl from another world."

Scilla didn't understand. Were there other worlds than Eryth, then? But where? And how did one reach them? Still, she clung to the promise.

Something rustled. Scilla froze. A duskwyrm emerged from the shadows, one of the few still free, and Scilla went boneless from fear. The wyrm's eyes locked on Scilla's. Its plated coils shifted from sapphires to emeralds to amethysts. It hissed, and Scilla grew lightheaded, knowing that its venom could kill her in an instant, her flesh blackening and shriveling in the space of a breath.

Once upon a faraway time, duskwyrms didn't bother with

faeries. They ate, grew, drew cocoons around themselves and emerged as dragons. Then they bothered anyone they chose. They had the rule of the land.

They never killed for sport, however. If someone was foolish enough to provoke one, or if hunger pressed and the usual quarry was scarce, then yes, a dragon would strike the fae. Not in Scilla's time, of course, but she'd shivered with childish delight when stories were shared of fearsome winged beasts throwing shadows on the ground, shadows that deepened and grew until—snatch!—a screaming faerie met her end.

If the faerie was lucky, she'd die on the spot, pierced through by sharp talons.

If she was unlucky...well. Again, these were only tales. It had been decades since anyone saw a dragon, much less a dragon's lair. But the old ones swore that a dragon, on the rare occasion of snatching a bleating faerie from the fleeing hordes, would beat its mighty wings and carry the poor soul for miles over the golden fields and jagged mountain peaks of Eryth until they reached their lair. There, it was said, they played with their prey. Taught their babies how to wound, how to maim, how to kill.

Or, because dragons were fickle, sometimes they kept the faerie alive for a while, but barely, feeding her berries and seeds and raw silver fish. Feeding a faerie kept her tethered to life, and the faerie's toes and fingers and delicately pointed ears did the same for the dragon, providing enough warm, salty blood to keep it going until a heartier meal was procured.

For days, even weeks, a dragon might slowly savor the faerie, or so it was said. Strips of flesh were peeled from limbs and torso. Nose, eyeballs, and tongue were ripped off with razor sharp teeth. Wounds were cauterized with fire breath to prolong the slow snacking, the faerie teetering between life and death until nothing remained but her organs, which the dragon saved for last.

Then came Wrenna, who subdued the dragons and brought peace to Eryth. Wrenna the Wrathful, as she was called in legends. And, true, dragons were no longer a menace. Wrenna, with her magic, manipulated the process of metamorphosis so that wyrms remained wyrms, earthbound and small, and grew to be dragons in only the rarest of cases. Scilla, in her thirteen years, had yet to hear of a single dragon sighting.

The stunted wyrms were the menace now. Trapped in their juvenile form, hatred sprouted where once they grew wings. Resentment pulsed in their forever slender tails, and fury replaced fire, coalescing into venom that burned from within.

The Sisters were immune to the duskwyrms' poison. But Scilla was just a girl, far from home.

The wyrm, less than two yards from her, swayed its diamond shaped head. It flicked its forked tongue, sampling Scilla's scent.

Scilla pressed her palms into the damp earth. Don't move. Don't breathe.

The duskwyrm's jeweled body tightened, then turned, slipping back into the shadows.

Scilla's shoulders sagged. She steadied her hitching breath. She lifted her gaze once more to the skull's hollow stare.

"Please," she implored. "We need her."

Chapter One, The Queen's Box

Willow smoothed her hands over her thrift-store gypsy skirt, willing the tiny bells not to tattle every time a party guest breezed by. She regretted wearing the damn thing and wanted desperately to dash to her bedroom and change. Only, she couldn't, because if she did, then Ash would win.

Yep, knew it, her sister's smirk would say. You can't stand the idea of being "normal," but even the smallest rebellion makes you break out in hives.

Even in Willow's imagination, Ash used snark quotes.

Although, seriously? A gauzy skirt adorned with tiny silver bells? Who did Willow fancy herself to be, a charming goatherd in a rustic and magical land?

(Well, yes, actually. Though maybe not a goatherd. And Ash could just shut up, even in Willow's own head. What Ash failed to understand was that there were other worlds than theirs. Better worlds. If Willow could no longer travel elsewhere—even if only in her dreams—she'd be completely and utterly lost.)

Willow had told herself, as she'd gotten ready for her parents' party, that she'd selected her outfit because she liked it. And she did! Her peasant blouse was embroidered with tiny blue flowers, and the collar was finished with twin lengths of soft blue cord, each tassel tied off with a knot. The blouse went perfectly with her gypsy skirt, and her strappy leather sandals—the ones her father called her "Jesus sandals"—tied the look together.

But now, with her back pressed to the wall of her parents' grand dining room, she felt ridiculous. She was nineteen, not nine, and pairing a tasseled blouse with a jingle bell skirt didn't make her a free spirit. It just made her feel like an idiot.

None of the party guests said anything rude, of course. None of the guests mentioned Willow's attire at all. The well-mannered men smiled with their perfect teeth, sipping bourbon and swapping stories about court cases and golf handicaps, while their wives widened their eyes at Willow before smiling awkwardly and glancing away. Still, Willow knew she was being silently evaluated and just as silently dismissed. Or pitied. Or both.

Her mother hadn't been silent, and whatever sympathy she'd felt for Willow after "that business with Mr. Chapman" had dried up months ago.

"Oh, Willow," she'd lamented when Willow descended the stairs, each step a tinkling affront to her mother's impeccable taste. "This party is important to your father. You know it is."

Willow had felt the familiar weight of unvoiced resentment drape over her. She was here, wasn't she? And she wasn't wearing a gorilla suit, for heaven's sake. Her long blond hair was twisted into a bun, no flyaways, and she'd spritzed herself with Chanel Cristalle in hopes of masking the lingering scent of patchouli that clung to her skirt. Shouldn't that be enough? Shouldn't she be enough, just as she was?

Her mother's sigh had put that question to rest. She'd swirled her hand to encompass the whole of Willow's ensemble and said, "Then why are you doing...whatever this is?"

"I'm not doing anything," Willow had replied, working to keep her voice level. "You told me to wear a skirt. I'm wearing a skirt."

"Yes, but..." She'd eyed the layers of colorful gauze. "It could be cute for a picnic, I suppose." Her gaze had traveled upward. "But that top! It does nothing for your figure, and you have such a darling figure. There's still a few minutes before our guests arrive. Won't you run back upstairs and change into one of your Laura Ashleys?"

Willow had grimaced. "Mother? The last time I wore a Laura Ashley dress was at my high school graduation. Under my robe."

"And you looked lovely at all the after parties."

"That was then. This is now."

"Well, yes. And yet here you are, aren't you?"

Willow had clenched her jaw, realizing too late that she'd walked into that one like a goatherd—no, a goat—into a lion's den.

Tonight was May fifth, 1988. A year ago, almost to the day, Willow had graduated from Braxton Academy. And what did she have to show for it? She'd put in one semester at Emory before dropping out. She'd gotten a job at Peaches, a record store in the neighborhood shopping center, but her boss kept cutting her hours. So here she was, still living with her parents in their enormous house on Habersham Road, still disappointing them day after day after day.

"Where's your drive?" her father had demanded just that morning. "Your purpose, your motivation?"

"You do need to figure things out, sweetheart," her mother had chimed in. "You can't be a wastrel forever."

A wastrel. Willow would have laughed if not for the fear that letting any emotion out would let all the emotions out, and then...well, yeah. Historically, letting her emotions out hadn't ended well. She had no desire to walk down that road again.

The only thing holding Willow together these days was Serrin, who came to her in her dreams. It was because of Serrin that she knew of other worlds. Of one world, in particular—a world that was most definitely not Atlanta, nor the known world of humans at all.

Serrin's world, that was where Willow longed to be. Serrin would save her from her sugared world of falsehoods and stolen innocence. But when? How?

It was complicated, loving a boy with pointed ears.

Willow slumped against the wall and watched Ash work the room like the pro she was. At sixteen, Ash was already fluent in the language of power and influence. She knew exactly how to let her parents' friends know that she was the sister who mattered, the sister who excelled, the sister who would earn their parents' pride forever and ever, amen.

She was welcome to it. Willow had eaten enough bacon-wrapped dates to last her a lifetime.

That said, Willow couldn't stand here like a loser all

night. She scanned the room for someone she could anchor herself to. Not her mother, who had claimed a migraine and made her disappearance forty-five minutes into the festivities. Juniper, perhaps? At eleven, Juniper was the youngest of the Braselton girls. She adored Willow's tales of faeries and dragons and worlds where magic still held sway. Once upon a time, Ash did, too. Once upon a time, Willow would make up story after story for the three sisters to act it out.

"You be the prince, and you be the princess, and I'll be the dragon!" Willow would say.

Sometimes Juniper wanted to be the dragon. Sometimes Willow let her.

But right now, Juniper was occupied by her role of party helper, passing around hors d'oeuvres on a silver tray.

Everyone knew their role in this mortal court. Everyone fit. Everyone but Willow.

She thought longingly of the "go bag" hidden in the farthest reaches of her closet, a backpack packed with a flashlight, two changes of clothes, and $1,000 in cash, stockpiled over the course of many months from her meager earnings at Peaches and the allowance her father doled out each week. $1,000 wasn't much, but it was enough to disappear. Or at least get her out of Atlanta.

Would she ever work up the nerve to leave?

Ash didn't think so.

"Your little adventure kit," she'd called Willow's go bag when she found it, sifting through the carefully folded clothes. "You love the idea of running away, but we both know you never will." She'd clicked her tongue. "You wouldn't last a week."

Willow had zipped the bag shut and shoved it back into the closet, furious. Later, lying in bed, Ash's words had needled at her. Was Ash right? Was this just a fantasy Willow clung to, the comfort of a make-believe escape hatch? Sometimes it felt as if she lived in two worlds at once: her real life—drab and cheerless—and her other life, the one that was meant to be. The one with Serrin.

She couldn't reach him on a thousand dollars, nor on a million. You couldn't buy your way to another world.

But staying in Atlanta, staying stuck, wasn't getting her anywhere, either.

Sick of the relentless party cheer, Willow sighed and shifted positions, making the bells on her skirt jingle merrily. Great. And yet, the sound called out to her, a thread pulling taut. She'd always been drawn to bells, to their clarity and their power to summon.

She touched one of the small bells and allowed the memory to stir: the chime of a tarnished silver baby rattle she heard more than a decade ago. That one chime rewrote the fabric of her life, proving that the world was stitched with unseen magic—and that she, Willow, was meant for something more.

It happened when she was seven. It was summer break, and she was bored, and she had nothing better to do than wander aimlessly around the house, opening cabinets and looking beneath beds, peering into the shadows where spiders and old socks hid out.

She found the silver rattle stuffed in the back of a drawer. When her fingers closed around it, the air was sucked right out of her. Then it rushed back, thick and cloying, while at the same time, the walls of the house thinned and grew transparent. She was pretty sure she'd gasped. She must have gasped. What other response was there to such a revelation?

But, strangely, she didn't remember being frightened. The whole recollection had a hazy feeling to it, as if sprinkled through with golden motes of dust, but through the gold filtered mist, she'd seen a woman standing at the edge of a forest. Her dress was dark. Her hair was long and wild.

The woman met Willow's gaze, and her eyes widened. She opened her mouth as if to speak, and then—

And then four-year-old Ash tugged on Willow's arm and called her name. Willow blinked at Ash, confused. Then she turned back toward the forest, but the forest—and the wild-haired woman—were gone.

"I said your name so many times," Ash complained, "but you didn't listen. And your face looked funny. I didn't like it."

Willow didn't tell Ash what she'd seen, not for a whole ten seconds. Then it tumbled out of her—all of it—wild and bright, like a secret too big for one girl to hold.

At four, Ash had idolized her big sister. And at four, she'd still allowed herself to believe in impossible things.

"But who was she?" she'd asked with huge eyes. "The lady?" She'd looked around. "And the forest, where did it go?"

"I don't know," Willow had answered breathlessly. "Back to where it came from? Ash, this is very important, and I need you to listen. Okay?"

Ash had nodded.

"I think it was fae magic," Willow had told her.

"Fae magic? What's that?"

"Faeries," Willow had whispered, and Ash's eyes had widened much like those of the lady in the forest, when she spotted Willow and Willow spotted her back.

"Can I try?" Ash had asked.

Willow had frowned, an uncomfortable itch of selfishness making her heart squeeze small.

"You're not old enough," she'd said.

"Am so!" Ash had said.

She'd begged for the silver rattle, then stomped her foot and demanded Willow share it or else.

"Ash, no," Willow had said, though she'd swallowed the words that tried to come next. It's mine. She'd held the rattle above her head and out of Ash's reach, prompting Ash to burst into great loud noisy sobs.

The ruckus had brought their mother, and when their mother spotted the rattle, all the blood had rushed from her face.

"Give it to me," their mother had snapped, and Willow, startled by the fear in her mother's voice, had handed it over. Whether her mother hid it or threw it away or melted it, even, (the thought did cross Willow's mind), Willow never knew. No matter how long and hard she looked, she never found it again.

Over the years, Ash had rewritten the incident and turned it into a joke.

"That dumb baby rattle?" she'd scoff. "Either you hid it, or, more likely, it never existed at all."

It had existed, though. Its chime left its imprint deep on Willow's soul.

It was after finding the rattle, and hearing its silver

chime, that seven-year-old Willow began to dream of the forest she'd so briefly glimpsed. Night after night, she dreamed of it.

She never again saw the woman with the long, wild hair. Years later, however, she saw someone else.

He came to her on the night of her thirteenth birthday. His name was Serrin—Serrin, the syllables lovely on her tongue, the name both foreign and known—and his blue eyes gleamed like sea glass, like the sweetness of a burbling creek. He had high cheekbones, a nose that was slightly too long, and a smile that was earnest and true.

He was other, her dream boy. The pointed tips of his ears made that. But it was more than that. Serrin wasn't like the boys she passed on the street, the ones who smelled of beer and aftershave and gazed at Willow hopefully, and he had nothing, absolutely nothing, in common with...

No. Her skin crawled, and she shoved him out of her mind, the teacher who taught falsely, the man who stole Willow's childhood.

Serrin wasn't like any rough, coarse human. Serrin was the glimmer at the periphery of a room, the flicker of movement just out of sight. Fae. Sometimes, in her dreams, he filled her with sunshine. After those dreams, she woke up believing all was well with the world. Other times, she woke up sweaty, her heart racing with dread. Something bad, something bad. It lurked in the darkness, this thing that was bad, but one day, it would reveal itself. And when it did...

Serrin.

He was the answer, the key, the shaft of light in darkest night. It made no sense. None of it did. Willow was many things, but she wasn't an idiot, no matter how often she felt like one. And because she wasn't an idiot, she knew, rationally, that...what?

Option one: She was crazy, as in cuckoo for cocoa puffs. As in, Bye, now. Off to the nuthouse. You take care!

Willow had been to the nuthouse once already. The name on the sign in front of the building read, "Mountain Crest: A Mental Facility for Teens," but it had been a nuthouse. Willow's shoes had been taken from her, because: shoestrings. Could someone really hang herself using shoestrings? The guards at the nuthouse hadn't wanted to find out.

Willow hadn't been sent to the nuthouse because of Serrin. No one knew about Serrin.

Was it possible that no one knew about Serrin because Serrin didn't exist?

There was a rabbit hole there to fall into, and it was a scary one. Willow didn't like peering into it. But—and this was a big but—before Serrin, there was the silver baby rattle, and with it, the vision of the forest and the woman with the wild hair.

Willow's mother refused to talk about any of that with Willow. Not the rattle, not what happened to it, and certainly not why her face went so white just before she snatched it out of Willow's hand.

Which meant there was something there.

Which meant (probably) (hopefully) that Willow wasn't cuckoo for cocoa puffs. Or, if she was, then her mother was, too. And that seemed unlikely. Her mother was a member of The Junior League. She did volunteer work at the library and took afternoon classes on flower arranging!

On the other hand, Willow's mother had gone through some stuff. Her own mother—Willow's grandmother—hanged herself when Willow's mother was a baby. It was so awful to think about, so awful to put those words together in that order. Willow's grandmother hanged herself, with deliberation and a rope and that final, irrevocable step off the stool or whatever it was she started off on to get to the right height. That plummeting moment that could never be taken back.

What kind of person hanged herself? A crazy person. Sure. Maybe. But also, maybe, a person who was made to think she was crazy, because, for whatever reason, she saw the world (or worlds) in a way that most people didn't.

That line of thought did lead to another possibility, which led to option two: There was something in their blood. Willow's, her mother's, and Ash's and Juniper's, too, if the math held. Something old and strange and rippling with power. Not madness, but...magic.

People who believed in magic were often labeled crazy, because, duh, magic wasn't real. But if the magic was real...

There were other rumors about someone in Willow's mother's past. These rumors weren't linked to Willow's grandmother, whose name was Wrenna, and who hanged herself. No, there'd been someone else—a great-grandmother? A great-great-grandmother?—who was seen as "off" in some way. Or different. Unfortunately, it wasn't just the silver baby rattle Willow's mother refused to talk about. Willow's mother—whose name was Mercy—dodged all discussions about her past.

Mercy had been raised by her adoptive parents, John and Elizabeth Ann Whitmire. Willow knew that. She also knew that the Whitmires had been extremely religious in that particularly southern way that overlapped with snake charming and speaking in tongues, and that the Whitmires' religiosity had collided with something in their adopted daughter's past.

Religious fanatics didn't much like magic. Or, if they did, it was only the baby Jesus kind of magic, and they didn't call it that. That kind of magic was divine grace, holy intervention, a miracle. Which, honestly, reinforced Willow's conviction that magic and craziness were linked for all the wrong reasons, and which made her feel better about option one, the possibility that she was cuckoo for cocoa puffs.

Willow was not cuckoo for cocoa puffs, and Serrin did exist. There. Those were her truths, and she was sticking to them. But that lurking danger she sensed...

What was it? Who was it? And how did it involve Serrin?

***

Ready for more?

Order *The Queen's Box* at celestesutton.com/the-queens-box or visit celestesutton.com to learn more. Oh, and hey! Subscribe to her newsletter to stay on top of giveaways, ARC opportunities, and drop dates for the subsequent books in the series! https://bit.ly/CelesteSuttonNewsletter

Acknowledgments

To readers everywhere: thank you. You are the reason *The Ballad of Baby Blue* exists, and I don't mean that in a vague, sentimental way—I mean it in the old-school, Mozart-had-a-patron way. I am immensely grateful for the support, encouragement, and magic of the indie writers and readers community, especially the generous souls I've found on Bookstagram. You've made this strange and wonderful journey feel less like shouting into the void and more like sitting around a glowing campfire, swapping stories. You make art possible. You are the reason I keep writing.

Thanks to Kiara Sibila, who helped me find my footing when I first dipped my pinkie toe into the Bookstagram waters. Kiara gently bowed out of the Celeste group, but for good reason, as she is hard at working writing her own novel.

Enormous squishy thanks to my AMAZING street team: Andrea Sweet, Haley Freeman, Jessica Martin, Jessica Snoots, Jessica Carroll (Team Jessica, woot!), Justine Estanislao, Kasey Darling (you darling), Kassidi Tidwell, Katelyn Wallace, Kathy White, Megan Killinbeck, Sam

McKnight, Sarah Lambert, Shilpa Vidyala, Skylynn "Ketta" Miller, Adelaide Jenkins, Belynda, Clarisce "Jammy Dodger" Roberts, Julieta Giraldo, Imtiaz Maham, and Tara Mathis. Y'all are crazy and wonderful and goofy, and our spiraling insta-chats that went verrrrrry quickly from books to, oh let's see: dogs, cats, pigs, Tom Hiddleston, Cookie Monster, animal science, googly eyes, back aches, Cujo versus Kobo, and...back again to Tom Hiddleston. So! Shout-out to Tom Hiddleston! Thanks, Tom, for keeping us going. We appreciate you.

Street Teamers, your energy and generosity make me want to bawl. Your posts, your creativity, your willingness to cheer on not just me but all of our funny little group— you're just the best. I am one lucky, lucky Celeste!

Thanks, too, to the wackadoodles who joined my Discord. Ermagawd, I didn't even know what a Discord was —and now I have one...? How did that happen? And we talk about books and indie publishing and kittens kittens kittens, and it is delicious. A lot of y'all are street teamers AND Discordians: Haley, Sam, Shilpa, Sarah, Katelyn, Kathy, Belynda, Justine, Megan, Adelaide, Julieta, Andrea, Kasey, Kassidi, Jessica C., and Jessica M., I love having two different ways to poke you! We also have Alexandra Gordon, Artemis McLeod, Haleigh Collier, Shannon Havel, and Nicaury Laureano, whose voices are so very welcome. Special Discord thanks to Justine Estanislao, who made things all purty and fancy for us!

To all of my early ARC readers, omigosh, y'all breathed life and hope into me as I sat huddled on my floor biting my fingernails to the nubs. Special super-duper mushy heart thanks to Tiffany Nock and Haley Freeman, whose early feedback transformed the book.

Justine? You get yet another shout-out, because thanks to rewriting the whole book (ahem, see above), I came to you in a panic, asking if you might possibly be willing to serve as a proofreader for the final FINAL draft. You came in like a champ, catching typos right and left, and all in the space of 24 hours! Amazebubbles!!!!

Thanks to my brilliant editor, Amelia Winters, whose insightful feedback made the book 1000 times better, and thanks to Amy Dudek for creating the stunning cover art.

And now—*gets teary*—a heartfelt thanks to my assistant, Jessica Carroll, who I swear dropped out of the sky (which is OBVIOUSLY Carolina blue) and stuck by my side through this whole ride. Jessica made *spreadsheets*, y'all. (I know. The horror.) She ensured that newsletters went out on time, she kept track of ARCs and ARC readers, and she acted as my fairy godmother when it came time to sending little pressies to Street Teamers. She brainstormed up a whole hurricane of brilliance, and, even as I type, she is probably putting together the most adorable fabulous PR boxes for Baby Blue that you have ever seen. Jessica went quickly from being my assistant to becoming a true friend, and her support has been invaluable. Jessica, let's keep putting books out into the world, shall we? Special thanks to Josh "Ducky" Carroll, too, who no doubt bore the brunt of things when Jessica needed to vent about me and my fear of all things spreadsheety. Jessica supported me, and Ducky supported Jessica. Therefore, Ducky = ☆.

Thanks to my Australian Sheila, Liesel, for being brilliant and wicked smaht and entertaining me when I needed distraction. Thanks to that goofball, Al, for inspiring our wicked smaht groupchat in the first place and for being wicked smaht and wicked entertaining, as well. Y'all make my heart happy. Speaking of happy, thanks to Ali P. for checking in on me every week or so, purportedly to make self-deprecating jokes, but in reality because he knows just how essential his cheerleading is. (How's that for an Edwinism, Ali?)

To my parents, all of them: thank you for my country mouse/city mouse upbringing. A little bit Blue, a little bit Evie, but barefoot all the way.

And finally, huge thanks to my husband and kids. I love you, I love you. (And, bonus, you provide such *excellent* material...)

About the Author

Celeste Sutton writes about enchanted realms, dangerous bargains, and the kind of love that makes you ache.

For two decades, she published novels the traditional way—books that found millions of readers and spent months on bestseller lists. But eventually, Celeste did what any fantasy heroine worth her salt would do: she opened the door to something wilder. Indie publishing called, and she stepped through gladly, joining a fierce, brilliant community of storytellers who believe magic is meant to be shared.

Celeste's love affair with fantasy began early, with the wondrous adventures of Edward Eager and the dragon-filled skies of Pern. Recently, thanks to her children, she rediscovered the genre as an adult—falling headfirst into Brandon Sanderson's intricate worlds of intrigue and sacrifice, Travis Baldree's cozy taverns where retired warriors serve cinnamon rolls, and Heather Fawcett's wild meadows of charming but dangerous fae.

She now writes immersive, addictive fantasy (with just enough romance) for readers who crave wonder, adventure, and high-stakes enchantment. If you, too, keep searching thrift stores for an old wardrobe—just in case—her books are for you.

You can keep up with Celeste by subscribing to her newsletter at https://bit.ly/CelesteSuttonNewsletter.

Want to read the next installment in the Her Dark Inheritance series, in which you'll find out more about where Blue may or may not have gone and what goings-on happen there...? We've gotcha. You can check out the book here: celestesutton.com/the-queens-box.

You can also always keep up with Celeste at https://celestesutton.com. She'd love to hear from you!

ad29b7dc-e157-4807-8c58-748cca407e14R01